'A drug-fuelled cross between *The Decameron* and
The Haunting of Hill House, *The Decadence* is Craig at her
unsettling, gothic best'
Hesse Phillips, author of *Lightborne*

'Thought-provoking, terrifying and startlingly intelligent,
this is a novel of horrors that hide in the shadows and those
that exist rawly in daylight for all to see'
Alice Ash, author of *Paradise Block*

'In *The Decadence*, lust and loathing wear the same skin,
and the houses are haunted by desire as much as any ghost.
An unflinching look at the destructive allure of belonging
and the perils of abandoning oneself to achieve it. You may
never find your way back'
Gianni Washington, author of *Flowers from the Void*

'Leon Craig has a keen eye for observation and a very
dark and distinctive imagination and this novel intrigues
and unsettles'
Sharlene Teo, author of *Ponti*

'If the idea of Iris Murdoch meeting Mariana Enríquez in a
country house during lockdown appeals to you, I urge you to
read *The Decadence*. It delivers on its promises in spades'
Victoria Gosling, author of *Bliss & Blunder*

'*The Decadence* filled me with horror in the best way – the
horror of a classic haunted house tale, but also the horror
of your twenties, with all its dead-ends, debauchery,
self-doubt, and longing'
Krystelle Bamford, author of *Idle Grounds*

Leon Craig's debut short story collection *Parallel Hells* was published in 2022. She studied English at UCL, Medieval Literature at Oxford and Creative Writing at Birkbeck. She has written freelance criticism for the *White Review*, the *TLS*, *Hazlitt* and the *London Magazine*, among others. Leon is based in Berlin.

The
Decadence

Leon Craig

Sceptre

First published in Great Britain in 2025 by Sceptre
An imprint of Hodder & Stoughton Limited
An Hachette UK company

The authorised representative in the EEA is Hachette Ireland, 8 Castlecourt
Centre, Dublin 15, D15 XTP3, Ireland (email: info@hbgi.ie)

1

A CIP catalogue record for this title is available from the British Library

Hardback ISBN 9781529371758
Trade Paperback ISBN 9781529371765
ebook ISBN 9781529371772

Typeset in Bembo MT by Hewer Text UK Ltd, Edinburgh
Printed and bound in Great Britain by Clays Ltd, Elcograf S.p.A.

Hodder & Stoughton policy is to use papers that are natural, renewable
and recyclable products and made from wood grown in sustainable
forests. The logging and manufacturing processes are expected to
conform to the environmental regulations of the country of origin.

Hodder & Stoughton Limited
Carmelite House
50 Victoria Embankment
London EC4Y 0DZ

www.sceptrebooks.co.uk

'Bind me ye Woodbines in your 'twines,
Curle me about ye gadding Vines,
And Oh so close your Circles lace,
That I may never leave this Place'

Andrew Marvell,
Upon Appleton House

'And only decades later, when roof and walls fell in upon
us, did we realize that the foundations had long since been
undermined . . .'

Stefan Zweig,
The World of Yesterday

For those who used to go a roving

They say a house ages five years for every one that it stands empty. By that reckoning, the time Holt House had been deprived of occupants already eclipsed Theo Mortimer's life span by three years. And yet, nestled in a green valley far away, encircled by hills and encroached upon by damp, the house drowsed on, scarcely registering such a brief interval of quiet in over eight centuries of existence. From little more than a squat and draughty hall, to a walled stronghold, to a crenelated folly tucked away from the modern world, Holt House took life and strength from all who passed through, transforming vigour into stone, spreading wider, stretching higher to reach its current incarnation. It had always known itself as the seat of the second sons of the Mortimer line, made itself a fortress against their premonitions of scandalous downfall and savoured their wildest dissipations.

It dozed fitfully, grasping down into the rich, red earth and biding its time until the rightful heir should come again. And as it slept, it dreamed of ages past, of revengers and rebels, scions sent to command foreign shores, the ledgers from ships laden with tea and sugar, schemes for advancement and industry. It dreamed too of darker things still to come, when the old ways would be no more and all that had once been familiar would be set ablaze. Time meant little to a house such as that, a trifle for the outside world. One of their number would return to resume possession, that alone was certain. Someone was coming soon.

1

The grandfather clock in the hallway chimed first, and then was answered by chimes throughout the house. Spiders laboured in the corners of the high ceilings, and beetles burrowed further into the beams and furniture. A mouse ran out into the centre of the Western drawing room and looked around, finding itself free to roam a little longer. A spray of dust fell in the attic and the door to the end bedroom upstairs swung open just a crack.

Like a starved dog which only forgoes its owner's flesh in the hope of better treats to come, Holt House waited patiently.

The First Day

'What harm could a week in the country possibly do?' Theo asked Jan, and took a swig from the white wine he'd brought furtively to her house, along with many bags of shopping and a holdall that looked far too small for the trip.

The curtains were drawn, but waiting in the panicky warmth of that long May morning, Jan could not help listening out for a fateful knock at the door of her parents' flat. What if one of the passing policemen who had been instructed to break up anything that might resemble fun, no matter how socially distanced, had seen Theo come in? It was too late to cancel now. The plan had been made, Jan had been cooking and freezing meals for the house party for the last two weeks and the others were already on their way. Kara lived in the same postcode as Jan, she couldn't be far off now.

'What if someone gets sick? What if we all get sick?' She reached into Theo's tobacco tin as it rested between them on the kitchen table, for once not caring about the indignity of being a perpetual scraper of small favours as his fortunes had risen and hers remained unimpressive.

'Then we just stay at Holt House a bit longer and wait it out until no one's contagious any more; we're all young and strong. Young enough, anyway.'

'You don't know that.'

'If it posed a serious threat to people our age, they wouldn't be discussing sending us back to work first. They

3

don't care about us and they never will, unless it's to make an example of someone.'

'That's the other thing I'm afraid of.'

'I've got it all worked out. Don't worry about it.' Theo was a past master at getting away with things Jan could never even dream of and had been ever since she'd first laid eyes on him at a house party during their university years, laughing and jostling with people from her course whom she was too shy to approach and who she later found out were largely his coke customers. He'd called her over, poured out two shots of neat gin and within half an hour they were discussing their favourite novels, which at the time were *Nightwood* (her) and *Les Liaisons Dangereuses* (him). They talked until 10 a.m. the next day and had kept up an edgy if sporadic text correspondence ever since, punctuated by world-obliterating benders with Ursie and Kara at his old place and later on at Jan's whenever her parents were away.

Jan lit her rollie and said, 'I don't know, this still seems like a really bad idea.' Opening the back window to let out some smoke, she looked up at the cloudless sky. Jan felt youth and summer speeding away from her ever faster, with little to show for them but an empty bed and a pile of unfinished marking. If she had to listen to her own uninterrupted thoughts much longer, who knew what would become of her?

'Nadya misses you. She needs this too.'

Jan relented. It had been far too long, and in a house of that size, certain opportunities were bound to present themselves. She thought she could smell Nadya's perfume on his shirt, fought the craving to lean forward to drink it in.

Her phone buzzed – Kara and Ursie were waiting outside for them. It was time. Kara kept the engine running while Theo helped her stuff all the freezer bags and boxes of spices into the car as quickly as possible. Ursie lay low in the back, texting rapidly. Jan only met Ursie's gaze as she slid awkwardly into the back seat beside her, unacknowledged.

They were not far into the journey but already they were consumed by the question of which places they would occupy. A few nights before, Nadya had given Jan instructions over the phone as to who should have which room, saying she knew Theo wouldn't care even if it was his house. As Jan wracked her brains trying to remember the correct configurations, her friends made up for lost bickering time.

'You said there's a lake, Theo. I want a room with a nice view,' Kara said, as she drove.

'The lake is hidden by the trees, so unless you're proposing we chop them all down that may be rather difficult.'

'I want a good one, though.' Kara threw a lock of tangled brown hair over her shoulder and swiped the lemonade out of Theo's hands to take a swig. Her long golden thighs glistened in loose denim shorts, faded mandala tattoo beaded with sweat.

'Can't we just wait till we get there?' Theo said.

She took a swerve into the wrong lane, the geriatric Audi spluttering towards a stall. 'Whoops!' Giggling at her own threat, Kara then steered them briskly onto Marylebone Road, past Madame Tussauds, the pavement outside empty for once of tourists thronging to catch a glimpse of its waxen horrors.

Which room was it? It was named after a colour, but the rising heat clouded Jan's brain. Nadya was going to be furious if she got it wrong and it wasn't like she could say why she needed it.

'The blue room! Please may I have the blue room?' she blurted out.

'Certainly, how do you—'

Kara braked abruptly again, having just realised she was about to blow right through a red light.

'Come on, Kara, keep it together! I thought we wanted a low-profile getaway?' Ursie was almost levitating with anxiety, as the jiggling of her leg increased to tarantella pace. Jan cursed herself for her lack of subtlety, and hoped for Ursie to distract Theo from asking further questions.

'How many rooms *are* there?' Ursie asked, still scrolling with one hand and applying lip balm with the other, as they waited pointlessly at the traffic lights on an Edgware Road emptier than Jan had ever seen it, even in the hours before dawn when the four of them had all been in halls together.

Jan scoured the pavement for signs of police presence and found none. Her parents had begged her to abandon the plan and said all her friends could stay over while they were still stuck in Italy with her aunt, but they didn't know what Holt House could offer her. They couldn't fathom the depths of her loneliness, how badly she needed the others to stick around longer than they would crammed into two bedrooms in North London.

Theo said, 'I can't remember off the top of my head, it's been a while, but there are enough for everyone who wants to have one of their own.'

Ursie yanked a braid out from under the seatbelt and sat up a bit straighter. 'It's not a castle, is it? What else have you not told us? Are there servants?'

Theo drawled from the front seat, 'It's not a castle, calm down. Your Twitter followers aren't going to come after you with pitchforks because you dared to enjoy yourself a bit.'

'I'm not posting anything about this, are you joking? I live off commissions, I don't need to get called out for being a mass murderer. I'm only just getting by on illustrating as it is.'

Kara asked, 'I thought we'd all agreed this would be kind of secret anyway? It's not like anyone needs to know exactly where we're going. If we stay for two weeks I think that's long enough to count as quarantine.' She flicked her window down and lit a cigarette, blowing a cloud of smoke out over the asphalt as they sped off once more.

Ursie said, 'Just no drama, please. I'm tired and overworked and I don't want to have a stressful trip. I'm really trusting you guys here.'

'Let's see how things go with the timings,' Theo said. 'It's been very busy. Business is booming, everyone's so bored. But it could be fun to stay even longer.'

Jan asked, 'You brought the stuff, didn't you?'

'Stuff? I have enough party favours in my bag to make an entire postcode see pink elephants for a week. Nadya is going to flip when she sees.'

Kara asked, 'Where is Nadya, anyway? I thought she was coming down with us?'

Ursie coughed and wound down her own window, sinking so low into the seat that her ears were almost level with the line of the door.

Theo said, 'Her lawyers messed something up, she'll join us later if she can.'

'Ah, right, hope she can manage it!' Kara said, in a tone that would have sounded fake to Jan even if she had not known that Nadya made a point of forgetting to invite Kara whenever it was even vaguely plausible for her to have done so. 'I'm sure she'll make them fix it for her pronto.'

Jan asked no questions about Nadya's absence, instead allowing disappointment to blow through her like a cold wind. She rolled her shirtsleeves down and stared out at nothing, as the conversation turned to gossip about who'd had to resort to sleeping with their flatmates or had been furloughed indefinitely or placed under house arrest by concerned parents. Outside, the sun glared down, while the hubbub from Regent's Park carried to them on the air, still filled with people despite all the admonitions of the constabulary.

After two months of picking over the faults in her lopsided thesis on curses in the legendary sagas while unable to access the university library and mixing increasingly stiff martinis to take for twilight walks along the canal, Jan was ready to go anywhere with her friends if it meant some respite from the enforced solitude. She didn't know what it would be like when they got there. Everyone had become so fractious, so difficult with all the years of sniping and competition impeding their once easy conversations. She hadn't seen Kara or Ursie since December, the silence accreting as months went by, thickening as lockdown was declared and then prolonged. But it was a relief just to be with other people again and, sometimes, adding alcohol did help.

The fear and uncertainty of those first few weeks, when everything had suddenly just stopped, had given way to a boredom that overlaid and muffled the terror that still coursed beneath its unshiftable surface. Estimations of normality's return were continually delayed as the toll of dead and dying climbed ever upwards. Neighbours who had been deliberate strangers now greeted each other with affability before returning indoors to twitch their curtains and make phone calls reporting untoward behaviour. Clusters of white flowers began blooming on street corners for lack of pollution. Rage surged online at anyone who dared to wring even a scrap of pleasure from this new era of isolation. Couples who did not live together were prohibited from visiting one another, park benches were taped off lest people ventured to sit on them, and police roamed the streets looking for citizens to apprehend for not having sufficient excuse to be away from home.

Jan had anticipated whiling away the latter part of her twenties with women, wine and literature before proposals, pregnancies and plans for house purchases outside of London tore through her social circle. This was the end of the world as she knew it and she still lived at home. Everyone around her had responded by leapfrogging a decade forward into a comfortable near-middle age while she stayed twenty-seven. Her own clock had been stopped for years, the passage of time perceptible only by the faint lines massing on her still-smooth forehead and the worsening of her hangovers as she crept towards thirty.

Jan had asked Theo, 'Can't we go to your parents' place instead? It's less of a schlep. I looked at Holt House online and it's right by the moors, so I bet it'll be full of damp. It

9

doesn't make sense for us to go all the way there; the drive will take hours.'

Theo asked, 'What's a schlep? I wish you wouldn't speak in Yiddish all the time. It's rather affected, don't you think?' Then he checkmated her. 'My parents don't want too many people around right now. They're both in their seventies and their health is fragile, so I can't blame them. Anyway, there isn't room.'

Now, the morning was already so warm the air felt swampy with pollen and dread. The car pulled over by a grand but strikingly empty hotel just before the Westway and Jan was silently shocked to see Luke lolloping towards the car, battered duffel bag in one hand, and lit joint in the other. Theo had not mentioned him to her as a possible invitee. He'd been bouncing around flat shares; staying on sofas or subletting for a month here and there and his current housemates wanted him gone. Jan had been under the impression that Kara wanted him gone as well, but apparently on the day of their departure the two of them were on good terms once again and so Nadya's space in the car had been allotted to him. Jan was unsure why Kara and Luke needed to be furnished with another chance for reconciliation at everyone else's expense.

Soon, all the friends were crammed together, hurtling out of London as fast as the old car could carry them, heavy with dreams of pleasant diversion, or at least a reduction in the intensity of their boredom. The smell of stale tobacco smoke filled Jan's mouth and nose, making her jab at the window button to let in some fresh air.

'My back's so cramped, can't I go in the front?' Luke reached out groggily to stroke a bare portion of Kara's neck and she swatted him away.

10

'Just wait till we get past the M25. You're going to attract attention, all of you in the back, so stay down and keep quiet.'

'Why don't you swap with Theo and come sit with me?' Luke was unrelenting despite the early hour and apparently oblivious to any irritation directed his way.

'Actually, I'd rather stay at the wheel, thanks. Theo's not insured to drive this car, even if he weren't probably already secretly off his tits.'

'He's only had a psycholytic dose of shrooms and one line of speed to pep him up for the journey,' Ursie said. 'You're being very unfair.'

The car erupted in laughter, and Theo denied nothing. Just for a moment, Jan allowed herself to forget that she was vibrating with nerves, not only afraid of being stopped by the police but also that they might prevail and make it to Holt House after all.

After scrabbling about on the floor, she had found the folder at last and was gripping it so tightly her palms were sticking to the plastic like two fat frogs.

Ursie asked, 'What's that?'

'A letter Theo got from the trustees confirming we're doing work on restoring the house.'

'You want us to work on your home? For free? I don't think so.'

Jan tried and failed to wrench the exasperation from her face before turning to Ursie. 'Obviously not. It's our alibi in case anyone asks what several unrelated adults are doing in a car together.' She gestured to the spirit level that was in danger of poking her in the eye. 'I also made him bring the tools in the back.'

Theo sighed and said, 'This is all so unnecessary. You and Nads got worked up over nothing and cooked this up

11

together. No one cares. We're not who they're looking to harass.'

Ursie said, 'Speak for yourself. What am I supposedly doing?'

'As an artistic specialist, you will be restoring the painted ceiling in the dining room,' Jan replied.

Ursie smiled and said, 'Just call me Michelangelo.'

Five hours later, irritable and exhausted from sitting crammed into the car all day, the friends barrelled down a series of lushly forested lanes where the trees curved overhead and the track grew bumpy. The heat continued bearing down on the roof of the Audi as they neared their destination, heavy and eager like the tongue of a great hungry beast, the elderly air con doing little to alleviate matters. The car bristled with bags of bottles packed tight among the summer clothes and stray limbs.

Theo's memory had guided them this far but gave out in the maze of near-identical, tree-shrouded lanes as they drew closer to Holt House. Kara jabbed at her phone, suckered to the windshield: 'It's not working properly.' The little blue dot wandered and jittered uselessly over the screen. It had already tried to lead them into a ditch and onto the outskirts of a small dairy farm. Now the map had frozen and would not reload, forcing Kara to pull over by a stretch of verge and get out to hold her phone up ineffectually to the sky like an offering. Jan stepped out with her to roll a cigarette and take stock of their surroundings, hoping to catch sight of some clue that might help to guide them the last part of the way. Over a low fence at the edge of a field, she saw two dark lumps on posts and found herself wandering towards them, trying to puzzle out what they could be.

Nailed to the wooden staves were a pair of dead black crows, feathers burnished green and blue, far larger than she'd expected. One seemed to stir a little, as if still alive. Jan drew closer, puzzled, then stepped back repulsed as a thin stream of squirming maggots coursed out of a wound in its neck.

She swallowed the vomit rising in her throat and turned around; she wanted to get as far from the grisly spectacle as she could. Hoping to shield the others from what she'd just seen, she spotted, between the overgrown trees on the other side of the road, a white-painted sign to somewhere called Hallow Hill.

'Not far now,' Theo said.

Jan slid her unlit cigarette back into the waist-bag her parents had insisted she start wearing after her phone had once again been stolen in a bar.

'Can't we ask someone?' Kara said.

'No,' Theo said flatly. 'The locals have never liked us, and it would be a terrible idea to draw attention to ourselves now.'

'How come you don't know the way? I thought you'd been coming here forever?'

'Not that often – it's such a pain to get to, I haven't been since last year.'

Luke said, 'I'm getting out as well, I'm dying for a piss.' He began clambering out of the car, looming over Ursie instead of using the door that opened out onto the verge. He had already managed to spill half a can of Sprite onto the backseat floor and Jan watched Ursie close her eyes with distaste as he manoeuvred his sticky boots over her knees. Luke ignored a conveniently placed bush and stood by the side of the road, letting out a steady stream as Kara giggled at him to put it away and Ursie retched. Ablutions concluded, they all piled back in the car and drove on in the direction the sign had indicated.

Jan said, 'I swear we've passed that hedge before.'

Theo said wearily, 'It was probably last time we went down this road and then turned back. Just go on a little further, Kara . . .'

They rounded another corner and a gap between the trees revealed itself, giving way to a gravel path shrouded in a dark canopy that curved round and away from the road.

'There we are!' Theo said, pointing at the words 'Holt House' carved into one pillar low by a pair of great wrought-iron gates, patterned with fruits, flowers and curling vines – and sealed fast against all incomers. On either side, the walls rose high and forbidding, topped with a row of iron spikes to keep out any prospective intruders.

Luke said, 'Oh, I see it now – why is it hidden?'

Theo said, 'It's not hidden, it's just not obvious if you don't know how to look. Can't you help, Jan? The foot-well's full of Kara's gut-rot prosecco.'

Jan wrestled with the car door and tumbled out, especially clumsy after hours of stasis. She walked over to the spot Theo described, a low-lying black rock behind which a little red metal combination safe lay half-buried in the dark earth and tried a couple of different combinations without success.

Ursie craned her neck out of the window. 'So, are you going to let us in?'

Theo said, 'Hang on, I remember this now, it's the date my great-uncle began work on the house; try zero six zero eight three eight.'

Luke asked, 'Thirty-eight? I thought it was much older than that?'

'There's always been a house here, but everyone adds something.'

Ursie asked, 'What did your parents do to it?'

'It was never theirs, Harold left it directly to me.'

'I can't believe you've had this place all along and are only just inviting us now,' Luke griped. 'We could have had so many cool parties.'

The box opened and Jan pulled from inside it a ring of keys of different sizes, selecting a large iron one with a curlicued head to match the trelliswork of the gate, but fitting it to the lock, she found that she could only turn it a little of the way before encountering a blockage she could not force past.

'It's so rusty I'm worried about snapping it in half.'

She pulled it out to peer into the dark mechanism, but saw no obstruction. A breeze above stirred the trees, blowing leaves through the gate to skitter around Jan's feet.

'Hurry up! I'm hungry. Let us in!' Kara shouted from the car.

Jan put her shoulder to the great gates and pushed, then jammed the key back. She twisted it a little further this time, but still could not make a full rotation. There was no way it would let her in.

'Maybe there's a knack to it I'm not getting?'

She felt the group's impatient gaze raking her face. It was unbearable when they were disappointed in her. Theo rooted around to secure the bottles then strode over to see

15

what the matter was. The path had absorbed so much sun she felt the hot gravel dust stirring around her ankles, though she was cold beneath the summer sky. Over the wall, the woods returned to stillness, not one trill of birdsong escaped. The key was icy in her hand as she offered it up for Theo to try once more. Jan felt herself overtaken by a wild, irrational reluctance to go any further. She suddenly hoped it could not be opened, that they would have to turn around and drive back through the night to London. Somehow their separate states of loneliness were preferable to whatever lay beyond.

The aged bolts groaned loudly and she heard something slide back as Theo turned the key. The gate swung away from them creaking with age and disuse. He hopped back into the car before it rolled past the threshold and stopped a little way inside, with Jan struggling to catch up. Perhaps it was the heat of the day, but just making it back to the others felt like wading underwater, each step was heavier than the last and she was panting by the time she regained her seat inside. She saw she'd left the gates unlocked behind them, though Theo appeared not to care.

'What are all these dark trees doing here?' Luke had wound down his window and was peering out at the copper beeches that lined the drive.

'Great-Uncle Harold was fond of them. An odd decision to put them all together like this, I know.'

The trees towered above, branches thick with dark red leaves, casting a venous shade over the sunbleached path and crowded together so thickly Jan could scarce make out anything beyond them.

'Wait, what's that?' Luke was peering out and pointing. 'I just saw something moving between the trees.'

The car jerked as Kara stalled it and Theo groaned loudly. Jan snapped her neck to look in the direction of Luke's finger, but all she saw was light playing over far-away trunks, winking and occasionally dazzling her.

Theo snapped, 'That's the sun reflecting off the lake. Don't scare Kara while she's driving. You can't see the water from here because it's quite low in summer.'

'That wasn't what I saw. I know what water looks like. Jesus, I grew up in Upstate New York.'

Theo said, 'Must have been a deer. I can't wait to get in the lake and cool off.'

'We could brew up some mushroom tea first,' Luke suggested. 'Did you bring any honey for the laaaarder, Gianetta?'

'Don't call me that, you know I hate it.'

A silence descended over the car and in it Jan could almost swear she heard Kara's teeth digging into the wet flesh of her tongue. Ursie was focused studiously on her phone, despite the lack of reliable signal for several miles.

'You need to help me unpack our things, Luke. You can go later.' Kara made a left turn and pulled them out of the woods to face the house.

Jan couldn't believe Kara had not only insisted on bringing him along, but was now annoyed with him already. Of course he wasn't going to help; at this point in their lives that was an absurd expectation.

'Let me out first, my legs are cramping so badly.' Ursie scrabbled at the door handle and leaped free.

The house stretched three storeys high and curled round into a wing at either end, clad in pale grey stone freckled with moss. The façade was divided in the middle by a set of double doors rising to a gentle ogee and, along with the hooded dormer windows of the attic, this gave Holt House the air of a slight smile, like that of a rich widow. Blue-purple wisteria draped from every lintel of the tall, narrow windows in jewelled ropes that swung with the faint breeze, while the earthy scent of early summer moved over the fields to caress the group with searching fingers as they stood, waiting to enter. The house sat poised and ready to receive them.

Kara said, 'So this is really yours, then?' Her voice a mixture of admiration and disapproval.

'My days, it's so big!' Ursie snapped a photo. 'You kept this very quiet all through uni.'

Jan said, 'Sorry, was he supposed to send you floorplans through the post?'

Ursie had made similar comments on being invited for dinner at the Rubins', though Jan's tall and narrow family home had little to compare with this.

Ursie faltered before replying, 'Don't be like that, it's just that you could fit my parents' flat in one of the downstairs rooms.'

'Their flat is lovely,' Theo said in mollifying tones. 'And a lot warmer in the winter.'

Jan asked, 'And we're the only ones here?'

'Who else were you expecting?' Theo opened the front door for her and turned back to get his bag.

'Hurry up, guys, the strawberries are going mushy. Ursie, you brought the Pimm's, right?' Kara had reversed the car as far under a tree as it would go. She was already out and tapping her foot.

Burdened down with bags of clothes and food, Jan shuffled over the threshold. Golden sun dropped through a
vaulted window and pooled on the black and white floor,
thick with dust, which rose a little, disturbed by the rush
of warm air and her footsteps on the tiles. It was cool
inside the house, and quiet after the clamour of their
arrival. A great wooden staircase dominated the hall,
curving up to the next floor and dividing the two wings,
the doors to which gaped ajar on either side. Nadya's
vague descriptions of weekends away with Theo ceded to
the sudden reality of Holt House, and its atmosphere of
watchful repose overwhelmed her. The maidens on horseback in the light-bitten tapestry gazed down on her with
serene disdain. Feeling shabby in her old leggings and an
oversized man's shirt, Jan tried to dispel the worry that she
had arrived somewhere for which her scant stores of
confidence and charm would not be sufficient.

Her friends stood behind her in the doorway, silent for
a moment, and then like a high wave breaking, surged
forth all talking at once and darting off in every direction
to explore. Kara spotted an old white fan on castors in
one of the open sitting rooms and went to slump in front
of it, while Theo wandered determinedly away from the
others to finally light the joint he'd been nursing for
hours, drawing vociferous protests from Ursie every time
he'd tried to spark it on the motorway. Curious, Jan
followed him along a dark panelled corridor and out onto
the terrace at the back of the house. The lawn stretched
all the way to the treeline and was overgrown with buttercups and clover, but large pink daisies and blue hollyhocks
still filled the flowerbeds and the effect was one of abundance rather than outright ruin.

19

As she was retracing her steps to retrieve the long-suffering strawberries from the boot of the car and hurry back towards the kitchen, Ursie swept past her, one pink trainer spilling out of her cloth bag and bouncing across the hall floor as she set her things down.

'It doesn't smell half so bad as I thought it would. Do you reckon someone left a window open?'

The air should have been heavy with dust and neglect, but all Jan could perceive was a touch of mustiness which could just as easily have been emanating from the waxy old Barbours hanging in one corner of the hall.

'I don't know. I don't remember if Theo said he had a housekeeper.'

'So, he does have servants.'

'I suspect they'd prefer to be called staff.'

Ursie snorted and headed right, skirting the curve of the staircase and into a drawing room filled with dingy oil paintings and porcelain ware to throw herself dramatically on the chaise longue and say with her most sardonic dead-pan, 'Welcome, to the lady of the house!'

A cloud of dust erupted from the cushions and reduced them both to coughs and giggles. The chaise longue creaked and sagged a little lower, so Jan put out a hand to help Ursie up and off it, but she shook her head and closed her eyes.

Jan had spent days constructing an elaborate menu of frozen delights after she'd agreed to help Theo with planning the trip. He'd affectionately described Nadya as 'domestically challenged' and flattered Jan's culinary abilities in such a way that made it difficult to refuse him. She knew she should be racing to rescue the cool boxes and decant their rapidly thawing contents into the fridge, but a different sort of urgency overtook her and she grabbed a piece of paper, Sellotape and a pen from the hall table. She scurried up the stairs to start staking out the rooms Nadya had chosen for them back in London. She'd been instructed by Nadya to reserve the rose-wallpapered bedroom at the back of the house, with its own bathroom and view of the orchard, for her and Theo – it had been his whenever he had visited his great-uncle as a child. Peeking inside, she saw a child's wooden sword resting in the corner of the room, as if it had just been set down. Closing the door swiftly, Jan went to stick her own name on the room at the other end of the corridor, the door of which opened out onto the landing. Jan fretted that not doing labels for the others would look odd – Theo had asked for her help with organising things after all, and the squabble in the car was a useful pretext. She quickly fixed Ursie's name next door to Nadya and Theo's, assigning her a pleasant, pink-painted room, with a little oval mirror and a view down into the inner courtyard where yellow roses sprawled and climbed around the base of the raised pond. Jan decided that if it had been up to her, this was the room she would have chosen for herself.

Crossing the cavernous open landing and giving the dusty pillows on the pistachio-coloured ottoman that stretched across it a quick thump, she scrawled Kara's name and stuck it to the door opposite her own, then selected the bedroom next to that as Luke's in case they broke up again later the same evening. The rest of the Eastern wing housed a large, damp bathroom and then another bedroom right at the end, the door to which was already slightly open. She paused outside, holding the pen and deliberating over whether she had made the right choices. A

21

floorboard creaked behind her and sudden anxiety spiked through her chest, making Jan turn back, newly abashed at her Nadya-sanctioned presumption.

Luke and Theo were hot on her heels. They drew level with Jan on the landing, peering down the two corridors on either side of the staircase.

Luke said, 'I knew it was big, but I didn't realise how quaint it would be. How long can we stay?'

Theo asked, 'Do you have other plans?'

He laughed. 'I don't think the Duke's Head is reopening any time soon, so no I don't. Plus, I'm pretty sure they know I've been helping myself to the liquor, everybody does it, but the new manager's such an asshole. She said if I did it again, I'd be fired.' Then, noticing, 'Why is my name on that door?'

'Because that one's yours,' Jan said. 'Nadya picked rooms for everyone.'

'What about one with a better view?' he asked, and looked over to the end of the Eastern corridor where the door to the end bedroom was now gaping slightly further open.

Theo said, 'That one's very draughty, it's the oldest bedroom in the house. I'd sleep in the one Nads picked out if I were you.'

'It can't be that bad. Better for the summer heat, surely? Looks like no one's claimed it yet.'

'The other one has a much more comfortable bed.'

'How do you know? You said you haven't been here in ages.'

He was walking closer to the door, which had a white porcelain handle patterned with little orange chrysanthemums.

'I don't want you going in there, Luke. I don't want anyone in there.'

He raised both hands as if Theo were attacking him. 'Alright, alright, it's your house. Chill out.' He stepped smartly into the room marked with his name and closed the door with what wasn't quite a slam.

Theo pulled the door to the end bedroom fully closed, then strode over to one of the enormous Chinese ornamental urns that flanked the landing staircase and lugged it in front of the end bedroom door, asking Jan to hold the lid so it wouldn't fall and shatter on the parquet.

'Let him calm down by himself instead of riling him up, alright?' Theo told her with a slight smile before he wandered back downstairs.

In Jan's bedroom, a midnight-blue embroidered quilt lay draped over the velvet futon at the foot of the bed. Family photographs in heavy gilt frames stood clustered on the gleaming mahogany chest of drawers: a couple who were presumably Theo's parents on their wedding day; distant relatives in sepia tones; his grandfather at Eton; and one of Theo himself, aged about eight, locks of brown hair falling into his glittering eyes, standing proudly in front of the same iron gates they had just passed through.

Theo had once told her that Harold had been immensely strict about proper behaviour and, on the rare occasions they met during Theo's childhood, Harold had always grilled him about whether he loved his country then bellowed at him to stand up straight.

'He always saw himself in me, I'm not sure why. I think it just made him happy to imagine it wouldn't all end with him. I had to take his name as a condition of the will.'

'Was he a confirmed bachelor, then?'

'Not in the way you're implying. Mum said he spent his whole life hung up on someone who died during the Blitz, a family friend I think. Would explain why he was so bloody miserable, anyway.'

Jan tried to imagine the weight of being handed something the size of Holt House to take care of, then opening it up to their friends. She shuddered, then went to lie on the bare bed. She gazed up at the ceiling, searching for and finding the little white-painted ring to the trapdoor that Nadya had advised her would be concealed within the ornate moulding. Good.

She was still furious with Luke. His new aura of calm collectedness fooled none of them, except perhaps Kara on a good day. And she had an inkling he'd been helping himself to more than just the top-shelf whisky at his old job – she'd seen the Duke's Head serving takeaway pints when she passed it a couple of weeks ago, which meant they must have taken him off the schedule. She languidly contemplated advising Theo to count the silverware but decided against it – she knew he wouldn't bother and Luke had never been much good at distinguishing what was of genuine value. He'd once asked her if an ostentatiously large diamanté necklace she'd worn clubbing was made with real diamonds and seemed surprised when she hadn't answered in the affirmative.

She opened the window and immediately the scent of the wisteria drifted in, loose green tendrils trailing into the bay window seat. She sat and lit her cigarette, ashing against the windowsill and looking out at the ragged flowerbeds at the side of the house, which teamed with purple, pink and white foxgloves. The rich colours reminded her of a jewellery box carelessly upended over the earth. Her mother had once told her that planning a garden was like writing a piece of music, one had to be acutely aware of harmonious elements like form and colour, provide counterpoints to enliven any potential monotony and maintain a steadfast grip on timing. The garden was a little overgrown but the artfulness of the composition had persisted.

It was strange to imagine all of this as Theo's in perpetuity. He had confided in her that his grandfather had been a baronet, a decorated war hero and a great favourite at the baccarat tables in Monte Carlo, where he had managed to lose several cars, most of his estate and the good favour of his wife, at least according to Theo. As his grandfather had sired only daughters, the title had passed down another line and his parents' lease on the dower house had run out when he was still at school. If it hadn't been for Harold dying without issue, Theo's inheritance would have consisted solely of his forebear's charm and appetite for risk.

She turned back into the room, but she could tell that sleeping in here was going to depress her, the vast double bed making her even more aware than usual of the absence of anyone by her side at night. She listened to her friends filling Holt House, the creak of iron-framed windows being pushed open far beyond their latches, the thump of the boiler stirring into action as Theo reminded himself how to start it. Jan lay back on the firm down of the bed and contemplated an afternoon nap but found her head so full of plans involving shortcrust pastry that sleep remained stubbornly out of reach. She quite distinctly heard footsteps walking up the stairs. There was no carpet on the treads of the main staircase, and Jan listened as someone ascended to the second floor, paused on the threadbare carpet on the landing then walked past Jan's door towards Ursie's room. She dragged herself off the bed and went back to the door to put her head out and explain about the urn, but the landing was empty.

The footsteps hadn't sounded like Ursie's, but Jan decided it must have been her, probably now sitting in the pink bedroom and feeling out of sorts. Jan wished she knew what to say that would set her at ease, but she worried even the effort of communication would grate. Where grandeur made Jan stand up straight and try to blend in, Ursie often shied away, fearing she would never be welcome. Still, if she had come, surely it meant she wanted to be here? Jan and Ursie had seen less and less of one another over the years as their lives diverged and Jan did not trust herself to call her back, to ask for closeness once again without confessing more than she meant to. The little burning flame of hope that never quite died, no matter how Jan tried to smother it, sprung up again. She wouldn't knock; she would go downstairs without pestering and let Ursie emerge when she felt ready.

Jan made her way to the terrace at the back of the house, where Theo was sitting with his arm tight around Kara, passing a bottle of the prosecco rapidly back and forth between them. They slid apart as she approached.

'Is that cold?'

'Barely. And it's not getting any colder.' Theo passed it to her by the neck for a swig.

'Fantastic.'

Kara said, 'I went to the freezer looking for ice cubes and it was completely empty except for some old peas.'

'I thought you hadn't been here for a year?' Jan asked Theo.

'Oh, I suppose I must have left the electrical things plugged in this whole time I've been away.'

Jan suddenly surmised that the practical questions of Holt House's existence had simply not occurred to him. For almost anyone else, the running of this house would be the focus of all their efforts, but instead it remained at the edges of Theo's conversation, the setting for a handful of childhood anecdotes but apparently never a matter of real concern. It would simply always be there, in one state or another. He was now spread out over the wooden bench, shoeless and tipsy, already in full possession of the space.

Jan asked, 'Do you not have someone local who keeps watch over this place?'

'My great-uncle never had much to do with the village. He kept to himself, really, apart from a gardener I think, though he must be ancient by now. I was wondering whether he still comes by occasionally to stop things from getting too out of hand, but I don't really know for sure. I saw a number on the notepad in the hall with "Adam" written on it.'

Kara said, 'He's not going to come here, is he?' She now sat at the other end of the bench; knees drawn demurely together.

'I should hope not.'

Jan said, 'I imagine he has other things on his mind at the moment. I'm surprised you didn't ask him to turn off the fuse box, though.'

Theo looked sceptically back at the house as if totting up the figures in his head, then shrugged. As someone of impeccable lineage he could be as blunt about saving or squandering money as he liked, in a way that would have had some whispering 'Shylock' under their breath at Jan.

'Such an eccentric family,' Kara said. 'Must be where you get it from.'

'What about all those drumming circles and astral projection seminars your parents dragged you off to?'

'That's just classic hippy stuff. You've met my parents and you'd never know they were into that if I hadn't told you. We don't sit around letting a big old house fall to pieces while we forget about it.'

'It's not good for somewhere to sit empty,' Jan said. 'You're lucky you don't have squatters.'

Theo let out a little chuckle. 'Somehow I find that hard to imagine.'

She took up the bottle from between them and drank a long glug of the prosecco before going to investigate the kitchen. Beyond a few gungy, unidentifiable jars and a small arsenal of decades-old appliances, all was in relative order.

She opened the fridge to see how much space they had. The reek was so sour and richly putrefactory she involuntarily took a step back. The shelves were dripping with a rank, frothy ooze and in the centre sat a hunk of rotten flesh, greenish and limp with flies erupting from what had once been its eye sockets. Fur clung to its sides in damp strips while the fridge hummed with the renewed effort of cooling the foul contents. She slammed the door shut and pulled the kitchen apart in search of rubber gloves to dispose of the half-liquidised carcass of what had once been a rabbit. Wrapping a tea towel she'd pulled from a drawer around her nose and mouth, she bagged the rancid mess, feeling it writhing slightly through two layers of plastic and then raced over to the back door to throw the thing outside before she could set to frantically cleaning the fridge with as much bleach as she could muster.

Theo came in and, after hearing what she'd found, took the bag further away to some outside bins Jan hadn't found yet, before returning with the cool box and calmly washing his hands.

She asked him, 'What the hell was that?'

'Well, I didn't buy it, I'm not much of a butcher.'

'Then where did it come from? It can't exactly have just wandered in.'

He pondered for a moment before saying, 'The gardener must have been culling them and forgot to come back for the meat. I'd ask if I can do anything else to help, but you look like you have it under control.'

'Well, I'm always at home in a kitchen,' she said weakly, stomach still turning at the stench, but remembering the bargain they'd struck – as many free pills and powders as Jan could stuff down her over the course of their stay, in return for her help with the practicalities of the trip. It would get easier from here, she told herself; that had to be the worst of it. She took out the glass shelves gingerly to wash them off in the sink and sponged bleach carefully along the rubber seal of the door, making sure to get into every crevice and kill any remaining trace of filth.

As he watched her, Theo said, 'It's such a relief to get away, being stuck at home alone was becoming really tiresome.'

'You weren't alone, you live with Nadya.'

He began to reach under her to scoop unidentifiable packages out of the cool box, emptying them into the freezer at last. 'You know what I mean. She was freaking out about us getting sick and never wanted to have anyone over, even though we're both young and healthy. Well, fairly young in my case.'

Theo was five years older than both of them, having crested his thirties a few years ago. In the time Jan had known him his brow had creased permanently from scrunching it when in deep consideration and his skin had lost some of the fullness of youth. The age difference had barely been perceptible when they had all first met. Theo had seemed excitingly raffish then, after flunking out of two degrees elsewhere because they bored him. Jan had never before known someone to switch paths with such understated casualness, such a lack of guilt at disappointing others' expectations. In his previous lives he had been a drystone walling apprentice, a Classicist, a Thai silk suit salesman, a banking intern and a sailing instructor before turning to the study of Biochemistry and petty drug dealing. A bit less of the latter, these days, since Nadya had put her foot down, though he still bought in bulk and supplied to their friends. Jan could scarcely imagine what his suitcase for this trip might contain. She had never had a friend before him in whom she felt so free to confide her most hedonistic longings and there find encouragement rather than condemnation. Nadya was a great many things, but the word 'friend' no longer fit the way it used to. It had been Nadya who wrote out emo lyrics on Jan's school folders in Tipp-Ex, who had been her first choice of companion for gallery trips, who had held her hair back after they partied too hard as teenagers, but now their pastimes were of another order.

Jan returned to exploring the ground floor. The kitchen led into a wood-panelled dining room; the ceiling richly but rather crudely painted with a scene of Hephaestus falling from Olympus. She watched through the french windows as a lone Kara continued her attack on the prosecco. Pushing through to the narrow corridor and along to the door at the end, she found herself back in the main hall.

Ursie asked, 'What do you think's in this one, then?'

She stood by the entrance, bathed in light streaming in from outside, tying her loose braids into a ponytail. She'd dug a pair of green leather slippers out from somewhere and was wearing them over bright white Adidas socks.

She pushed open the door opposite Jan to reveal a pair of gold damask divans, low dark wood tables inlaid with mother of pearl, a selection of broken statues of dancing Indian goddesses and several large hanging prints of mountains and flowers. In a bracket high on the wall, an antique dagger lay gleaming in its engraved silver scabbard and Jan wondered in passing whether it was still sharp.

'The Eastern drawing room, I suppose?' Jan surmised from the décor.

'As opposed to the Western one? How very Orientalist.' Ursie picked up a small chalcedony snuffbox sitting on the mantel and unscrewed the top, finding nothing inside it.

'True.' Jan sighed and drew a finger along a red lacquer side table. 'It's also very dusty.'

Ursie said, 'I'm still feeling kind of intimidated by it all, to be honest. This is a long way from Hackney.'

'I'm so happy you came, though.'

'It's not that, it's just places like this . . . I feel like I'm being watched.'

31

'I know.' Jan tried another tack. 'Nadya said there was a library, shall we try and find it?'

'There's a library? Like in *Beauty and the Beast*? Next you'll be telling me Theo has a troupe of singing teapots as well.'

Ursie trailed Jan around the foot of the big balustraded staircase and down the narrow corridor of the Eastern wing. The library contained three entire walls of books, a big desk looking out over the flowerbeds on that side of the house and a sliding ladder of the sort Jan would have found irresistible as a child. A grandly labelled marble bust of Boccaccio observed the room from a high alcove built into the shelves. Ursie began poring over the spines and taking books down at random.

A large illuminated manuscript sat open on a lectern, unshielded from the light. Jan wiped her hands on her leggings to remove any grease from the journey and leafed through it carefully, coming across a page that depicted a hauberked Templar Knight with white tunic and crimson cross, wielding his sword and sat astride a black warhorse. Peering more closely, she realised it was a thirteenth-century chronicle that seemed to be describing the bloody deeds of one Godfrey de Mortimer, already historic at the time of writing. This was presumably an ancestor of Theo's, though Jan's Anglo-Norman was extremely rusty as she'd been focused on other languages during her PhD.

She thought she recognised the word 'Judeu' and was about to take a closer look at the crabbed hand when Ursie exclaimed, 'This is the full Loeb collection! These are so old! And this!' She eased out a leather-bound book of Homeric hymns and began leafing through it.

Jan asked, 'Still haven't had enough, hmm?'

'After finals I couldn't look at so much as an upsilon for a month without wanting to puke, but these are so stunning I almost want to dive back in. Maybe that would be a good lockdown project.'

'I never learned Greek, sadly, only Latin. Our feeble female brains apparently couldn't take being taught it at the same time as the boys.'

Ursie said consolingly, 'You still could, you know. I think my old tutor runs an online summer school.'

'Perhaps another time. I'm having enough trouble translating all the passages for my thesis. Someone should have told me they actually expect you to understand the Old English cases for postgrad. I hate it. I really don't know if I can finish.'

Jan paused to rap the desk just in case.

'Oh, shut up, you'll pass with like no corrections. You're so lucky you could keep studying. I had to take on more shifts at the bar right after undergrad. I couldn't go back to Mum and Dad's, they had to put Great-Aunty Marie in my old room and I couldn't afford to rent near them any more. What do you think's in this?'

Ursie had wandered over to an old leather trunk in the corner of the room, firmly sealed with a built-in lock, which she jiggled.

'No idea,' said Jan. Ursie straightened up and cast a disapproving eye around the room. 'Doesn't any of this bother you? All this stuff, this whole house, was just handed to Theo by his grandparents, for doing absolutely nothing.'

'I think it was his great-uncle's, actually.'

'Whatever. I didn't get anything from my grandparents except some old photos and their wedding rings. Did you?'

'My great-grandfather made silverware,' Jan said quietly, 'so that's been handed down.'

'Yeah, you were quite literally born with a silver spoon in your mouth.'

'And that was all he left us. When he fled the pogroms the only thing he had was a talent for metalwork. He was basically a refugee.'

'When was that?'

'The eighteen-nineties.'

'My grandparents came to London from Dominica in the sixties with one suitcase. It took them a decade to bring my mum and aunt over,' Ursie reminded her. She looked away, out of the window, then asked, 'Do you know where Luke's got to?'

'I think I saw him wandering away into the woods earlier.'

'Cool, so I expect we'll never see him again then.'

'I don't know.' Jan shrugged. 'He's probably gone to do lines off a log and talk to the soil.'

They left the library and Ursie tutted as Jan wrestled with the latch to the door that would allow them onto the terrace at the back of the house.

'Why don't you go sit with the others and I'll fix us some drinks,' Jan offered. 'G&Ts okay?'

Ursie pulled out a Marlboro Gold and lit it. 'I'll keep watch for Luke in case he comes back. Hear what the soil has to say for itself.'

Jan kept her smile pasted on as she hurried towards the kitchen. Rummaging for clean glasses, she began chewing over all the things she could not say to Ursie, who had often made comments about Jan's background but had seldom before seemed to take issue with Theo's ancestry or Nadya's money. Nor for that matter, Kara's claims to working-class identity, despite having attended what was effectively a highly selective grammar school and her parents owning a four-storey Edwardian house. Pouring water into the ice cube mould for later and cutting cucumbers to chuck into the highball glasses, Jan briefly contemplated whether the questions Ursie had asked her over the years were because the crimes required to build and maintain somewhere like Holt House were so long obscured as to be almost invisible or because as a racial other herself, perhaps Jan's own circumstances felt more easily within reach. Ursie was certainly no stranger to being treated as a curiosity by the sheltered and the socially inept; either way, her directness was infinitely preferable to others' unstated assumptions.

Outside on the terrace, she found Kara smoking a rollie and sneaking glances at Luke in a disgruntled fashion.

'So which room did Jan put you in then?' Kara asked Theo.

Before he could reply, Jan jumped in. 'It was Nadya's idea, so people don't get lost at night.'

Kara said, 'I keep forgetting you've never been here. You seem right at home.'

Theo said, 'She's read a lot of novels. And I'm in the rose room.'

'*The rose room*.' Ursie imitated him and laughed. 'Is that the master bedroom? You going to try and put me in the maid's room then?'

Jan said, 'I thought you'd already found the one she picked for you?'

'You lot made such a fuss in the car about the rooms.'
Ursie sighed, 'I thought I should leave well alone. Me and
Kara were wandering about downstairs trying to get a
signal.'

'You didn't come upstairs?' Jan decided the footsteps
must have been Theo checking on something.

'I found a corner in that room with the pool table
where if you stand on the armchair, you can get two bars
for a bit. Wanted to tell my mum we arrived safely. Doesn't
seem to be there any more now, though.'

'That's a billiards table,' Theo said. 'And the walls are so
thick they block everything out. I was down here trying
too, but it hasn't changed.'

'Oh great.' Spurning the iceless G&T, Ursie had another
go at the open wine bottle.

'You have Wi-Fi, right?' Luke asked Theo.

'I'm afraid not, Harold never wanted it in the house.'

'Awesome! This is such a good opportunity.'

Kara raised an eyebrow at him. 'What do you mean?
You'll go mad without the internet. I've seen you backhand a PlayStation for being too slow.'

'I was high and it was a piece of shit, it wasn't letting
me save my FIFA settings. But seriously, this is great, I'm
going to get so much done. Why have you never invited
me down here before? We could have done a creative
retreat!'

Luke had designs of being a great actor, stymied only
by his aversion to work and his attraction to powders.

Ursie, who actually lived by her art most months,
smiled thinly.

'The timing was never quite right,' Theo said. 'How's
your thesis going, by the way, Jan?'

36

There were a few secrets Jan still kept from Theo and one of those was the curious stasis that had crept over her in the last months when it came to her PhD. She had never asked for an extension before in her life, and the fact she had done so now sent her into paroxysms of shame. That Theo must know how she'd judged him for his unfinished degrees made her self-recriminations even more painful.

'It's going. What does everyone feel like having for supper?'

'It's far too early for that, isn't it? Let's just have some more wine.'

'By the time I've finished cooking you'll be ravenous.'

She watched Theo upend the bottle into his and Luke's glasses.

Kara said, 'I know you have complicated menu plans, Jan, but I'm really not that hungry. Can't we throw something simple together?'

She and Ursie headed towards the kitchen with Jan trailing after them. When she entered, the two had already begun shaking salad out of bags into a large bowl.

'Is your mum going to be okay if you can't get through to her?' Jan asked and began flinging open cupboard doors at random, turning up a series of wooden salad tongs, an ornate but tarnished silver goblet and a tin of tuna marked 'best before 2005'.

'She'll be fine,' Ursie said. 'Keeps saying this whole Covid disaster proves I should have gone into the law.'

'Are *you* going to be okay?' She watched Ursie's face for the shadow. 'Don't answer if you don't feel like getting into it.'

'It's alright. I've had a few decent commissions recently and I've been doing online workshops. I thought it was all going to dry up, but it seems like some institutions unlocked special funding. Mostly I just feel bad I'm not doing more to help people. There was a mutual aid group for my area but it just turned into my BoBo gentrifier neighbours curtain-twitching about suspicious homeless people.'

'Sounds tedious.' With a twinge Jan recalled the flyers shoved through her door which she had ignored in favour of gazing helplessly at her computer screen, her ideas still failing to crystallise into anything resembling a coherent argument as the time ticked away.

'What's BoBo?' Kara asked.

'Bourgeois Bohemian.'

'Oh.' After a long pause, Kara continued, 'I'm still on furlough, thank god. They were trying to get us to work anyway, but my friend Marieke threatened to report them and they stopped.'

Kara had been let go from several jobs for, as far as Jan could tell, turning up late and spending most of her time crying in the loos. She now did admin for a firm of under-writers three days a week and spent the other four break-ing up with Luke. Her parents had given up on banning him from the house at this point and had begun offering her money to go abroad and 'experience new things', none of which had stuck.

'That's so illegal, good for her. I really hope if one thing comes out of this it's waking middle-class people up to the fact that businesses and landlords are not on their side.' Ursie dug a large ceramic salad bowl triumphantly out from under the sink and brushed off a thick veil of dust.

Jan said, 'It's a disaster that this had to happen now, when social services and the NHS have been stripped to the bone.'

'Well, we've had ten years of the Tories and people still keep voting for them,' Kara said. 'They don't want change; they just want more of the same. I never thought we'd be here right now, after last year. It could all have been so different. Imagine what a Labour government could have done for people in this situation.'

Kara had spent all of the previous winter flyering for Labour and avoiding Jan's eyes when they met at parties. It was only after the election had been decisively lost that she began texting her directly again, asking to hang out.

Jan tuned out the subsequent eulogising, cutting the cucumber very fine and shredding the rotisserie chicken into a bowl. Kara wandered away upstairs halfway through, insisting she still needed a shower, while Ursie chopped the tomatoes next to her in silence.

Jan's fears during the Corbyn era had grown and solidified with each new revelation: the East London mural, filled with obscene imagery intended to resemble people like her; the hijacking of Holocaust memorial events with other unconnected tragedies; the foreword praising a 1902 book that attributed the European banking system to a conspiracy of Jews; the strenuous denial from those whom she had once trusted that any of this should signify. And after all of that, staring down at the ballot paper, she still could not live with choosing any other party and hadn't.

Ursie had been sanguine at the time, pointing out that the party had a long history of mistreating its Black members as well and that any useful work was best completed outside of a party-political framework, but Kara and others in Jan's circle had remained steadfastly convinced that all claims of antisemitism were merely scaremongering with no shred of veracity. At the same time, Kara had been growing ever thinner and more miserable as the situation with Luke worsened, giving up on applying for less drudgerous work in favour of videoing herself singing off-key with her guitar and picking vicious fights with strangers at parties. It was hard to confront Kara when her anger made Jan frightened not only on her own behalf but on Kara's too. And so, after it was all over, they had drawn close once again, without discussing what had gone before.

A piercing shriek came from upstairs and for one brief moment Jan found herself hoping for disaster before realising they would all be obliged to deal with it.

Hurrying up the back stairs, she noted a framed engraving of a flowering blackthorn branch hanging at the top of the staircase. Something flickered across the glass very fast and Jan barely had time to dismiss this as a reflected ray of evening sun before a cold blast of air almost knocked her bodily back downstairs. Like a wall of icy wind, it blinded her with its intensity. So freezing cold it chafed her skin and froze her bones to splinters, solid as a gut punch. She wheezed and reeled, clutching for the banister, not daring to look back behind her. A damp and bedraggled Kara now stood at the top of the back staircase, wrapped only in a small green towel, lip wobbling. They all rushed to investigate the source of her screams.

'Was there a spider? I'll kill it for you, Kara,' Theo said, reaching down to start taking off his shoe.

'There's something wrong with the bath.'

'What sort of something?' Jan asked. 'I don't understand.'

'I don't know . . . I was topping it off with more hot water and blood started coming out of the tap. It stinks.'

'You're dripping everywhere, why don't you go to your room and dry yourself off before you get a chill?'

'Don't believe me? Fine. See for yourself.' She pushed the door open and exclaimed, 'Look, it's disgusting!'

Jan and Theo peered in. Smeared all over the bottom of the tub was a layer of reddish-orange dirt, which stained the water pink and reeked of iron.

Luke peered in over the tops of their shoulders.

'What IS that? Is that period blood?'

Jan groaned. 'Of course it's not. Why would Kara be scared of her own period, you idiot? There must be a dead bird stuck in the pipes or something. I saw a hawk earlier today, maybe it dropped its prey in there.'

Theo pulled Kara in for a hug and said, 'I'm pretty sure it's rust. You'll be fine, you just had a bit of shock.' And then to Jan, 'It'll go away if we run the taps for half an hour, used to happen in the dower house pretty often before the new plumbing got put in.'

Kara, still quivering, asked, 'That's really it? Are you sure?'

'Hundred per cent. Sorry your bath got spoiled.'

Still hugging her, he snapped over the top of Kara's head at Luke, who had ever so innocently begun to wander down the corridor of the West wing, 'Don't even think about going in my room to help yourself.'

Luke raised his hands in protest. 'I wasn't doing anything. I was on my way to the kitchen to get a beer.'

Jan swallowed the bile welling up from her empty stomach and turned away briefly before she said, 'Dinner's almost ready. I can take the food outside if we're eating there?'

Ursie, who had been waiting at the foot of the stairs with an expression of martyred patience, drifted out onto the terrace, rolling a cigarette. Jan went back down to the kitchen and poured herself a generous glass of Sancerre. She watched it cast a pale golden gleam over her hand as she turned it and tried to breathe normally again. She drizzled vinaigrette over the salad before taking it through the garden doors and round to the terrace. Theo's worn copy of *À Rebours* lay on the table, covered in loose tobacco after being used as a rolling surface. It was still warm outside and the sun was just beginning to set, swathes of pink and orange trailing through the cool violet of the evening sky. The forest sat dark on its haunches around them, exhaling steadily. Little rustles and sighs could be heard softly issuing from its edge, far away across the lawn.

She picked up a rusty metal bell with a wooden handle that had been left behind a stone eagle on the terrace and rang it.

Ursie, sat at the other end of the outside table, lifted her head from her phone.

'Is there a fire?'

'Nope, just dinner.'

'Do you need a hand? I thought we were done, sorry.'

'Nearly! Can you nip into the dining room for me and grab the yellow citronella candles I saw sitting out, plus some of those net pyramid things to keep the gnats off the food?'

Jan watched her hurrying inside and added, 'Please can you bring out some plates for us as well? The plain set if possible.'

'We can't be trusted with the fine china, then?'

'It's more that I don't trust myself with it, you know what a klutz I am.'

'Sure.'

'What's this? It looks great, Jan.' Luke emerged from round the side of the house, clutching a bottle of bourbon he'd liberated from the shopping bags and of which he had already managed to drink a third by himself. He sat at the head of the table, rolling another cigarette.

'Before you light that, can you get us some more wine please? There are two bottles in the fridge.'

Jan saw Theo hunched in the doorway peering and jabbing at his phone, shirtfront full of cutlery.

'Any news of Nadya?' she asked, keeping her voice as casual as she knew how.

'No idea. It's pretty much bricked. I'll try again upstairs later.'

She turned back to the table and set about lighting the candles Ursie had brought out, marking the perimeter of the terrace with them in tall glass holders so no one would fall off it in the dark, before realising she hadn't taken off her apron. On the way back to deposit it in the kitchen, she crossed paths with Kara, seemingly recovered after the bath experience, and humming a jaunty little tune to herself that Jan couldn't quite place.

'I'll just bring the chicken and then we'll be good to go.'

Kara asked, 'Everyone's outside, aren't they?'

'I reckon so.'

Kara went past her to peer out of the french windows. 'Yep, that's all of us; I keep thinking we've forgotten someone.'

Jan had the same strange sensation, as if a guest had been forgotten and at any moment would take their place at the table alongside the five of them, but she put it down to her anticipation of Nadya's arrival, tension building in her stomach, each nerve exquisitely sensitised while the familiar sensation of holy terror gathered in her chest. Her skin prickled, hairs rising on her arms and she felt her cheeks flush with a mixture of longing and fear that after all this time apart, Nadya's desires might not be so easily sated.

She made plates for everyone while Ursie returned to the table and began pouring the wine. The heat had lessened a little and a breeze came over the lawn from the lake. Kara shivered for a moment and Luke pulled her close to kiss the side of her long white neck.

Theo said, 'It's such a clear night, look at the stars,' and pointed upwards, where the first bright specks were beginning to emerge in the dusk. A faint wash of pink played over the lower part of the sky, but above that the darkness was prevailing. 'We might even see a meteor shower later in the week if it stays like this.' Theo knew these sorts of things, though Jan had no idea how. He moved through the world as if everything were well known to him already, his fate as readily predicted and encompassed as his past.

The friends were silent for a moment while they ate, amiably passing second and third bottles of wine back and

44

forth to drown out the day's arduous travel while a selection of house music played from Theo's phone over the powder blue speakers someone had rested on a low stone pillar at the edge of the terrace. All of them sat shielded by the forest and the high stone walls from the chaos of the world beyond, where the old certainties were crumbling one by one. With bellies filled, their thoughts grew hazy, their pulses slowed and the house creaked a little in the cooling air, shrugging itself into a more comfortable stance, ready to welcome them in and hold them close.

Ursie asked, 'What are we doing tomorrow? Are we staying here all day?'

'What did you want to do? It's not like anything will be open.' Theo was stacking the empty plates ready to take to the kitchen.

'I don't know, I've never been here before but I'm getting restless already, I want to go out. Can we go on a walk or something? Somewhere we won't get hassle.'

Theo said, 'We could go to the moors, there are wild ponies and a stream. We said we'd do a picnic, right, Jan?'

Jan, mentally reshuffling the meal plans she'd spent two weeks working on, made a noise of assent.

'Wild ponies? Sign me up!' Kara was upright and animated again, shrugging off Luke's arm to refill her glass.

'They're very sweet but quite bitey. Don't put your fingers in their mouths.'

Kara asked incredulously, 'We can feed them?'

Jan said, 'I can go see if we have any sugar lumps in the pantry.'

'Speaking of sugar and other associated powders,' Theo said, 'what do you say we go indoors in a bit?'

'That's my boy! Let's get the party started.' Luke was already draining his glass while Ursie's face wore an expression of barely disguised scepticism. Jan looked over to Kara to see how she had received Luke's rallying cry and, noting no especial resistance, gave up on intervening directly.

'There's no need for that,' Theo said to Kara, taking the cutlery she had been gathering out of her hands. He fished an origami-folded envelope of blue-patterned paper out of his chinos and handed it to Kara. 'I'll do it. Why don't you two go rack up?'

Jan drifted into the dining room after Kara, who was already pulling a stack of books off a low shelf in the corner to examine them in hopes of finding a good surface. The stack comprised of a selection of faded modern classics and one book that seemed to have nothing written on its plain, dark spine, which piqued Jan's curiosity. Before she could examine it, Theo came in after them and took the books out of Kara's hands. He said, 'Not in here, please, the games room is much better for that sort of thing. Open the french windows so the smoke doesn't linger.'

When they looked puzzled, he said, 'It's in the other wing, all the way to the end.' He began gathering up the books to replace them as Jan trailed out after Kara towards the main hall and round to the other wing.

Newly installed in the games room, Kara divided the mound into five lines, then shaved off the bottom edge of each one in a different direction. She quickly divvied that up into two baby bumps, saying under her breath, 'Just for us. I'm so glad we all made it!'

'Thank you for driving us. I didn't realise Luke would be coming too. Is he okay?'

'Oh yeah, he's in a much better place now; the first month of lockdown was hard on both of us but I think he's really learned to pace himself at last.'

Jan quickly absorbed her spoils and sat back as Kara continued raking the five big lines back and forth to neaten them. When the others came in from the terrace, she passed round the note to each of them. Adding the second fat line set off a prodigious drip at the back of her throat that made Jan's bile rise again for a moment.

Ursie began telling a story about going up to her step-uncle's place in Yorkshire to see her aunt and watching fat, dazed grouse bashing into the windows.

'He made it big in the City years ago, doesn't have much to say for himself but he treats Auntie Michele right and that place is lush. The grouse are so funny, they just wander up to the glass and try to walk through.'

'They're literally arses with a brain stem. I swear the ones near us just see cars in the road and decide to run in front of them,' Theo said.

Ursie turned to him. 'Have you ever been shooting?'

'I went once with a friend from school. Didn't like it, it was so wasteful. His little brother was a creep as well, he kept bragging about trying to fist a girl in a jacuzzi.'

Jan said, 'Oh dear god, that is so dangerous if you do it wrong.'

Ursie blenched. 'There's a right way to do it? I thought it was just a porn thing?'

'There's a right way to do most things,' Jan continued. 'Think about it, if it can push a baby out, then a hand shouldn't be too difficult.'

'I guess not, but wow. No thank you.'

Jan remembered too late that Ursie could be oddly squeamish about sex in conversation, though her art was often provocative and daring.

Jan said, 'Hang on, I know who you mean, the little brother was in my year at Tothill. Jack Oldcastle? A jet ski fell on him after finals?'

'Oh yes, that was him,' Theo said.

'He was the worst; he bullied several guys I knew back into the closet. He called me a fat Jewish dyke and then ran away when I tried to kick him in the shins.'

'Did you see the picture of his arm after the jet ski?'

'Afraid so. It was so mangled. He kept posting pictures of it complaining about having to wank with his left hand and then bragging about getting pity hand jobs for life. Nadya hated him as well, ask her.'

Ursie wiped the table with her thumb, dabbed the coke residue onto her gums and sighed heavily at the prospect of school stories, before reaching for the nitrous cracker and a blue balloon.

'We haven't done too badly,' Theo said, now pouring prosecco into a set of crystal coupes he'd brought from the dining room and determinedly steering the conversation away from public school reprobates they had once known and loathed. 'I think that was a pretty smooth getaway, considering all the scare stories of police cars waiting on the road. No need for your dossier, Jan.'

'I'd still rather have had it than not.'

'Never knowingly underprepared.' He patted her shoulder with one big flat hand, and Jan resented herself for finding that soothing in its easy masculinity.

'Depends who you ask. My parents were convinced it would be a disaster.'

Luke asked, 'They didn't want you to go?'

'No, they kept saying we'd get arrested or turn up here to find the house broken into. It happens to empty houses in Italy a lot, according to my mother. Everyone is stuck living with their parents, so teenagers use them for assignations.'

'I want to have sex in an abandoned Italian villa,' Ursie said. 'Sounds romantic. It's been ages for me, I've probably got cobwebs down there. And now it's even more impossible with the lockdown.'

Jan felt Theo's eyes flicking over her face, waiting for some reaction to the comment, but she held her expression steady.

'I don't think that anything's stopping people, if they really want to,' Jan said, and she watched Ursie drain her glass.

The night stretched and blurred into a long ladder of powder and gossip and prosecco, each step of their descent punctuated by the hissing of balloons and pauses for the frantic, ecstatic inhalation that always made Jan's teeth feel oddly fuzzy while plunging her into brief moments of subaquatic calm. Theo measured out many more rounds of lines, drinks were refilled, at one point Ursie and Kara went out for a night walk and came back excitedly saying they'd seen a badger through the trees but couldn't get a proper look, though when Theo asked them about it their description sounded too large to be quite right.

Ursie asked, 'Are your parents still in Italy?'

'Yes, they're staying with my aunt; it was only meant to be for a week, but they've got pretty comfortable out there. They keep sending me pictures of themselves hiking up the mountainside.'

Kara said, 'That seems like a bad idea, what if they get sick out there?'

'I told them that and they said I was being alarmist.'

'I wonder where you get that from,' Luke sniggered to himself. Registering Kara's hand on his leg, he added, 'I think we're going to turn in.'

Jan had no skill for knowing when to call it a night – she and Theo were always the last ones standing – but when she saw Kara and Luke getting ready to retire upstairs, she forced herself to follow them. All the lights were still on and she was suddenly too exhausted to go round switching some off. She checked her phone and found nothing, one small bar flickering in and out of existence.

Ascending the stairs, Jan heard a swell of laughter from a few rooms away and felt a sudden clannish upsurging of joy. They were almost all here, her favourites, maddening in their own ways but present and persistently alive. It could all be mended, conversations long delayed could finally be had, gently and with renewed understanding in the face of all this death and chaos. Perhaps the fearful boredom of the last few months could finally be turned to good use.

She paused by the big bay window overlooking the front steps to gaze out on the moonlit drive through one opened section. The front lawn rolled down to meet the forest at its edge and surge away into the darkness. The stream that fed the flowerbeds and burst up through the fountain in the garden coursed softly past on its meandering way, cool susurrations rising on the breeze to reach Jan's ear before dispersing bodiless into the night.

She pushed back the door to her room, ready to fall down into the sweet embrace of sleep, if it would take her tonight. It so often didn't, confining her to hours of waiting in the dark, worrying and wishing she could finally make her thoughts and limbs lie still. The wide bed was lumpy and furrowed by generations of Mortimer sleep, but it was time to try again. She sloughed the dirt of the day from her face and went to lie beneath the covers. As she tried to settle herself, too tired to even fetch a glass of water for the bedside table, she noticed every framed picture atop the chest of drawers had turned to face the wall.

The Second Day

Jan rose early to find the bedclothes wrapped around her face and body as tightly as a winding sheet. She fought halfway out of the sweaty casing and flopped mermaid-like onto the floor. After a few minutes of disoriented, uncaffeinated writhing, she strode over to yank open the chest of drawers and swept all the framed pictures out of sight.

Theo and his ideas of comedy were sometimes rather slipshod and she needed to take this one on the chin. Too many cokey nights together had led her to confide some of her worst fears about her place in the world and, not sharing them, perhaps he would believe them fit material for practical jokes. She was not unwelcome here, that was the comedown talking.

After rinsing off the worst of the night's struggles she reached into her suitcase, finding nothing but shorts and summer dresses she felt too ashen-faced to wear. She pulled open the chest of drawers again. Rows of primly folded shirts sat enshrined in tissue paper, wafting camphor into the room. She took out a blue and white striped one and, finding it mercifully soft, slid it over her head. At five ten and big boned in a way that made it nearly impossible for her to be considered thin, Jan was often happier in men's clothes. Increasingly, the effort required by femininity no longer felt worthwhile, its prizes intended always for someone else and its creative pleasures dwarfed by the fear of her failures inviting further judgement.

As yet uncertain of her destination, Jan was about to set off down the main staircase, but just as she turned, she found her gaze drawn straight to the end of the Eastern corridor. The urn was standing against the wall, rather than the door, as innocently as a valet stepping aside to let his master pass. The white-painted door hung slightly open, a gentle light illuminating the room beyond. Knowing how annoyed Theo would be at the incursion, Jan reversed her course up the stairs and stomped over to the door, cursing Luke under her breath as she went. He and Kara had been given separate rooms so they didn't have to interact if they were fighting, and that should have been plenty. But clearly, he was determined to make sure he really had been offered the best of what was there. Jan had learned unwillingly that often when you told men calmly that a thing was not intended for them, they would whine and dispute and rage until they prevailed. Or, if you withstood their entreaties, the moment your guard was down they'd take it anyway, even if they hadn't wanted it all that much to begin with. And if they were halfway intelligent they could make it seem like something you'd colluded in. All this she had been taught, reluctantly, at Tothill and it had cost her dearly in time spent slapping away gropes and circumnavigating double entendres. She could still hardly bear for Theo to hug her hello or pass out next to her, lest he suddenly betray her too, and so Luke's easy, sneaky sense of entitlement to whatever took his fancy made her almost wild with rage.

She paused on the threshold of the end bedroom, and as she did a little gust of air swept past, scented faintly but unmistakably with the rancid sweetness of decay. Her nasal passages were much abused by the traffic of recent years, but the smell hung on the air for a moment, seeping into her lungs as she unwillingly inhaled. Jan averted her eyes and pulled the door to smartly, then scrabbled to push the urn back into place before turning on her heel and hurrying downstairs.

Jan slammed the coffee pot around the kitchen, noticing as she did so that the old silver goblet stood empty at one edge of the sideboard, stem flaring gracefully at the bottom and sides engraved with some obscure design Jan barely glanced at. She shoved it back in the cupboard as she hunted for the sugar. The kitchen was somehow both poky, with the handle of every cabinet jutting out to catch her hips and a small side table which always seemed to be underfoot, and yet also too spacious, with a long passage leading to a pantry that should have had a window but didn't. The room got very little light and even in the full glory of the May morning it was damp and cold.

Looking out over the kitchen garden, scrubbing away the whorls of chicken fat and vinaigrette shellacked onto the plates while the four-person coffee pot she'd brought whistled gently on the stove, Jan felt herself swell with pride that her first instinct had been to attend to the day's preparations. Perhaps this was her rightful place, taking care of the others before they even knew what it was they needed. Outside the sweet peas ran wild, while filmy white butterflies flitted in and out between the leaves. Two bushy bay trees framed the gap in the hedge that led to the wider garden beyond. She could happily stay here and watch the seasons turning, her hands growing knobbly with age and use, the years counted out in stews and puddings . . .

The coffee began to bubble over and noisily broke her from her reverie – what on earth had she been thinking? She was an academic, not Theo's hired help.

Ursie wandered in, rubbing the grit from her eyes. 'I still feel like I haven't slept right in months. Shame though, it's a good hard mattress, none of that Tempur nonsense.' She fetched down a cup and stood waiting for the coffee to brew. 'Do you have any condensed milk?'

'I can look. Are you planning a baking project?'

'Nah, it's an island thing. Makes the coffee really sweet. You've never seen me drink it like that before?'

'I've only ever seen you drink it black with sugar. I bet it's delicious though.'

'If you find some, maybe I'll even make chaudeau – it's not the season but you should try it at least once.' Ursie cast an eye over the dishes as Jan dried them with a raggedy white towel. 'We all need a bit of sweetness round here. Don't know why I agreed to come to this place.'

Jan slapped down the towel. 'Nobody forced you to come. You could have stayed at home in your flat.'

'Theo told me it would be so cosy, with all of us together again, but the atmosphere is exactly how I imagined it.'

'And what did you imagine?'

'I don't know, just . . . I woke up this morning and my stuff was everywhere, thrown about all over the floor.'

'How fucked up did you get last night?'

'I can't go as hard as I used to. I went to bed just after you did. Do you not get what I'm saying? It wasn't *me* who made the mess.'

There was no door to the pantry and the blind corner created the feeling that anyone might be listening just out of sight among the old cereal packets and bags of mouldering rice.

'Do you think we could have this conversation outside?' Jan asked her. 'It's a bit cramped in here.'

Ursie looked at the empty space around them doubtfully and shrugged. Then they settled themselves on the terrace table, wooden chairs still fresh with the morning dew.

'What is it?'

Jan leaned in, lips almost grazing Ursie's ear. 'You do know Luke has stolen before, don't you?'

She pulled away sharply. 'You can't just say stuff like that, Jan, that's really serious. Anyway, I checked my wallet and my money's still there. Someone came into my room and threw everything around like confetti just because.'

'I was next door and I didn't hear anything, you must have been drunker than you thought.'

'It wasn't me! Someone decided to mess with me just because they can. Maybe Luke, maybe one of the others. You know how Theo likes to play pranks on people sometimes. Remember the time he nearly gave that girl who was on acid a breakdown? He convinced everyone to hide when she came back from the toilet and put houseplants where they'd been sitting. This place lends itself to that kind of foolishness.'

Hearing her own worries from another mouth made them suddenly absurd to Jan; they were both fretting over nothing.

She said, 'So the problem is the atmosphere?'

'It's creepy. All the granny furniture and the ugly masks on the walls and the draughts. Sorry, but that's my opinion.'

'I think those masks are from Papua New Guinea. And I happen to like the furniture.'

'I don't know, it's just not right him having a big empty house all to himself,' Ursie insisted. 'Several families could live here, farm the land as a collective or something. Theo should sell this place; buy somewhere he'd actually live.'

'You want him to sell the house his family have lived in for generations because you feel the vibe is off?'

'I don't know; it might help, he seems kind of stuck. Frankly, you all do and it worries me. He's living off Nadya, and you and Kara won't move out of your parents' places. You both have jobs, sort of, but he doesn't.'

'I really don't think that's fair, Ursie.'

'Just giving you a little bit of advice. Nothing wrong with that. Don't you want to be independent? You're lucky you can live at home, but surely it's not a forever thing?'

'Of course I want to move out but I'm saving up. You know that perfectly well.'

'None of you are poor.' Ursie gestured around at the rolling lawn and the mullioned windows rising above them. 'Take some control of your life.' Ursie stared at her dead on, perfectly symmetrical face golden-hued in the morning sunshine.

'What do you think I've been trying to do? I'm finishing my PhD.'

'You don't have to be living at home for that. You'd be so much happier standing on your own two feet instead of trapped with your parents, all resenting one another. It's so dysfunctional.'

'It's not that simple.'

'Yes, it is. I left when I was eighteen, never moved back in. Lived in some shitty flat shares for the first few years, but I made it work. All you need's a little bit of determination.'

'Well good for you, Ursie. So, I should live somewhere with black mould and pay £850 a month in rent for a room when I don't have a proper job?'

'Plenty of high-paying jobs you could get if you looked, with your connections. I just don't see you working in academia; I hate to say it, but it's an exploitative dead end. Why do you think I didn't keep on with Classics? I don't earn loads but I get to be my own boss.'

'Where is this coming from? I haven't even finished my coffee.' Jan was trying not to cry because it always irritated Ursie, who thought crying was something you had control over and got angry at other people for doing it. She said it was manipulative.

Ursie put her arm around Jan, which ordinarily Jan would have enjoyed with a piercing stab of libidinous guilt. She continued, 'You're so talented, you could do anything and instead I see you doing nothing with your brain, except a degree I know you don't care about any more. When are you going to choose a path that actually touches other people's lives?'

Jan's brain filled with the unmatched halves of sentences, rejoinders too spiteful or too close to truths they had tacitly agreed never to voice. It clogged and jammed and then the reply that did emerge was so limp as to be even more humiliating than silence.

'I don't have anything to prove to you.'

She threw the grounds of her coffee onto the grass at the edge of the terrace and stalked off, scrabbling about in her waist-bag for the makings of a cigarette to roll as she went, her back turned stubbornly to the house. The forest was cool and quiet, the murmur of the stream blending with the birdsong and aggravating her more. She wished she still listened to the bands of her adolescence, to any music that still had the power to move her, but the time for discovery was past. Her life had been in stasis long before England and the world had ground abruptly to a halt.

But all she had to do was hang in there a little longer, finish what she had started before making any new decisions. She couldn't just throw almost a decade's study out like it was nothing. She'd loved it once, the cryptic lines of ancient poetry about mead halls and limbless kings, the sealskin manuscripts and the sense that lurking somewhere in the back rooms of time were answers to the mystery of how all the legends connected with each other. But now her life was coddling hungover undergraduates through the Dream of the Rood, each class more disaffected than the last, marking exam papers for pennies and applying for conferences in Aarhus and Tübingen she didn't even care to attend, just so she could say she'd been. She didn't want to teach; she just wanted to read and think and be left alone by the great machine of the world that insisted everything she did should somehow be shiny and monetisable. What did it matter to Ursie that Jan did not have a job per se? It wasn't as if they were together or ever could be; Ursie had made that plain enough.

Jan found herself in the kitchen garden, peering at dead tomato vines looping dryly around their wooden supports and clumps of what she thought might be wild strawberries spilling over into a patch full of bolted cabbages. If there was still a gardener, perhaps he had been using the space as his own allotment, a practice which could hardly be begrudged given Theo so rarely visited.

Without a real job or the prospect of finding one right now, moving was an entirely theoretical question anyway. Could she live here and look after the house for Theo? If she were able to get the internet connected, maybe she could find something remote that would pay just enough for her to eat and read the rest of the time. It wouldn't be so bad to retreat into a hermit's existence surrounded by the moors. But what would she do for sex? The old urge stirred unquenchable; she yearned for other bodies, the promise of losing herself in someone else for a while.

There had been that first night with Ursie, between their second and final years of university, when Jan had thrown a huge and raucous party at her parents' house. Coked up as they'd ever been, she and Ursie were fixing their makeup in the upstairs bathroom when Jan lifted her skirt to show off the riding-crop marks already purpling her thighs. Ursie had stroked them admiringly with one soft finger and later that night asked to sleep in Jan's room rather than making the trip back to Leyton. She had asked Jan to plait her braids, and then when that was done, she plaited Jan's hair and began to kiss her neck, first tentatively and then with more force when it became clear Jan liked what she was doing. Before her lips touched Jan's flesh, Jan had not even known of her desire for Ursie. It felt so forbidden as to be utterly imponderable, to want someone she had believed to be entirely straight. In that moment it struck her like a tornado, turning her inside out and rendering her unrecognisable to herself.

Ursie asked Jan to do those same things to her, to bruise her and fuck her as roughly as Jan liked being fucked, then said no more. The only words that passed between them were breaths of pleasure, the only interludes provoked by reaching desperately for water. The summer night stretched endlessly as she swam between the perfection of Ursie's thighs, caressed her lovely belly and drew her nails across the glory of her back.

She wouldn't even look at Jan the next morning. Jan had texted her asking if they could meet and talk. For a few brief hours, Jan had lived in happy anticipation of a future where she made Ursie's dinners, rubbed her shoulders at the end of long days and listened to the stories of her week – all triumphs and disasters would be theirs to share. Ursie read the message but didn't reply until a week later, saying she was busy. Jan lay bed crying for two days and then went out to a masked queer party where she had allowed anyone there to do anything they liked to her, because she was afraid if she didn't she would never be able to stand someone else's hands on her body ever again. To become nothing more than a body, to receive pain in a way that finally made her interior monologue go silent and the moment unfold like a blessing – this was the one place she felt free from both others' judgement and her own. She could not let Ursie take this from her and, the more meaningless she made the act itself, the further away from any sense of violation she hoped to travel.

Jan had been madly, coldly furious with herself for believing that something might come of it. She had looked up to Ursie ever since the first day of university when Ursie had come into the lecture hall just before the humanities library induction. She had nervously asked if it was okay for her to sit next to Jan and struck up a conversation where Jan had been silent and adrift. During their lunch outside in the square later that day, little details of how Ursie had spent her gap year doing an intensive life-drawing course and training with her parkour troupe began to trickle out and Jan realised she was in the presence of someone both talented and determined. It was Ursie who won an award for her paintings normally reserved for BA Art students, Ursie who was profiled by the campus magazine, Ursie who knew a huge number of different people in other years somehow, and Ursie who was invited by her tutor to adapt one of her third-year essays on Catullus into a conference paper. Once, before anything at all had happened, the two of them had been lying drunkenly on Ursie's bed at a house party and Jan had murmured something like, 'If I'm just a footnote in your biography, I think that would be alright, you know.' And from the corner of the room Theo had laughed and said, 'Why don't you two just finger each other already?'

Ursie, for her part, had never initiated a conversation about what had passed between them. They didn't see each other after that night until Theo's birthday several months later. Ursie had just come back from a trip to Helsinki with a delegation of young climate artist–activists and Jan was smoking outside with Theo, who said, 'I'll leave you to it,' and disappeared. All Ursie asked was 'Are we good?' and Jan had found it impossible to reply anything other than that they were, so as not to cause a scene and ruin Theo's party, ruin the whole of third year by making it awkward for everyone.

Her whole life had splintered into closed compartments of secrecy and rejection. She could move between each one, but was never fully understood in any of them. Always, some aspect remained unacceptable, unspeakable, and she must go elsewhere to attend to each of her defects in turn. To be the entirety of herself in one place, at one time, would mean admitting to unbearable loneliness.

Every so often they would find themselves in the bathroom or an unlocked bedroom at a house party, and Ursie would look at Jan a certain way and draw her in. And Jan would find herself gladly drowning in the majesty of Ursie's supple, shea-scented body, fingers clutching and curling inside the way she knew Ursie liked it. Longing for the sensation of Ursie's own corresponding hand around Jan's throat, which haunted her with every moment of its absence.

It had happened less and less often over the last few years, and in parallel to this Ursie had begun ignoring Jan's platonic requests to meet for coffee or the theatre, or saying she couldn't make it and then failing to reschedule.

Jan remained bound in a vortex of uncertainty as to whether the end of their dalliance was simply due to Ursie's career ascending to ever more illustrious heights, or a product of the discovery Ursie had made about Jan the first time they had touched with any real intent. Jan was, in fact, someone who could be used and discarded easily, and she would be grateful for any attention she received. Ursie was not the first of Jan's friends to learn this.

Jan had felt herself corroding from envy, and then from her subsequent self-disgust, as Ursie went on to make a great deal of her life from not all that much, while Jan had been handed almost everything but so far had done precious little with it. Before that night she had successfully alchemised her lust and resentment into pure admiration, but afterwards this proved impossible. The disappointment became so poisonous that Jan felt she could either transmute it into rage or die.

Jan wandered through the door of the kitchen garden and came out into an orchard where ripening apples thronged the trees and a first few cherries clustered on the bough. An old stone well divided the edge of the orchard from the forest line. To her right was a vast box hedge with a chain-link gate set into it, through which she could just about make out a tennis lawn. She unlatched the gate and walked out into the middle of the court where an old, half-collapsed ball sat abandoned. She hurled it at the fence, which groaned as the ball failed to bounce back, landing with a soggy thump at the far end. Instead of rescuing it, she ambled through another gate at the far end, coming out onto the sloping lawn behind the house. The table on the terrace was almost empty, except for a pink linen shirt of Theo's that had been draped over one of the garden chairs and was now sodden with dew. Someone else had left their baccy out overnight and there was a dead fly floating in one of the wine glasses.

Uphill, the fountain was stagnant; a moss-encrusted maiden scarcely covered by her robes was pouring a trickle from a near-empty urn. Jan stood on the dew-flecked lawn, looking down into the house. On the ground floor, to her left, she saw Ursie and Kara in the games room, horsing about with cues and preparing to play a game. In his bedroom, she spied Theo in profile, sitting on the edge of his bed, watching something on his phone. A jerky movement in the other wing caught her eye and she raised a hand to her brow, peering closer. Was that Luke in the end bedroom again? Abruptly, a curtain was drawn shut, blocking off her view.

Jan turned her gaze towards the green and golden acres of hillside, far beyond the high wall that separated Holt House from the rest of the world. In the distance, Hallow Hill rose high into the blue, the ancient black cairn on top just visible in the early morning mists. Culver Lake, the far bigger sister of the one at the foot of Holt House, gleamed grey-blue with reflected sky in the dip between them. According to Theo, the river ran underfoot and underfield all the way from Holt House down into the Culver before widening out to become a colossal reservoir where locals liked to fish and tourists went windsurfing. The buttery bright morning induced a craving for a second cigarette, though she was keenly aware this would make her sick as she'd been chaining the night before. Her legs were wobbling like she was trying to balance on rolling pins and she could still smell the ash in her hair.

A cuckoo called out and, without meaning to, Jan broke into a run. She needed to move, to wake herself from the glum torpor that had overtaken her. She raced around the back of the tennis court hedge, along the thin margin of grass that separated it from the woods, and then onto a faint trail almost grown over after the steady traffic of long-dead feet. Her lungs wheezed and for a moment she thought she tasted blood, but her thighs pistoned and

66

her feet found their rhythm soon enough on the over-grown path. For a moment she abandoned herself to the joy of her body working just as it should, her youth coming back to save her from long, wanton nights of snorting and shots. It was time to make contact with the earth, the turning world, uninterrupted for a while. Clumps of bluebells had persisted through the vernal warmth and wild garlic grew thick and pungent in dappled patches of light from above. The very last cowslips still dangled yellow and shy.

She reached the lake and made her way around it, feeling light, springing over the carpet of leaves and twigs towards the open bank on the far side. It was so inviting. She ripped off her clothes and kept running, feet slick with mud, until she was up to her waist and then she dove in. The water was cloudy from the silt she'd stirred up, little fishes flashing silver around her and the depths illu-mined peridot by the sun reaching in from above. Abused lungs bursting with saved breath, she swam down deep, shoulders scything her into the silky green cool. She kept her eyes half-open, stinging from the water. A thick black line scored her vision and she realised it must be the girder holding up the lido deck at the lake's centre. Carefully adjusting her course so as not to bash her head into its underside, she shot up towards the light, kicking her legs with the energy of one soon about to rest. As Jan neared the surface, she saw a pair of white cylinders protruding from the edge of the lido deck.

Swimming closer, the cylinders resolved into legs with feet. Very familiar looking little feet with high arches, finely formed toes and dark, red-painted nails. Then, with a sudden splash, a swirling column of bubbles appeared before her in the water, resolving into a figure. Two icy blue eyes met hers in the green gloom. Nadya reached out one hand to Jan's neck and grabbed it, before the other snaked around to join in, choking her. Almost out of air already, she tried not to panic as Nadya forced the remaining breath from her throat and gave a sly underwater smile. Jan kicked frantically to try and prevent herself sinking further down again, as Nadya clasped her slender legs around Jan's waist and locked her ankles, forcing Jan to exhale. Glistening bubbles streamed from her lips, heart thudding like a war-drum. Just as she began debating whether to try and fight Nadya off for real, the legs and hands let go. Nadya calmly grabbed Jan's wrist and towed her up towards the lido, placing one hand onto the grainy stone surface, so Jan could heave herself out and lie gasping for a moment at her feet.

Two thighs slick with lake water straddled her ribs and Nadya peered down, brushing a strand of hair from Jan's face. 'Did you miss me?'

She coughed and grinned. 'I usually rather enjoy being able to breathe, so not especially.'

'That isn't what you said last time. I distinctly remember begging.'

'I go back and forth on the matter.'

'Yes, you are very indecisive.' Nadya was easing off her sodden cotton shorts and underwear, lifting one leg and then the other, then replacing them so she sat directly on Jan's chest, skin against skin. Jan looked down quickly and then looked up to face her. The sun behind Nadya's head picked out each tendril of wet blonde hair, dipping it in bronze, her meticulously plucked eyebrows raised in mocking delight, wide pink mouth stretched wide. She leaned forward, one small hand pressing hard into each of Jan's wrists.

'I can't . . . When did you get here?'

'Shut up.' She straightened for a moment, moving herself the final distance to sit on Jan's face and the world went very quiet for a time. Nadya would take and take, and her relentless pursuit of new humiliations for Jan transformed them both, a determination surpassing even lust, pushing them into a symbiosis of mutual perversion. No matter how she might struggle against it, Jan had always been Nadya's creature and all her professed reluctance did was sweeten the eventual surrender. Jan needed only to feel the shadow of Nadya's hand to anticipate its sting and lean in a little closer.

Once Nadya had finished, Jan asked about the meeting that had delayed her arrival. Nadya had handed in her History of Art PhD thesis last year and then discovered right afterwards that her lawyers had misadvised her on what she needed to do in order to remain in the UK. British schools and universities had been happy to take her father's roubles, but obtaining a non-student visa had turned out to be another matter entirely. However, Jan only heard about these tribulations once all of them were at least three lines deep, so she was never entirely certain how much things had worsened or improved.

'I should have them shot; they have ruined my life.'

'If the lawyers made a stupid mistake, they're going to have to pay you a lot of money.'

Jan stretched out on the dry concrete, basking in the sunshine and Nadya's renewed attention.

'I don't need their money, I want them to fix it, and I don't think they can.' Nadya narrowed her nostrils before shuffling over to lay her head on Jan's stomach. Her long, wet hair tickled Jan's thighs and Jan had to resist the temptation to comb through it with her fingers.

'Can't you do another master's and buy yourself some more time? A second PhD if you have to?' Jan found it almost unimaginable that Nadya could not buy her way out of this one and the possibility of failure was too painful to contemplate seriously.

'In order to get onto another master's course I would have had to apply back in November. The only places that will take me aren't worth going to, and what's more my father won't pay; he's already pissed I turned down that summer job working for his friend.'

'That was a rather questionable decision.' Feeling Nadya about to boil over, Jan hurriedly continued, 'I thought you found a stopgap, anyway?'

'My father won't budge on any other options. I was trying, but he'd rather I went to join Mama in Geneva.'

'We'll find a way to keep you here,' Jan said. 'This can't be the end of the road.'

'Theo keeps asking me to marry him.'

Jan tried and failed to relax her muscles so Nadya wouldn't feel her tensing up.

'He keeps saying we don't have to tell anyone about it but at least that way I'll be safe. The secrecy is so insulting. He should be proud of me or not ask at all.'

'So you want him to do it for real?'

Nadya held both hands up to the light, screening her eyes from the sun but clearly also imagining a sizeable ring welded to her slender fourth finger.

'He chooses the worst times to ask. Over the phone. While we're eating shitty pizza. When I'm on the toilet.

It's like it's a joke to him. I'm worth a lot more than that.'

'I really don't want to hear about this.'

Nadya sat up and turned to face Jan. 'If he's serious, he can book a restaurant and do it again, properly. I want nice pictures.'

'You really want that?' Jan's face flushed with barely concealed worry at the impending possibility she had not fully believed in until this moment. The teleology of Nadya's life as a seemingly straight woman stretched out from this one stumbling block onwards to children, grand-children and the grave. As her other ties and obligations multiplied, there would be no room left for Jan.

'Yes, every girl wants that. Everyone but you. Do I have to explain everything to you?' Nadya was shaking with rage, her tiny shoulders stiff and drawn up as Jan tried to put her arm around her.

'Get off. You're crowding me. We've been here too long; the others are going to see my car if we don't hurry up.'

As the two swam back in silence from the lido to the further shore, where Nadya had slipped in, she said simply, 'Wash your mouth out.'

'This isn't drinking water.'

'Do I need to drown you again? Perhaps I'll hold you down for longer next time.'

Jan splashed her, then took a mouthful of the lake water, swilling it over her tongue, tasting rain and mud and leaves, before playfully spitting it out in a jet just to the left of Nadya, who retaliated by splashing her back, then taking one cupped hand and drenching Jan's face. Jan, newly relaxed by Nadya's attentions, let her do it.

71

'There we go. All gone.'

'I know which taste I preferred and it wasn't lake.'

'Don't be like that, it's very annoying and I don't have patience right now.'

They were picking their way to the shore now, where Jan spotted a pair of silver flip-flops discarded among the flag iris. How ever had she missed Nadya on the way in?

'You put us in the bedroom I told you, right, the one with the rose theme?'

'Yes, Nadya, it's labelled for you.'

'Good. Theo is probably still asleep, knowing him.'

'I think he's up, actually. How about I go fetch my clothes and come back to the house in ten minutes?' Jan suggested.

'Make it fifteen. And then you can brew me some fresh coffee while you're at it.'

Jan watched as Nadya slipped her shorts back on and pulled a dry tank top over her wet bandeau bra, petite frame swamped by the white cotton hanging at her sides. Jan leaned in again for a beat but before she had so much as parted her lips, Nadya gave her such a withering look that she withdrew. Of course Nadya would go to him. Now was as good a time as any to give him what he always wanted, when the work of getting her ready had been done by someone else.

Strolling away from the lake, Nadya called over her shoulder without looking back, 'You'd better have left some towels in our room!'

Jan laughed, as titillated as she was demeaned, and pondered swimming back to the lido to finish what Nadya had started, but the day was advancing too fast for that to be quite safe. How would she explain it to the others if they came upon her *in flagrante delicto*? She picked her way round to the heap of her own clothes, walking mainly in the shallows of the water to enjoy the cool malleability of the mud around her feet. Dressed, she wandered a winding path through the trees, deliberately idling while gathering flowers to assemble in a rough posy on her return to the kitchen. Distantly, she heard a car door slam, marking the time Nadya must have begun her journey into the house and upstairs.

Small brown sparrows fluttered through the trees above as Jan sat for a moment between the roots of one of the larger beech trees, and spat again discreetly. Her mouth was still silty. Nadya loved catching her off-guard, she took Jan's reserve as a personal challenge and relished creating situations where she would be forced to react without the chance to think anything through. When they had been teenagers, this tendency had been the source of arguments, if Jan refused to show her face in public without makeup or answer honestly when asked if she was annoyed. And then Nadya would do something to wrest back control from Jan, like telling her loudly she needed to buy trousers that fit her, or finding Jan's teenage diary in her bag and reading it aloud to their friends, or sitting in some metalhead guy's lap at a house party to watch Jan squirm out of the corner of her eye. She always won and so Jan began to give in pre-emptively; she came to regard her own subservience as part of their understanding. Perhaps Nadya's mooted engagement with Theo was another one of her whims, to remind Jan of her place at Nadya's feet. But it didn't feel like it was.

They had only started talking because one lunchtime at school when they were both sixteen Jan had inserted herself into a conversation on the merits of bourbon versus scotch. She emerged briefly from the fug of nerdery that surrounded her as a scholarship girl to volunteer the information that she drank from her parents' cabinet alone in the evenings. Nadya, confined to the girls' dorms at weekends, had seen her opportunity for escape into the less supervised mode of London life that the day pupils enjoyed and she jumped at it. They had been inseparable ever since, bar a short period during university when Jan had tried to wrest herself away and look for a real girl-friend. But her encounter with Ursie and the subsequent certainty that she was good for one thing only had sent her back into Nadya's orbit. And not long after that, Jan threw the party where Nadya met Theo. The next five years of her life had been spent waiting and going behind his back and hoping for something, anything to change. Jan fixed a smile to her face and retraced her steps as slowly as possible back the way she'd come.

Jan had taken a hot shower in the ensuite to drive out the chill of the lake and was downstairs whisking a vast bowl of eggs when Nadya wandered into the kitchen and greeted her as if they were meeting for the first time.

Waving an ancient grey remote held together with sticky tape, she asked, 'Do you know how to make the TV work?'

'No idea. Why don't you come have breakfast outside?'

'Why do English people love being uncomfortable?'

'Boarding school. Didn't work on you, though.'

'At least it's not too hot here. It's been boiling in Moscow for weeks, apparently.'

'You going back at all this year?'

'Even without the Covid restrictions it would be a bad idea. My dad says he's not needed there right now and my mum's in Switzerland with my brother. Geneva's a shithole, no character, the most boring people you can imagine. All they talk about is skiing and boats. If I wanted that I'd still be hanging out with everyone from Tothill who liked that sort of thing.'

One evening at the depressingly beige flat in Knightsbridge that Nadya's parents had bought for her, she had recounted to Jan the story of being woken up at 3 a.m. years ago by one of her father's bodyguards and told to pack what she could fit into a suitcase. She had groggily taken some of her best clothes and jewellery but had left all her diaries and Polaroids behind, later realising these had probably been destroyed. Her father had chosen the wrong person to award a lucrative contract to and Moscow was no longer a safe place for him to keep his family, even with all their existing security. Nadya had grown up in a sea of transitory private tutors, overindulged Borzois and trampled luxury handbags, covering her face for digital photos if there was half a chance of being recorded doing anything compromising. A would-be kidnapper had got as far as the front door of their home when she was sixteen, holding a bag she'd later been told contained zip-ties, muscle relaxants and a knife, and that year Nadya had been sent to England, where no one understood her accent or wanted to play chess with her.

Nadya asked, 'Do we have to go to the swamp today?'

'Sorry?'

'You know, the picnic. Theo told me that was the plan. He's snoring like a pig; I left him upstairs.'

Jan laughed for a moment and said, 'Oh you mean the moors.' Nadya stared at her hard, hating to be corrected, until Jan added limply, 'I'm so hungover I feel like I'm drowning in mud. So no, we don't have to go if you aren't up for it.'

Nadya muttered something grim-sounding in Russian and went over to the large coffee pot resting on the sideboard to pour herself a cup. Jan noted she had a new ring, a lustrous dark green stone in a chunky silver setting, rather at odds with her casual summer outfit and minimal makeup.

'Be careful with the Moka, it's leaking from the middle. It stained my shirt earlier.'

'This family. I bought Theo's mother a little gift of soap in a dispenser, I think it was Chanel but I don't remember. She's never used it, they just have these gross old bars that get thin and cracked, in every bathroom in the house. So English.'

'Well, a certain sort of English. Not the most hygienic, I agree, but I can't make myself use any other kind either.'

'And the separate hot and cold taps. It's weird. I asked his father to turn the heating up once and he just offered me a big woolly jumper covered in dog hair.'

'I thought you got on with them?'

'Yes, they're kind people. His dad is so funny. You know, he looked up Russian customs and brought out bread and salt to welcome me the first time we met. But it's not a well-designed house.'

'Have they ever met your parents?'

'Not yet, but maybe they will soon. Ursie!'

'Heyyy. Do either of you have a painkiller, I feel like pure shit.'

'I found some in the boot room,' Jan offered. 'But I don't know if they're in date.'

When Ursie looked puzzled, Jan pointed at a nearby door. Having both Ursie and Nadya in one room was almost more than Jan could bear. Thanks to the pandemic she'd forgotten how tense it made her. Analgesics obtained, Ursie returned in time to be handed a second mug of coffee by Nadya and to begin heaping sugar into it, still bereft of condensed milk.

Ursie said, 'Don't cook all those eggs, Jan. The boys can scramble some themselves and they'll get rubbery if you do a load and leave them.'

Jan, doing her best not to slam the fridge door, said, 'Let's go sit outside with the breakfast in a minute.' She poured a glug of the egg mixture into a pan and prodded it haphazardly.

Kara, emerging bleary-eyed in a big black hoody and bare legs, got swept up in the rush to the terrace.

Jan asked her, 'How did you sleep?'

'Not brilliantly, I kept dreaming that I was crawling through a dark tunnel on my hands and knees. You were ahead of me, Jan, but I couldn't see your face. There was something behind us as well but it was too tight for me to turn around and look.'

'Can I have some toast?' Luke strolled onto the terrace and began drinking from Kara's mug of coffee while still standing up.

'Yes of course, there's a rack here.'

Luke smiled without saying thank you and sat at the other end of the table, grabbing a butter knife and two slices.

'Hey, leave some for us, we were here first!' Ursie took the last piece and began loading it with globs of egg from the pan.

Nadya said rather loudly, 'I've run out of juice,' and held her glass up, knowing that Jan would instinctively rush to take it and refill it.

The rest of the morning passed in a blur of refilled coffee pots and cigarettes. Jan sat nursing a beer for hair of the dog while Ursie ate a tumbler of plain ice cubes. Kara did her hair up in a braid crown to keep it off her neck in the heat and Nadya snapped at her that it was wonky. Theo attempted to pacify them with a family-sized bar of Dairy Milk which he distributed as meticulously as he had the powders of the night before.

It occurred to Jan that she never heard Nadya laughing any more, and had not for a long while, even before the trouble with her visa started. In the beginning, the same sly sense of the absurd had enlivened all their interactions, poking fun at the stern pronouncements of their teachers, the pretensions of their peers and the way that their lives seemed constructed to funnel them all towards various banal ends. Now that humour only surfaced in Nadya's invention of new torments to occupy her snatched moments with Jan.

Jan buttered a rough-hewn piece of toast and retreated into the Western drawing room in search of a moment's quiet. Perhaps Holt House was beginning to grow on her in all its fusty splendour. She briefly smiled at the mental image of their group taking tea on the low sofas and handling the sugar cubes with silver tongs then realised with a shudder that she'd pictured Nadya as lady of the house. The battered brocade footstools, sunbleached silk curtains and Meissen-style curios seemed to regard her with puzzlement, as if waiting for the real heir to come and put them to proper use again, but Theo remained outside in the sunlight. She wondered, not for the first time, whether Theo's curious blindness when it came to Nadya was merely a symptom of having so many fine possessions that he need not care for what happened to them so long as they all remained his.

She took a big bite out of the toast, pools of salted butter melting on her tongue, the sourdough pleasantly chewy. In a far corner of the room, she saw the edge of a framed piece of embroidery that had been pushed almost out of sight behind an armchair. In the top left corner of the quartered shield, she recognised the heraldic symbol of the Moor's head. Ursie had been more right in her dislike of the décor than Jan had given her credit for. With her lips pursing in distaste, Jan was walking closer to examine the piece when Luke walked into the room, midway through rolling a cigarette.

'Got a light on you? I've lost mine and Kara won't share hers. She's in a mood.'

'Here you go – but not in here, please.'

'Why not? It's not like anyone's here to stop us.'

'Because you're going to stink the whole room up and it already needs a deep clean. This place could be really wonderful if Theo were bothered to throw out some things or give them to a museum.'

'It's big but isn't it a bit of a gloomy old pile? All these honking great cupboards, I constantly feel like something's about to jump out at me.' Luke put the finishing touches to his cigarette, seeming determined to ignore Jan's scruples. 'Who's this, for instance?'

He pointed up at the framed portrait on the wall. A tall, gaunt man in a grey suit with two whorls of white hair at his temples and an oiled moustache peered down at them with an expression of supreme hauteur.

'A relative of Theo's, presumably.'

'He looks like he's just about to condemn me to the workhouse.'

'Wrong era, I reckon, look at the suit. But not the most cheerful face, I agree. I wonder if this is Great-Uncle Harold himself?'

'Well thanks, now I feel like an idiot. Look, he's got Theo's chin.'

Jan went to look more closely at the painting. Harold's hand – if that's who it was – was gripped tightly around the wing of a brass lectern fashioned in the shape of an eagle. His expression of dour serenity tugged at something queasy in Jan's core. Depicted on the table by Harold's other hand were two hourglasses, pale sands running low through their pinched waists.

'Let's go outside, it's rather stuffy in here.' She suddenly felt abashed to have been ruminating over her morning exploits with Nadya right under Harold's painted gaze.

They walked back through the house. Wandering past the dining room, with doors flung open and dust motes dancing in the streams of noonday sun, Jan saw a glint of reflected light where there should be none. At the far edge of the long sideboard in the corridor, the silver goblet sat on the polished wood, as if it had just been set down by a guest. She snatched it up and peered inside.

'Were you drinking out of this?' Jan sniffed the cup but caught no scent of wine or any other drink inside it.

'No, looks too fancy for me. Is it special?'

'None of this silver is worth anything, it's all plated. Feel the weight.' She hefted it experimentally then remembered how her morning had started and added tersely, 'You can stop going in the end bedroom, as well. Theo already told you to stay out of there.'

'I don't know what you're implying, but I haven't been anywhere near that room since he pitched a fit about it yesterday. I'll be outside if you want to smoke.'

Jan stomped back into the kitchen to replace the goblet at the back of the cupboard, tucked away behind the plainer wine glasses. Then, without thinking too deeply about why, she wedged the heavy granite mortar and pestle in front of the cupboard door and walked out. Ursie could ask Luke herself if she had questions about who'd ransacked her room, Jan didn't want him to completely lose it on their first full day here.

The golden sunshine of the morning had given way to a clear, greyish light in which the dilapidation of the house and gardens was far more apparent. Shingles were missing from the roof, the paving stones on the terrace were cracked and perilous, while the woods seemed to have encroached even closer to the house overnight; there were little striplings sprouting beyond the boundary line and tree roots bulging under what had once been a flat, orderly lawn.

Jan slumped in a garden chair next to Luke, rollie burning indolently in her hand, and rested her eyes on the trees. How long would she need to sit in this chair and wait before the forest came to meet them? Before it grew thick all about her, ivy entwining her legs and birds nesting in her hair, while it continued its march into the vast belly of the house? When the first grasses sprouted from the floor and deer roamed inside, all striving would be at an end. The house and its surfeit of gewgaws felt like a fragile shell filled with brittle toys, soon to be swallowed by the encroaching green. She sat unseen in remotest nature and all around her countless creatures were eating and dying and dissolving back into the soil.

This was cousin to the vertiginous terror that sometimes gripped her in the streets of London where, buffeted by the city, she felt her self sitting so lightly upon her that in an instant she might give in, strew her keys and clothes and name upon the ground and wander lost forevermore. Sometimes she longed for such an unveiling, when her mind would break open at last and the struggle to render herself comprehensible would finally be over.

'What are you thinking about?' Luke asked her, all apparently forgiven.

'Lunch. I'm trying to work out what I can make with what we brought.'

'Come on, let people forage. I'm fine with a tin of tuna, honestly. Maybe some potatoes. Just relax, you've been completely wired ever since we got here.' He started rolling another cigarette immediately after stubbing the old one. 'I know Theo asked you to be den mother or whatever, but it's not like we can't fend for ourselves.'

'*Can* we fend for ourselves, though? We're all getting older and we just keep doing the same things over and over again.' Jan looked at his sunken cheeks and nicotine-smudged fingertips as she said this and remembered too late that men could also be pathologically vain.

'Sure, when you put it like that, we are getting older.' He brushed his hand reflexively over his still thick white-blond hair. 'But you're nearly done with that PhD, Ursie's doing amazing things with her paintings, and Kara's achieved so much, I'm in awe of her, even if she thinks I don't respect her music or whatever. None of what you're doing is quick or easy to finish. As they say in NA, you've got to take things one day at a time.'

Last night he had put away line after line with the rest of them, regaling them with his tired theory that almost all the great works of humankind had been performed by men because of their libido, that this was the reason so few suspension bridges, classic plays and the like had been created by women. Jan had laughed in his face and then set about tearing the argument apart. But when she got onto the portion of her rebuttal concerning the suppressed desires of women, he'd grown irritable, insisted Jan was an outlier, how could she know what most women wanted? Fearing the force of her own riposte to that with Kara and Ursie in the room, Jan had faltered. Now she wished she'd gone ahead and asked what Luke believed the women who passed through his bed were seeking, if not satisfaction of their own.

He had briefly slept with Ursie during first year, after he and Kara had begun seeing one another, but before she and Kara knew each other properly. The entanglement had ended when Kara had come knocking on the door of Luke's room in halls to tell him she was heading to the basement to do laundry, and please could he give her back the fitted sheet she'd lent him. Ursie, astride Luke and now incensed, had clambered off and walked out in a fury at being made party to his cheating. Ursie and Luke had never been too close after that, but had developed sufficient camaraderie that it hadn't been a problem to invite both of them to the same parties.

She asked, 'Are you still going to NA?'

83

'On and off. Not as much as I should, especially not lately; it's shit over Zoom. But yeah, I do go sometimes and it helps. You ever been?'

'I don't think I have quite the same relationship to drugs. Anyway, isn't all that twelve steppy stuff based in Christianity?'

'I know someone whose higher power is her cat. It depends which chapter you go to. I find that stuff difficult because of my dad, you know, but I think for me it's Marlowe.'

'As in Christopher? That's your higher power?'

'Yep.'

'I wasn't sure if you still auditioned for things.'

'All the time before lockdown. I'm not saying I got many parts, but it's something.'

'Kara said you burned your acting notebooks.'

'I was feeling very low.' Luke blew out an extravagant cloud of smoke. 'Anyway, they had a lot of stuff from the Cambodia years when I basically gave up. It got really bad out there, I was so fucked up all the time. I don't want to remember it now; it got pretty dark. If I hadn't been forced to leave, I would probably be dead.'

'I thought you just got fed up and came home?'

'Come on, you know this, I got deported,' Luke said, sounding angrier than Jan had expected. He continued, 'I got caught with weed, of all things, in a fancy hotel. We used to break into the pool at night when the good bars closed and usually they didn't care, but one night the porters got really fed up and called the police. Either I could pay a massive bribe, which I didn't have, or come back. I don't know if this counts as home, though. It's not Upstate, but it's not London either. Lockdown is such bullshit; they just closed the whole city to keep a few old people safe. I mean, are the theatres closed for good?'

'I'm not enjoying it either, but that's going a bit far. What about the cancer patients?'

'It sucks for them, but I don't see why we should have to put our entire lives on hold. There must be another way around this because it's not just going to disappear. Are we going to be doing this forever?'

'I honestly don't know.' Jan looked out across towards the trees. 'I was thinking of leaving maybe, going somewhere like Lisbon or Copenhagen before it's too late, but now that seems like an insane idea. My aunt's still trying to get those Sephardi-Portuguese apology passports for her kids, and maybe I'd be eligible for one too.'

'You've got savings?'

'Some, I don't know how much I'd need to start over. It'd be pretty expensive, right?'

He looked at her with an odd expression she could not read.

'It's not as much as you might think . . . I'd recommend South East Asia, actually. I'd still be out there if I could. But there's no way they're letting you in now with the pandemic. I thought you were dead set on being an academic anyway?'

'Back when I thought it was about reading books and studying. I haven't touched the undergrad theses I'm supposed to be marking. And I don't want to go to Aberdeen on the train three nights a week and sleep on someone's sofa to get paid less than I'd earn working in Starbucks when you add up all the overtime. It's not living. The students expect you to be their counsellor now rather than actually teaching them anything. I had

85

three undergrads come into supervisions last year and tell me they were suicidal. I had to refer them all to the Student Mental Health Service, who I know are totally useless because I've tried using them myself and just got put on a waiting list.'

Luke nodded, but didn't reply. He looked up and Jan saw a familiar profile heading down the corridor towards them through the french windows. 'I'm going for a nap,' he announced. 'I think it's better to let her keep on cooling off.'

He strolled away around to the front of the house and was long gone before Kara appeared on the terrace.

'Luke was just out here, where did he go?'

Jan shrugged. She was not going to tell Kara or directly refuse to tell her, and thus become further drawn into whatever conflict was consuming them today.

Kara sat in the chair Luke had just vacated and stared sullenly towards the treeline, where Jan caught sight of Theo and Nadya re-emerging from the wood, Nadya talking animatedly to Theo as he kicked along a saggy old football he must have dredged up from somewhere. They'd made themselves crowns of ivy, Theo's sitting at an angle on top of his smooth, dark hair. They looked the perfect couple. The sight of Nadya holding his arm twisted Jan up with rage and frustration. During her seclusion in London, she had somehow managed to forget that having Nadya around meant seeing her climb all over Theo. The two spotted Jan's plume of smoke and waved, yelling for her to come over to them, but she just shook her head and forced a smile.

Nadya asked, 'Where's Ursie's room?'

Jan pointed left and laughed, watching Nadya draw out her phone, realise she still had no signal, then pick up a lichened twig that had fallen at the border of a flowerbed on the lawn and lob it expertly through Ursie's window. At least she'd had the sense not to throw gravel.

'What the hell is this?'

Jan couldn't see Ursie but could hear the laughter in her voice.

Theo shouted up, 'Come down and hang out with us! There's a stream and we put beers in it, we can go paddling and get drunk at the same time.'

'Guys, I was having a nap; you woke me up!'

'We can make you a crown too! Sleep is for the weak, come on down, we're going to the moors!'

Evidently persuaded, Jan heard the sound of Ursie's window closing. She felt her heart compress, beats skipping sideways with fresh panic at the two women's proximity.

<hr>

The gorse flowered cadmium yellow, dotted all over the hillside among the bright green bracken, giving the impression of a roughly stitched quilt laid over the landscape. The great green hills rose and curved, lulling the river between them as it ran for miles, burbling and spilling over rounded grey stones. Atop the greatest of these, pointed out to them by Theo as Hallow Hill, a black cairn jutted up into the sky. This was one of the few peaks where locals had not yet succeeded in erecting a stark wooden cross to loom over the slopes below.

Jan had been leafing through the books in her bedroom and had come across an account in a collection of folk tales from the area about a particularly fearless Mortimer forebear, a scoundrel who had travelled the world only to return in penury and disgrace, at risk of losing Holt House. This adventurous man undertook to spend one night waiting in the cairn, in the hope he might exchange his soul for worldly riches in the place where evil was said to dwell. But the inhabitants long-buried there stirred in their sleep, reaching out bodiless to seize at him and frighten him away from striking such a foolish bargain. They had scarce repelled the foolhardy man to the threshold of the tomb before the Devil gave chase, pursuing him all the way across the moors through scrub and briar, right to the lip of the gorge, where he dangled above the churning waters below till a servant came with the dawn to rescue him. And so the cairn had been shunned ever since, still open to the sky and visited only by the stars passing overhead.

When Jan tried to tell her friends about this, Nadya had remarked that he must have been a superstitious man to begin with, if he went up to the cairn hoping for a bargain. The thread of meaning Jan was trying to pull out from the story became snagged with justifications for an encounter she had not even personally experienced.

Theo said, 'It was probably sleep deprivation that made him feel like that.'

'Can't you allow for any possibility there might be something more?' Kara asked him. 'Some wonder left?'

'I can, but that detail is pretty hard to ignore. I know about altered states – you can make people see things that aren't there.'

Jan pointed out, 'The story didn't say he saw anything exactly, it was a feeling. In a way, the land saved him from himself.'

Ursie said, 'I don't know, that sounds a bit blood and soil to me.'

'Only if you think loving something means making a special claim to it.'

'So, in his case, probably yes?'

Luke said, 'I don't why we're all arguing about this. We weren't there and we can't know for sure, that's the point of faith.'

Sensing that Luke was about to get started on a circular dismantling of the catechism he'd had beaten into him, which would as usual end in a surprising degree of agnosticism for a staunchly rationalist atheist, Theo turned instead to Kara and asked, 'Do you want to hear a family story? I don't believe a word of it myself, but it's the sort of thing you'd like.'

'Go on.' She smiled and took a step to draw level with him as they walked along the grassy path over the low curves of the valley.

'When my mother was a girl, she and her sisters were so bored at Holt House they made a Ouija board and started asking it questions in the end bedroom. Mostly silly stuff, like whether boys they knew liked them and how many children they would have. It gave a few unhelpful answers like 'maybe' and it got the quantities of future children completely wrong, like saying my aunt would only have one child.'

'What if the spirit was really sexist?' Ursie asked.

'Possibly, but it also said my mother would have none, which really upset her. They asked the board who they were speaking to and it said "M", so they started teasing it, asking if it meant "Me" or "Ma'am" instead. It got annoyed and kept moving the planchette to say "no" and then repeated "M" several more times before it stopped replying. My mum is convinced it stole some of her lipsticks afterwards and crushed them. She said that doors kept opening randomly when she was the only one in the room and she always felt like she was being watched. I'm sure it was just her sisters playing pranks on her, though; she's quite impressionable.'

Jan said, 'Did anything happen after that?'

'No, but my mother and my aunts refused to go in the end bedroom ever again and they wouldn't tell Harold why. He'd have been furious with them for being so silly.'

'Who was M?'

'No idea, I'm afraid. Presumably a relative, given the initial.'

Nadya asked, 'Can we visit the ghost room? I want to see it.'

'There's nothing to see in there, it's very boring, really.'

Nadya gave a disappointed little sigh and fell back to take Theo's free hand. Theo was wearing a ragged Paul Smith shirt and trousers that looked too heavy for the heat. Jan's backpack full of salad dressings was beginning to pull at her shoulders, while she observed Theo trying to walk as if the old wicker hamper Jan had insisted upon in a fit of theatricality were not the most unwieldy method possible for transporting plates and glasses.

Jan still cringed at the conversation she'd had with Theo in third year when he'd made a reference in passing to an ancestor who had been persecuted by Elizabeth I for not converting to Protestantism and she had asked him if he 'had any names he didn't use'. He had thought she meant his father's surname until she repeated the question several times, feeling sillier and sillier at her euphemistic method of asking whether he had a title.

The group straggled along the side of the stream, weaving in between black trees bent double by the winter winds and gaps in the grass where white boulders pushed up like exposed bone. A hawk flew high overhead, coasting on the updraughts and scanning for its lunch.

Watched by throngs of blue-daubed sheep who apparently roamed the moors unshepherded, Ursie was peering intently at the landscape around them for possible threats, having expressed concerns on the drive over that they could be apprehended. Kara had brought a very expensive-looking old camera along with her, which she was pointing indiscriminately at the sheep and surrounding hills. Luke was walking along kicking at outcrops of moss, the sleeves of his Joy Division top pulled over his hands.

'Please can I just have a bump?'

Theo said, 'We're about to eat lunch, can't you wait?'

'I'm not hungry.'

Jan said, 'I have strawberries. And fried cauliflower bites.'

'Please can I have some K? I'm really not feeling good, it'll balance me out.'

'Ugh fine,' Theo said, 'it's in my back pocket. Nadya, can you grab it for me?'

'No. You've had more than enough for now, Luke. We can do it back at the house with the scales if you need your own private supply.'

'Since when were you his business manager? I thought you didn't care about sharing with friends.'

Nadya's mouth tightened into a line. 'His business is my business. Maybe you'll understand that one day.'

'He's not a fucking drug baron, it's a few lines. Chill out.'

'No, you need to chill out. You're bringing everyone else down and . . .'

'Nadya, stop, please,' Theo said and turned to Jan, 'I think we're almost at the spot. Just over there by the stepping stones.'

They had come to a bend in the river, where seven dove-grey boulders protruded from the coursing waters, forming a sort of partial dam before the river twisted again and got deep enough to paddle. A pair of dragonflies, glinting metallic blue, danced over the current, locked tightly together. The cloudless sky above almost matched their brilliance, so wide and high it felt momentarily oppressive to Jan.

The picnic blankets finally laid and the wine uncorked, Jan began levering out slices of quiche and cold potato salad onto their plates.

Ursie said, 'This is honestly like something out of *Brideshead Revisited*.'

'I don't especially fancy playing the role of Anthony Blanche. Spinach and courgette or tomato and mushroom?'

'A bit of both, please. I have always found that final scene in the chapel very moving, despite everything.'

Theo said, 'You can take the girl out of Catholic school . . .' and Ursie chuckled.

Nadya interjected, 'Every year at Oxford some guy decided he was going to be the new Sebastian Flyte and carried a teddy around with him for a few weeks, before he got talked out of it.'

Jan said, 'Didn't you carry around a dead hamster for a bit?'

'That was for a taxidermy project, it was completely different.'

'Do you remember Ollie and Ben who used to hang out in the art rooms with us at Tothill?' Jan asked. 'Laura G told me they got sent to jail for selling coke and heroin.'

Nadya looked sharply at her and asked, 'How long did they get?'

'Not sure about the sentence. One of them got out after two and a bit years, I think the other one is still in there for some reason. It's really sad, he got into a top conservatory in St Petersburg for violin and couldn't go.'

'Well, it's probably for the best he didn't try that in Russia. You know what a petukh is?'

Luke said, 'I saw a documentary on that. It's wild in there.'

'They think you're weak, they tattoo circles on your knees so all the other prisoners know you should be sucking dicks for as long as you're inside.'

'Did you watch it too?'

'No, my bodyguard told me about that. He was a sweet guy, though I had to bribe him sometimes to let me go on dates with boys. He had twin daughters and used to show me pictures of them on his phone.'

Ursie asked, 'Do you ever hear from him?'

Nadya shook her head. 'I had to leave my phone behind so we couldn't be tracked. Lost all my contacts.'

'That must have been scary.' Ursie took a big bite of the quiche and gestured enthusiastically at Jan, who was torn between satisfaction at her verdict on the dish and the sick unease that came whenever Nadya and Ursie interacted directly, which thankfully was not often.

'They didn't really tell us what was happening, and I was half-asleep. I'd just come back from a party at my best friend's place. You remember Galina, right, Theo?'

'The one who threatened to have me castrated if I wasn't nice to you?'

'She was only joking. My old boyfriend was such an asshole.'

Kara asked, 'What did he do? You never talk about him.'

Jan silently remembered Nadya's youthful insistence that she be signed out from Tothill under the pretence of spending weekends at the Rubin house, only to fly off to Paris with Dmitri, having given the school a convincing fake passport and kept her real one. The interminable YouTube videos he wanted to show them about different types of hunting rifle. The flagrant cheating. Nadya calling her from bathrooms around the world promising she'd really leave him this time, asking to stay over at hers. The final swift backhand, for arguing with him in public when Nadya saw him give his number to a waitress, who must have been at least twenty-five to his eighteen.

Nadya said, 'It was a long time ago. I moved on to better things.'

Theo cut himself a second slice of the spinach quiche before he said in a loud voice, 'We have an announcement. Nadya and I are engaged.'

No one else knew Nadya well enough to catch her swallowing her surprise, but Jan saw it bloom across her face, to be quickly replaced by a seraphic smugness as she poured a fresh glass of wine for herself and then topped off Theo's as well.

Jan said weakly, 'That's wonderful, congratulations,' and clapped Theo on the back, her mind collapsing with fury and disappointment. So, this was what she'd chosen, after everything.

Silence fell for a moment as they variously reflected on the towering arguments the pair had had over the last few years. Nadya had often held herself aloof from parties she was not hosting on the basis of their grotty locations, bad music or boring guests. Theo's last rare victory in persuading her out had culminated in her telling him that if he did not leave immediately and take an Uber home with her, he'd find his things on the kerb. This was not the first time she had threatened to turn him out on the street for displeasing her, though Theo tended to treat it as a harmless joke.

Kara, who had hitherto opposed all marriage as a bourgeois institution designed to oppress women and who had declined to give anyone wedding gifts on that basis, asked with a disturbing brightness in her voice, 'Have you already set a date?'

Nadya said, 'We're not sure when weddings will be allowed again, but very soon I hope, once my parents are allowed to come over from Geneva and stay for a bit.'

'Probably a winter wedding then,' Kara said. 'Do you have a ring? Can we see it?'

Theo said, 'I thought we might use my grandmother's ring' – then added hurriedly when he caught Nadya about to glare at him – 'That's for Nadya to decide, though.'

Jan's entire body was numb. She braced a hand against the grass to stop herself falling face forwards into the quiche. Perhaps Luke had had the right idea in agitating for chemical reinforcements before the picnic.

Kara played absentmindedly with a loose cauliflower floret while Jan noticed Ursie inclining towards her, mouth pursed in a shocked O and clearly longing to gossip.

Ursie asked, 'Do your parents know?'

'I called her father last week. More informing than asking permission, but he was still very happy. I think he's sending vodka and flowers to Nadya's place.'

Jan noted that Theo still referred to it as such, despite having lived there for two years, ever since he had been evicted from his last place along with all his housemates for throwing giant parties.

Luke had been sitting at the edge of the picnic blanket mashing one of the quiche slices into paste with his fork and picking out the mushrooms to leave on one side. He asked, 'What's the hurry? You're so young, don't you want to wait?'

Nadya replied, 'I'm twenty-seven, that's pretty old for Russia. My parents got married in their early twenties.'

'I guess when you know you know.' Kara's brittle smile was too big for her face. 'Shall I take a picture?'

'Oh really, you don't have to . . . okay then.'

Kara directed Theo and Nadya over to an old hawthorn tree that stood near the river and Nadya hopped onto a low curving branch at seat height, while Theo stood clasping her hand rather awkwardly. He was doing a good impression of easy charm, but Jan could see his knee bouncing in the way it did when he wanted to leave a noisy bar or exit a tiresome conversation.

'Smile! Gorgeous! I'll send you the prints when I've developed the roll.'

Nadya said, with an edge to her voice, 'Please keep it to yourselves for now. I want to do a more official proposal later, but Theo was just too excited to wait.'

Luke said, 'Your secret is safe with us. We're going to celebrate tonight, right?'

The group settled themselves once more, with Nadya scooting back onto the blanket and draping Theo's arms over herself. She assumed a satisfied expression, craning up to kiss his chin.

'Of course we will.' Theo trailed a hand up Nadya's thigh, moving her diaphanous skirt to reveal the upper inches of pale flesh toned by daily Peloton workouts. She smacked it lightly and giggled.

Jan had seen this routine many times before. She had no idea whether Nadya behaved like this when she wasn't around, but it never failed to rile her. During a group dinner for one of their old school friends, Nadya had canoodled with Theo for the entirety of the first course and then asked Jan to come with her while they refreshed their makeup. She had commanded Jan to get on her knees in the stall and set to work, though the climax had been marred by someone outside knocking impatiently, and they had ended by flushing the toilet several times while Jan playacted as the drunken friend whom Nadya had been helping to throw up.

It occurred to her that this engagement would be but one among many, that all of her straight friends would have weddings which she would be compelled to attend until they started having children, at which point she would cease to be of any interest or relevance to them except as a source of amusing but – *sotto voce* rather tragic – hedonistic anecdotes once every six months. She would be happy for them, and bring gifts and dance until late in the night, but it would be the end of something. She would stand, dateless, at Nadya's wedding one day soon, watching her promise to be faithful to Theo forever.

Jan was already in her twenties when it became legally possible for her to marry someone else in the UK, though this option felt so far removed from her current existence as to be entirely abstract. When Jan tried to picture her own wedding, to some faceless woman from the future who apparently liked her enough to go along with it, the jumble of concerns overwhelmed her. What could she promise another person, in the mythical future when Nadya no longer had a claim on her? She and Ursie used to say that if they were still single at forty then they'd marry each other, but it was a joke that Ursie had long ago ceased making.

After the pistachio marzipan had been devoured and cinnamon coffee from several thermoses savoured with a joint, they paddled a little while in the cool eddies of the stream and then by silent consensus began packing up. On the walk back to the cars, Kara looked even more glum than before, trailing a little behind the rest of the group, while Ursie attempted to hang back and whisper to her about the news. Jan feared talking because she wasn't sure she could adequately compose herself. She strode on ahead, mind fixed on returning home; her chest was leaden and her stomach felt dangerous. Perhaps an hour or two alone in the great soft expanse of the bedroom would fix everything.

As they gathered around the cars, Nadya took her hand. 'Why don't you come back with us? I feel like I've scarcely got the chance to talk to you this holiday.'

'That's sweet of you, but how about we have a drink together this evening in the hammocks? I think I should probably help Kara with directions back to the house.'

Kara, catching up to them, said curtly, 'It's okay, we can follow on behind you guys.'

Not knowing how to refuse in front of the others without a ruckus, Jan gave her assent.

'Shoes off inside the car, please.' Nadya's Jeep was pristine, it still smelled like new leather and air freshener. Jan could barely believe her eyes as Theo removed his own trainers and put them in a cloth bag – this was the man who couldn't see a block of cheese without reducing it to rubble and had once voiced the belief that caring whether laundry was dry or not was tragically middle class.

Enclosed in the upholstered environs of the back seat, Jan leaned back wearily as the car set off down the lane, narrowly avoiding a procession of alpacas wearing floral wreaths at the other end of it.

Theo said, 'They're always up to something weird here.'

'Where are they going?' Nadya said. 'Shall we follow them?'

'It'll be some sort of godawful village fete, let's just go home.'

'But they're so cute! Look, that one is trying to eat his flowers.'

Theo, who was driving Nadya's car, gave no indication of being prepared to follow the alpacas, for which Jan was profoundly grateful.

'I thought I'd seen it all after all those rotting scarecrows on the way down,' Jan said, 'but I suppose not.'

'Cousin-fuckers.'

Jan laughed and said, 'You're one to talk. I thought aristos loved marrying their cousins.'

'Now that Nadya has done me the honour of saying yes maybe we'll be able to skip the webbed feet for another generation.'

'But not the congenital insanity, clearly.'

99

Nadya asked, 'Do you think Kara and Luke are going to be a long-term couple?'

Jan said, 'He's only been back a year and they're already having trouble again. She's in denial about that, though. I tried to talk to her about it last night but she shrugged me off.'

Theo kept his eyes fixed to the road. The closest they'd ever come to an argument was when Jan had suggested that he should stop selling to Luke as a matter of ethics. He'd pointed out that if he started judging whether people had a problem or not, he'd go out of business. And besides, Luke would just get everything he wanted somewhere else.

Nadya said, 'I don't know, it just seems odd, they've never seriously dated anyone else but he doesn't seem that excited about the idea of commitment. He's only really excited by one thing.'

'Do you think we should have talked to his parents? I still feel so guilty for how it all turned out, him just taking off like that.'

'No. His dad and stepmum are super Evangelical and insane,' Theo said and turned off the tree-covered hollo-way onto an A road dotted with mud-splattered cars.

'Shouldn't we still try?' Jan persisted. 'He's their son, he's basically homeless and has no job or any prospect of getting a new one because of lockdown. They should come and get him when it's allowed, I really don't think he can cope with London.'

'And do what with him? They'd probably put him in some sort of Christian rehab in Utah, as if that would help him,' Theo said. 'He's tougher than he looks. Remember that time he locked himself in the bathroom at a party then climbed out of a tiny window and round the side of the house onto the balcony?'

'That was terrifying. I've seen Luke drink three quarters of a bottle of Jack and hold a conversation with a ticket inspector. He didn't even get fined or anything,' Nadya added.

'The man had a job teaching English in Cambodia and yet he didn't even finish his English degree. Like life, Luke will always find a way,' Theo concluded.

Nadya returned to her original theme. 'It still strikes me as kind of immature that they're rushing straight back into it without talking about any terms or what they actually want. I mean, I'm sure Kara wants a house and kids and all of that, but your twenties are for getting the stupid stuff out of your system and I don't think Luke's finished yet.'

With a sadistic thrill, Jan heard Nadya remember too late that Theo was in fact already well into his thirties, and thus, by Nadya's standards, also hopelessly behind.

She said, 'By that rationale, you two should be all finished, since you're engaged.'

Theo said mildly, 'There's still a lot for us to explore.'

'Like what, bungee jumping?' Jan regretted acquiescing to this gambit the moment the words left her mouth.

Nadya giggled and peered back over the seat to look directly at her. 'No, though I would like to try that one day. I meant the kind of stuff you can only do when you really trust each other, I'm sure you can guess.'

Theo said, 'We started talking a lot after the lockdown and Nadya realised she's bi. It would be really hot to watch her enjoy herself like that with another woman. Maybe you could give her some tips, Jan?'

101

Jan was so filled with despair she did not know whether to laugh or cry at Nadya's hypocrisy. A year ago, when the two of them had been fighting because Theo was out raving so much he barely saw Nadya, she and Jan had gone to a private party in a gay men's sauna in Soho. She had assumed they would enjoy the party together, but Nadya had disappeared with a Brazilian couple into one of the big shower stalls, leaving Jan to occupy herself with a forgettable blonde in the jacuzzi, as she waited hours for Nadya to re-emerge.

Nadya said, 'It's so funny, everyone was so weird about it at school even though we kept making out with each other whenever there was a party.'

'Really, Nads, you never told me that?' Theo sounded surprised.

'Oh yes. It was like the last days of Rome.'

'I didn't,' Jan said. 'None of you would make out with me because I was already out as queer.' This had been one of Nadya's finest bits of acting, publicly rejecting Jan so she could do whatever she pleased in private.

'Turns out we're all queer!' Nadya proclaimed.

Jan sat seething. It was not inaccurate for Nadya to call herself that, but Nadya hadn't had to train herself to look only at her feet in changing rooms lest someone accuse her of being predatory. Nadya didn't have to google which countries were safe for gay tourism or worry about being affectionate with Theo in the street.

'What about you, Theo? Are you going to experiment a bit too, maybe there are some men you find attractive?' Jan asked.

He laughed uneasily. 'I don't think so. I can't even tell when men are hot, I wouldn't know what I was doing.' He paused. 'But I want to watch Nadya.'

'Just don't turn into one of those Tinder couples that only have a picture of the woman and then try to bait and switch at the last moment. I really hate that.'

There was silence for a moment and Nadya said, 'Oh no, of course not.' And Jan knew she was making a mental note to block Jan's profile on sight.

Theo laid his hand at the top of Nadya's thigh and squeezed. She grazed her fingers over the back of his hand.

They were rolling down the drive now and Jan was desperate to get out of the car. 'I really need to make a start on dinner,' she said. 'We stayed on the moors way longer than I planned.'

Nadya said, 'You're so caring, I'm sure you'll make someone very happy one day.'

'I'd like to meet the fool willing to try.'

She had spotted something white attached to one railing of the gates and snatched it through the window as they drove past, thinking it must be a flyer or some bit of rubbish blown there by a passing car, only to realise that what she held was in fact an official-looking envelope. She yanked open the car door and strode, half-sprinting, to the front door. Looking back at the driveway for any sign of the other group, she saw Theo and Nadya leaning against the car, making out furiously, Nadya's hands clasping his chino-ed buttocks.

Jan turned reluctantly to call for Theo to give her the keys before realising the door to the house was unlocked, swinging open at her touch. She traipsed through to the kitchen, the dining room, the games room. Every entrance had been left unsecured, the others must all have assumed that someone else would see to it. It was probably only the intricate design of the gate that had prevented whoever had delivered the envelope from advancing up the drive to the house where they could easily have wandered in.

Alone in the kitchen, Jan uncorked the wine and hunted for a glass. Someone had moved the mortar and pestle away from the doors and the goblet was gone from the cupboard again. Not stopping to look for it, she poured herself a brimming tumbler and drained it in one. She knew Nadya enjoyed riling her, but that had really been something else. Even though Nadya was already having her cake and eating it, the thought of her persuading Theo that it would be a positive development for their relationship to start having threesomes was astounding. It was bad enough to be around Theo on a normal day, to smile politely while corroded with guilt for betraying a friend. She had wanted to tell them both to stop, that other women were not toys that could just be picked up, played with and conveniently put away. It was one thing to be outcasts, deviants together, but the idea of Nadya casually obtaining what Jan had suffered and deformed her life for made her dizzy with rage.

When Nadya had first realised she might have trouble remaining in England a few months previously, she had unleashed the fact casually on Jan, over coffee at her flat while Theo was out buying orange juice for brunch after a big night. As soon as she realised what Nadya was telling her, Jan had fallen to her knees and said, 'Marry me. Get as many prenups as you need, but marry me and stay here.'

Nadya had laughed and said, 'That's so cute. If I marry you for the visa, I will not need a prenup because my father will disown me.'

104

Jan had tried one last desperate bid, knowing in her heart that it would fail. 'So what? You can get a job. We can be together and be free.'

And Nadya, who had not moved from her high stool at the marble counter, said, 'Free is just another word for poor. And the poor are not free, not really.'

While Jan was gasping for a reply, she snapped, 'Get up before Theo comes back. You're being ridiculous.'

Jan poured another large measure of wine and went to sulk in the Western drawing room. She sank into the old leather sofa, and pondered the case of faded morpho butterflies on the opposite wall, pinned and preserved forever in iridescent mid-flight. Finally ready to examine the letter, she saw through the cellophane window that it was headed with the emblem of the local police force. The glue sealing the flap shut was weak and she pried it open to take a closer look, fearing the worst. Printed on headed paper, the letter claimed there had been a report of someone coming here who did not reside in the county and, owing to the ongoing crisis, they insisted that this person or persons return to their primary residence with immediate effect.

She read the letter several times in shock, before she found herself pacing the room beneath Harold's liverish gaze, panicking and plotting. A new and stubborn reluctance had ignited within her after their return from the moors; despite everything she wanted to stay here. As soon as they had driven over the threshold, she had felt strongly how much she needed to be at Holt House, how the world beyond its walls became more irrelevant every moment that passed. If she could just stay, nothing would have to move forward, perhaps there was even time to dissuade Nadya from tying herself to Theo forever.

There must be a way to change one's primary residence, it was probably something to do with council tax or where you were registered to vote. If Theo managed it somehow, then surely they couldn't insist he had to leave? They already had the letter from the trustees. It was probably something he could do online, if they could only get reliable internet for ten minutes.

Her mother would know the relevant legislation, but she hadn't wanted Jan to come here in the first place and, cautious lawyer that she was, would advise Jan to leave regardless. She poked the letter back into its revealing position and pinched the envelope shut before marching reluctantly upstairs to knock at Theo and Nadya's door.

'What is it?' Nadya asked impatiently from inside.

'I think we have a problem.'

The bottom of the door was not flush with the carpet and she heard Theo say under his breath, 'Make her go away.'

Nadya called out, 'Now isn't a good time, can't you wait?'

'It's urgent; come on, guys.'

The door opened. The air was fuggy and the windows were closed, a bottle of gin resting on top of the nightstand while Nadya had wrapped the entire double duvet around herself, clearly naked underneath. Theo sat shirtless on the corner of the bed. He took the letter and read it quickly. Jan waited, thinking she saw for one moment a nascent expression of indecision before he straightened up and said with a new tone of calm derision in his voice, 'This is just classic countryside nonsense. One of my

106

neighbours clearly has it in for me. Did anyone see you take the letter?'

'Not as far as I know. The drive was empty apart from us. Isn't there a gardener who still sometimes works for you? Maybe it was him?'

'So much for feudal loyalty.' He yawned and stretched, then affectionately yanked Nadya's foot to tease her. She kicked him and turned over.

'What are you going to do?'

'I doubt the constabulary are going to come here and break down the gates with a battering ram, even they're not quite that old school.'

'The house can't be seen from the road, can it?'

'It certainly can't. That's always been part of its appeal.'

Nadya said grumpily, 'Sort it out, Theo. Bribe the gardener to go away or something.'

'No need. Just reseal the letter and tape it back where you found it. They can't prove we ever read it and if we leave it, they might end up believing we were never here in the first place. It buys us some time anyway.'

He rootled in his jeans pocket and took out the key. 'You should close the gates as well while you're at it.'

'So, we just ignore the letter?'

'Yes. They're busybodies and this is my house. There's no legal grounding for any of this nonsense anyway,' he said. 'My friend Raff's just qualified as a barrister and he told me most of the stuff they're doing is unenforceable.'

'But what about Nadya's car? If they were waiting round the corner and took down the licence plate, it's in her name.'

'I wouldn't worry about that.'

'It belongs to a shell company,' Nadya said, finally upright. 'The government cannot take it. Same as my apartment.'

Jan said, 'You're such a criminal, I love it.'

Nadya said, 'Only if they catch me. Go put it back up.'

'Alright, alright, I'll go.'

Now that Jan had become compliant, Nadya pulled her into a hug. As Jan tried resolutely to avoid the obvious wet patch still drying in the middle of the bed, Theo enfolded both of them in his wingspan, stinking of sweat and weed.

'Nadya's my little crim, eh?'

Jan asked, 'You're absolutely sure this isn't going to bite you in the arse with immigration stuff? I thought you had to be extra careful.'

'It's all going to be fine, and once we're legally married they can't touch us,' Nadya said.

Jan thought that despite his recent decision Theo had a pained look at the mention of the wedding, like a man who has sunk up to his waist in quicksand and is sure he has further yet to sink before all is silent.

He added, 'We haven't even started planning the party, but naturally you'll be a guest of honour. My best friend Will from school will be the best man – you won't mind being in the bridal party, will you? Or do Nads and I have to fight over who gets you?'

Visions of curly penis straws and £350 pink tulle bridesmaid creations in a size large swam before Jan's eyes, but she dismissed them. Knowing Nadya it would probably be a piss-up at a private members' club or a weekend away in Venice. Whenever any of them were allowed to fly regularly again, which seemed a prospect easily relegated to the distant future. Jan's grief congealed in her stomach as she extracted her arm from beneath Theo's.

'Seriously, go tape that notice back on before anyone sees and lock the gate. This is the master key, don't lose it. They haven't put a penalty on the letter, so you know they're simply trying their luck. And don't tell the others, they'll just panic.'

Jan sprinted down the back stairs, scrabbling for sticky tape in the boot room drawer and grabbing a nondescript green jacket as she went. Mission completed, after carefully retaping the letter and locking shut the gates behind her, she was slinking back over the lawn, still on high alert, when she heard the sound of heated conversation coming from Kara's window.

'Can't believe it . . . yes I know, I heard the whole thing this morning, they were making so much noise . . .' Kara's voice resonated.

Then Luke's throaty laughter.

'Her voice! The headboard was bashing the wall so hard this morning I swear the plaster was going to crack.'

'They're still at it, huh? It's been what, five years?' Luke asked.

'You've seen them, they're like teenagers. When they told us today, he was all over her. The constant PDA makes me sick.'

'Hey, I'm happy for him, he's still my closest friend in London. It'd be nice if you'd show me some affection like that once in a while, you know.'

'I went down on you for ages only last night and you couldn't even finish. My jaw still hurts, you ungrateful pig.'

'So I get a blow job once a month and that's it? That's my lot?'

'You're just selfish, you're obsessed with sex like all men. Can't you be the least bit romantic?'

'The last time I bought you flowers you got so mad: "Who was it this time, Luke? I know you cheated on me so just tell me who it was with." I saw them in the supermarket and thought you'd like them.'

'You bought me supermarket flowers? You're so cheap. This is exactly what I mean.'

'Baby, you know I don't have a job right now. I think this is all getting a bit overheated. Come here.'

'Don't touch me, don't you fucking touch me!'

The sound of loud sobbing followed, along with murmured reassurances from Luke, who was presumably still touching her.

The disaster had rumbled on for so many years that Jan no longer knew whose side she was on, if there was even a side or merely fragments of what had once been a relationship. When Luke had returned from Cambodia after over four years of near silence, the two had startled everyone by immediately resuming their antics, slightly less frenetically, but with a growing, evident rancour on Kara's end that had begun to terrify Jan with its venomousness. She ranted frequently to Jan and Ursie about how much she hated Luke, yet was suspicious of any new women who came into his orbit, believing them to have designs on him, and flirted with guys in bars whenever she and Luke were on a break, only to get embroiled in vociferous arguments about their politics. The one thing of which she could not accuse Luke was being insufficiently left wing, especially when he always poured

110

triple rum and Cokes for her and her friends at whichever pub he washed up behind the counter of.

***

Back in the kitchen, Jan eased the tray of defrosting lamb
meatballs out of the fridge and set them in the oven to
thaw before she could pan fry them, then quickly sliced
the tops off some red and green peppers before brushing
them with oil. Jan worked with practised ease, washing
and wilting handfuls of fresh spinach and cubing tangy
feta cheese, to stuff inside the peppers along with giant
couscous and a sprinkle of preserved lemon. Once the
peppers were properly baked, she would drip arterial
pomegranate syrup over the top and scatter a handful of
flaked almonds and coriander leaves over the tray.

Cooking had always calmed her down. Long weekends bumbling around alone in London while her parents
were away in Italy visiting her aunt had necessitated
learning domestic skills she might not otherwise have
acquired in her teens. She often wondered whether she
ought to have picked culinary school over academia – the
hours were much the same and she would find out faster
if her efforts were worth anything. Making food appealed
to her perfectionist tendencies and serving it gratified, if
only briefly, the unquenchable longing for approbation
she felt.

Jan sang 'Lovely Joan' as she worked, out of tune but
happy, knowing no one could hear her. Her lack of musi-
cality enraged and baffled her father, who could sit down at
the piano and break out into Ravel or Beethoven without
thinking anything of it. Her body was stiff and unbending,

like she had a solid rod for a spine. Luke had once asked in all seriousness if she'd been taught to carry books on her head as a child after one of their first-year Western Canon lecturers had shown them a clip from *My Fair Lady* while telling the class about *Pygmalion*. Years of being barked at to sit up straight, because slouching made her look 'untidy' meant Jan could move the mass of her lumbering body through the world with a kind of iron grace that resulted in ticket inspectors unthinkingly calling her Madam, but she had no ability to abandon herself physically unless Nadya forced her to.

The meatballs were sizzling promisingly and small gusts of steam crept out of the lightly charred hats of the peppers. She was prodding one with a fork to check the texture, when a muffled banging came from upstairs.

Jan rolled her eyes and ignored it, assuming that Kara was still angry with Luke, and turned on the kettle for the couscous. She was waiting for it to reach boiling point when the banging came again, louder this time and radiating through the floor. She raced up the back stairs and found Nadya waiting outside the bathroom near her and Theo's room, yanking on the handle and looking exasperated.

'Jan! Jan? Where have you been? I've been calling you for ages. Ursie's trapped in there and she's flipping out.'

Trying to collect herself, Jan forced the old air out of her lungs and took a deep, shivering breath. Ursie was shouting incomprehensibly from inside and hammering at the wood.

'Where's Theo? Doesn't he have a key?' she asked

'Don't know. I think he went to do something on the other side of the house. She sounds pretty desperate though.'

'Let me out!' The hammering intensified. 'I'm going to faint! This isn't funny!' Jan heard her ram her shoulder against the door, her breathing fast, bordering on panic attack.

'Hold on, Ursie, I can get to you!' She sized up the door and took a step back, preparing to break it down.

'Wait, wait!' Theo had appeared behind Nadya, looking puzzled by all the commotion. 'Let me try first before you do that.'

A strand of dark hair flopped over his brow and he pushed it back irritably. He put his hand to the knob and turned it experimentally, seeming as surprised as any of them as the door opened with ease when he pulled at it. Ursie tumbled out, almost knocking Jan over, before shoving her away to stand with her hands braced against her thighs breathing heavily, trying to stop the towel falling away from her body.

Theo put one hand gingerly on her bare shoulder. 'What's wrong? Did you lock yourself in somehow and get scared?'

Nadya gave Jan a sidelong glance and went over to turn the knob of the now-opened door back and forth quizzically.

'I was having a shower in that disgusting tub and thought I heard the door open and someone come in, but I couldn't see with all the steam. I told them to leave me alone but didn't get any reply. When I got out to yell at them some more, the door just slammed shut. The heat must have made me dizzy. I got really panicky all of a sudden and my hands were wet. She shuddered. 'I couldn't get it open.' Now glaring at Nadya: 'Why didn't you do it? I was so freaked out.'

113

'It wouldn't turn, I thought you'd locked it from inside.' She said to Theo, 'Why do you even have keys for these anyway?'

'I don't think we ever used them for the inside doors, I've got no idea where those are kept.'

'That reminds me.' Jan fished the key to the gates from her waist-bag and handed it back to Theo for safekeeping.

'Good girl,' he said. 'I wondered where that got to.'

Ursie said, 'Is there a knack to the handle?'

Theo answered, 'I don't know, it's just old.'

Nadya harrumphed and returned to her room to finish dressing, while Ursie stood on the landing, still in her towel and looking uncertain. She pushed the door to the bathroom further ajar and looked back into the steam anxiously. Theo pushed past her, insistent upon opening the small window above the toilet to prevent mould. Looking past the damp shower curtain yanked hastily to one side above the bath, Jan found her gaze travelling over to the mirror, which was fogged with condensation. The surface was curiously smeared as if with frenetic writing, but even as she peered in, trying to work out what it might say, Theo took an old towel and cleaned away any remaining trace. Jan was about to ask Ursie whether she'd noticed the same thing when a delicious, citrusy scent crept up the stairs to fill her nostrils.

'The meatballs!' Jan raced back down to rescue them from burning in the oven, all thoughts of doors and mirrors forgotten for the moment.

Promptly after dinner, Theo began depositing bumps into the divots of a mancala board with his tiny golden spoon. A cluster of pre-rolled joints sat in a little Willow pattern bowl he had taken down from the sideboard.

'There are six of us, right?' He laid a pen midway across the board to mark the border between one substance and another, while Nadya was decanting the luxury Finnish vodka she'd brought into dessert wine glasses.

'It's a betrayal of the motherland, but I really think this might be the best you can get here. Did you bring any pickles, Jan?'

'Of course, let me go slice them.'

'You going to bring out some gefilte fish as well?' Luke asked.

'No, but you can always be chopped liver.'

Ursie asked, 'So what are we doing here, exactly?'

Theo said, 'You know Ring of Fire? This is Inferno, the enhanced version. Diamonds are coke, spades are two puffs of one of these, hearts are shots and clubs are K.'

At the same moment Ursie laughed and said, 'Good god,' Jan said, 'Please no, I always K-hole and I hate it. Also, you should balance out your uppers and your downers.'

'Alright, clubs are speed. Lucky I brought some, I don't always.' Theo started scooping the K-bumps back into the packet and replaced them with slightly yellowy, chalky-looking speed.

'Is everyone clear on the original rules?' Nadya asked.

Luke said, 'It's been a while since I played, can you remind me?'

Theo reeled off the complicated rules about who drank when and why. 'Normally for Ring of Fire you'd just pour some of your drink into the King cup and the last King drawn has to down it. Since this is Inferno, you just put whichever substance you would normally take onto this little tray and we save it for the unlucky fourth King.'

Kara said, 'Can you write all those down on a bit of paper? My head hurts hearing about these again and I actually know the rules.'

'But forgetting them is the fun part.'

Jan said, 'She's right actually, there's already plenty of opportunity for penalties even with the rules written down. And what if you're the most gone, Theo?'

'Ugh fine.'

Ursie said, 'This is some of the dumbest shit I've ever heard of and I'm very into it.'

Nadya began shuffling the cards with a practised hand and separated out the jokers and aces.

Kara was the first to draw a two of diamonds and picked Luke.

'Baby, you know it's a penalty, not a favour?'

Kara giggled and passed him the coke straw. All the guys had to do a shot and then Jan was thumbmaster with the five of clubs, catching Kara out.

'You sure I can't have K instead? Speed makes me feel really weird and spacey.'

'Do you think you might have ADHD, Kara?' Nadya asked.

'Don't know. I never got checked for anything except dyslexia, which I definitely don't have. Maybe.'

Theo said, 'Dr Stoyanova is in the house tonight. It's your turn to pick a card, Nads.'

She drew the ten of spades, 'Okay, categories. I'm stuck here.'

116

Theo suggested, 'Dog breeds?'

'I don't know the English names for those.'

Ursie said, 'Sexual fetishes?'

'That's a good one!' said Nadya. 'Okay, feet.'

Ursie said, 'Latex,' Luke said, 'Shoes,' Kara said, 'Voyeurism,' Jan said 'Troilism,' Theo said, 'Uh . . . what the hell is Troilism? . . . Piss?'

Ursie shouted, 'Drink! You paused so you have to drink.'

Nadya said, 'No, he has to smoke this. What is Troilism, Jan?'

'You know, like Troilus and Criseyde.'

Ursie snorted but Nadya cocked her head to one side, 'I need a bit more to go on than that.'

'It's a fetish for seeing the person you love with someone else.'

Nadya, fiddling with her ring as she worried the large green stone around and around her finger, said, 'Isn't that just a fancy word for cuckolding?'

Ursie said, 'Hang on, isn't that basically the same as voyeurism?'

'No, it's a very specific subset of voyeurism.'

'And you'd know, would you?' Nadya asked.

Jan shrugged and tried not to grin, her memory of that morning resurfacing to thrill her once again with its obscene daring. Nadya could throw her freedom away if she was determined to, but clearly there were certain itches Theo simply could not scratch.

'Enough!' Theo boomed out. 'All of us have to smoke the joint and then we move on.'

Ursie said, 'Please tell me you haven't made this insanely strong.'

'You're lucky I didn't roll a Camberwell Carrot for the occasion.'

The game continued, with Ursie consistently missing the cue to point at the sky, Nadya taking every opportunity to dose people as a penalty and Theo successfully quibbling his way out of most of them. The girls had just done another round of shots when Nadya pointed and asked, 'Who's that in the picture, Theo? It's super creepy.'

'That would be Great-Uncle H, himself,' Theo said. 'The man whose largesse you're enjoying.'

They all looked over at the oil painting above the empty fireplace which had caught Luke's eye earlier that day. Jan realised that the artist had rendered the proportions of Harold's body ineptly, making it far more muscular than was really appropriate to a man in his seventies, presumably to flatter him.

Out of the corner of her eye, Jan saw Nadya dart out a hand over Theo's drink and pour a quick stream of powder from her opened ring into the glass. Catching on quickly, Jan asked in a loud voice, 'Can anyone else see the buttons of a jacket behind the lectern thingy? It looks like that was painted in a bit later, maybe to cover something up.'

Luke got up and went over to peer at it. 'I guess there must have been another figure next to him at one point. Look at this big rough section by the side.'

With the overhead light shining on the canvas instead of sunlight from the window, a darker shadow to Harold's left had become visible. It reached from the bottom of the painting to about the height of the top of Harold's head. The outline of the smudgy silhouette made Jan suspect it had once been a woman, but she had no way to prove the theory.

'I've no idea who that might have been. He never married and didn't seem to have many friends left when we knew him.'

'You never talk about him, what was he like?' Kara asked. 'I want to know more, it's his house after all.'

'A recluse, mostly. I barely saw him after we stayed here one night when I was twelve and I got really sick from food poisoning. I don't think my dad ever forgave him for that.'

Nadya's hand had safely withdrawn. She said, 'You should try to find out who the other figure was, it's sad not to know more about your own home.'

Kara said, 'Aren't you the expert?'

'Not in paintings from the twentieth century, no.'

Ursie said, 'I wish there was a portrait of me by someone else. I always wanted one. Doing my own is not the same.'

'No doubt there'll be a portrait of you one day when you get knighted for services to the arts, Ursie,' Jan said, her stomach twisting with admiration and resentment.

'I would never. Order of the British Empire? I don't know, my mum and aunty would be really proud, but I'd be so uncomfortable with it.'

Theo said, 'Fair enough, titles all flow down from the Queen anyway. You know most of Lancaster and Cornwall are owned by the Crown, right? They have loads of special rules about driftwood and farming. I remember Harold used to tell me about it.'

Kara interjected, 'Half of Scotland's closed off for toffs to play blood sports on. Let's guillotine the lot of them and get it over with.'

'And will I be spared? The baronetcy passed down another line, after all.'

Ursie grumbled, 'I guess so. But I still don't think anyone should own land.'

'Or private property in general. That goes for your parents' house too, Jan, and mine.' Kara sniffed with martyred satisfaction at the consistent nature of her edict and did another bump.

'So, what happens to holiday homes?' Nadya asked.

Ursie jumped in before Kara could. 'People should still be able to go on holiday. The whole point of socialism is to make people's lives better. I just don't think anyone should have more than they need, including property.'

Nadya said, 'We tried that. It didn't go so well, remember? You still got special treatment if you knew the right people.'

Theo said, 'Guys, this is so boring, I hate listening to people argue about politics.'

Kara said sharply, 'Everything is political. Literally what else is there to talk about?'

Before he could answer, Ursie kept going, 'The Soviets failed because their agricultural plan was a disaster. They tried to specialise different crops in different regions and then corrupt locals kept skimming off the top. And the weather was shit. I have read about this, you know.'

Nadya was looking at Ursie like she was a piece of gum adhered to a suede boot. 'I can't believe you're arguing with me about the history of my own country.'

Ursie continued, 'Just because the USSR didn't work out as a project, doesn't mean that everything was bad. What about all the African nations who got Soviet support in their struggle for independence, like Angola? And I challenge you to tell me a single thing about socialism in the Caribbean.'

Jan tamped a moistened finger over the powdery table and left them to it, fearing what would happen if she inserted herself directly into an argument between Nadya and Ursie.

'Where were we with the game again?' Theo asked. 'I think it was my turn. Jack of diamonds. I get to make a new rule: no more politics tonight, and anyone who disobeys has to do a big bump of ket.'

Kara said, 'But—'

'Come on, you can fight about it in the morning if you're that desperate. Pick a card.'

She drew a three of clubs and proceeded to work away at the joint, scowling. Jan introduced a rule that anyone who drew a card had to get up and run widdershins around the table, which they constantly forgot because they were so reluctant to do it. Theo had to refresh the mancala board and Nadya refilled the shot glasses. The game grew ever sillier as the rules became more convoluted and everyone more drunkenly insistent on awarding penalties. Caribou was looping in the background – as the frequent soundtrack to their revels, it had the curious effect of making Jan feel high all by itself, and worked as an intensifier in these sorts of situations. When Theo drew the final King, the rest of the assembled group whooped and jeered with relief.

'Much nicer than a big cup of mixed liquids, I have to say,' he said as he twirled the straw between two fingers and set about clearing the tray as his reward for losing.

Moments later, he had his eyes closed and was mumbling incoherently. Nadya scooted over to him and put her hand on his shoulder. 'Are you okay, my love?'

'I'm fine . . . just . . . very tire . . . wet coins?'

121

'Theo, open your eyes.'

'Yes?'

She held his head back a little, trying to get him to look at her. 'Are you asleep?'

'Maybe.' He shook himself. 'I'm not feeling so good.'

'Let's go to bed.'

'No, stay here.'

'You can't stay here; this is the sofa.'

'Okay then . . . broccoli.'

'Oh Theo, you're so high. He's really overdone it this time.'

Luke said, 'He's dreaming with his eyes open. He's totally gone. Let me get him under one arm.'

'Thank you. I'll get his shoes off now.' Nadya collected up his things and they slowly led Theo away and upstairs. She turned to give Jan a look over one shoulder before the group passed out of sight.

Kara said, 'Are all your boarding-school friends Tories, Jan? Or just Nadya?'

'Mercifully not. But generally going to people's houses and talking about how they should be repossessed won't get you the most receptive audience.'

'We were talking theoretically.'

'You made it pretty personal. You're lucky Theo is so chill.'

Ursie tried to make a joke of it. 'It'll be okay. When this place is seized after the revolution, I'll try to swing it so we can all still hang out here. We can have a community garden.'

'And in this fantastical world after the rain, who's going to come and take my family home from me? You two?'

122

After a pause, Kara said, 'I guess so. There's no need to be so *conservative* about it.'

'Are you fucking serious?' Jan was practically spitting now, fighting the urge to get right in Kara's face. 'In what way is not wanting to lose our only home conservative? My great-grandfather fled Russia when he was basically still a child, with all his worldly goods sewn into his coat to escape being murdered in the pogroms. I also want higher taxes and civil rights for everyone, but do you have any idea why joking about taking my house is not funny? I'm sure *you'd* be fine, but we wouldn't. Or does your knowledge of Communism not stretch to the Doctors' Plot?'

'This isn't Russia, or nineteen-thirties Germany. Are you seriously telling me you don't feel safe here? You're being kind of dramatic and self-victimising.'

The rage that Jan had been bottling up since the previous year's election cycle spilled over.

'Are you even aware that Jews were banned from Britain from almost four hundred years? Do you have any idea how it feels to walk past the cemetery in Oxford they destroyed and built a fancy garden over? To see you all congratulating yourselves over the Kindertransport when you let the adults die? The school Nadya and I went to wouldn't even allow Jews until the seventies.'

'Calm down, Jan, Jesus.' Kara relit one of the half-smoked joints and inhaled. 'People not being admitted to public school is hardly a tragedy, but you made your point.' She slid the mancala board and the little spoon in Jan's direction.

'Sorry,' Ursie said. 'Though to be fair, my grandparents were not around for most of that.' Then she asked, 'So they spoke Russian?'

123

'Yes, and Yiddish. But they didn't teach my grandparents, so it was lost.'

Kara asked, 'How come you didn't learn Yiddish?'

'And talk to who with it? The Jewish Labour Bund are mostly ashes. I should have learned Hebrew instead, as that might actually be useful if I ever have to leave the country.'

Ursie, choosing to divert the conversation before it became even more explosive, said, 'Yeah, I reckon I might turn in. Has anyone seen my hoody?'

Jan found it on the back of an armchair and, still feeling badly for yelling at her, held out her arms to Ursie and said sorry in return, not looking at Kara as she did so. Ursie stepped forward to be hugged.

She said, 'You know, if there is a revolution, I'd want you on my side. You're pretty scary when you're angry.'

'You too, Urs. Good night.' Jan kissed the top of Ursie's forehead, before she went to grab her phone and tobacco pouch. Jan watched her head upstairs, longing to call her back, to try and listen to her side of things without defensiveness. To ask questions instead of reacting. But it was all too late, and if Ursie did not stay of her own accord, Jan could not force herself to beg.

Luke came back downstairs and draped himself beside Kara on the couch.

'The lovebirds have gone to bed. Theo was in a bad way. I thought Big Boy could hold his drugs better than that, but he's dead to the world. Someone change the song.'

Kara stroked his blond curls and said, 'He must have been tired out from the picnic, still. They're such an odd couple. How long have you known Nadya now, Jan?'

'Since we were sixteen. I can't believe they've been dating for five years; I was the one who introduced them as well.' It was one of the enduring regrets of Jan's life that she had reflexively invited Nadya to her master's thesis hand-in drinks, thinking Nadya wouldn't want to hang out with Jan's university friends.

Kara said, '*I* can't believe he's going to marry a Tory.' Jan internally noted how she gave Theo a pass, perhaps because he never fought with her directly, or she simply liked him better than Nadya. When Jan and Kara first met in halls, she'd been entirely apolitical in a gently hippyish way, but gradually she'd started attending demos and circulating petitions along with Ursie. But unlike Ursie, she also got caught up in fierce rows with random people on social media, broke things to prove obscure points and cut off old friends for trivial differences of opinion. Jan wanted to believe Kara was enlivened by a new zeal for justice, but it largely felt like an overflow of the rage she could not aim squarely at Luke for fear he would leave again.

'I've known her for almost half my life and I don't think that's quite fair, if you listen to what she actually said.'

'Yes, but it's the way she said it, you know how girls like that are. She only likes fancy places and fancy people.'

'She's so stingy at the moment, I don't know what's gotten into her.' Luke licked a finger and ran it round the divots of the mancala board to gather up the residue.

Kara said, 'I've never been allowed to have a proper conversation with her and ask about her beliefs, if she even has any. Theo always butts in and changes the subject; you know how he hates conflict.'

Jan felt the tug of an invisible string, as fine as spider silk but stronger than steel wire, tugging her upstairs. She

prayed she'd interpreted Nadya's parting glance correctly.
'I think I'm getting sleepy.'

'You've done the most gak after me, there's no way you can sleep now.'

'I have Valium. Don't have too much fun without me, guys.'

'You know we will.' Luke blew her a scornful kiss, eyes already on the thick margin of powder clustered inside the speed baggy that had fallen from Theo's pocket to the floor. Jan headed up the staircase, mindful not to hurry in case her tread against the boards was audible from the Western drawing room.

She turned, shot home the bolt to her room and pulled a little antique library chair that folded out into a stepladder towards the centre of the carpet. Was she really going to go through with this? Trying not to capsize onto the floor, she stretched up and on her second attempt managed to hook a finger into the ring for the trapdoor she had located the day before. She pondered briefly how bored Nadya must have been to discover this feature on her last visit – she had said Theo spent the entire time there on mushrooms, crawling about downstairs like a worm. Jan yanked the trapdoor wide open and shucked off both shoes to haul herself up into the musty dark of the attic, phone tucked into her bra as the only source of light. Treading carefully over the rafters that stretched out above Ursie's bedroom, she made her way slowly through the Western wing of the house and rapped three times on the ceiling roughly where she'd been instructed Nadya and Theo's room would be.

Waiting in the pitch black, surrounded by the mouldering accoutrements of generations of Mortimers, Jan struggled not to laugh. At least it would keep her from weeping. Because she had loved Nadya, more or less consistently, since she was sixteen, a woman who would never love her back, who had always treated sex with her like she was gratifying some vile need of Jan's. (And yet she kept returning.) Because she was, despite all that, lying patiently in the dust waiting for the newly engaged Nadya like her faithful dog. It was too much, all too much.

The hatch opened and Nadya shimmied up from the linen closet in the en suite bathroom below.

'You didn't need to knock so loudly; I almost fell out of bed.'

'How's Theo?'

'Fast asleep. He woke up again and I thought he would never go down.'

'A poison ring, really?' Jan felt Nadya shrug in the darkness.

'Be nice and I'll tell you where I got it. It's great for clubbing.'

'Come on.' Jan wrapped a hand around Nadya's wrist, emboldened.

'Get off! I'm coming.'

She crawled back to the ceiling over her own room, Nadya close behind her. She waited, on her knees, before she felt a hand push her face first down into the rough wooden flooring, her forehead furring with dirt. Then Nadya pulled up the skirt of Jan's dress and dragged her fingernails along the upper part of Jan's thigh.

She said, gloatingly, 'That's right, kneel for me. Keep your face down.'

Jan felt Nadya lifting the dress higher and higher, soft cotton draped back over her shoulders, as Nadya's nails raked her waist and hips, digging in so sharply they drew blood. Nothing else mattered but the ragged nerves in her back, as she bore it silently, gratefully.

She saw faint light from a distant window gleam over an old set of silver candlesticks, richly adorned with bunches of grapes and curling vines, forking branches interlaced to curl over and under one another. They stood abandoned in the attic, their dust cover fallen away to reveal the casually abandoned treasure. Theo really didn't take care of his things.

Nadya said, 'You can touch yourself if you have to,' as she moved on to pulling handfuls of Jan's hair, pausing to cram her fingers into Jan's mouth so she had to lick the blood off them. 'Does it hurt?'

'Very much.'

Nadya ran her nails across Jan's back again, tugging at the cuts she'd just inflicted. She trailed one hand around to reach into Jan's bra and seize the nipple with a bolt through it, twisting till Jan saw prickles of light at the edges of her vision. Nadya had an unerring instinct for the sort of pain that Jan most feared and so badly needed. Her tolerance scared other lovers, but Nadya scorned its limitations.

'You're such a mess. It's a pity it's so dark in here that I can't see the pathetic look in your eyes when I do this to you.'

Jan tried to keep herself from moaning, but one small sound escaped.

'Shut up. Just shut up and do what you have to in silence,' Nadya whispered and wiped her newly bloodied hand on Jan's dress, then after a few moments pulled Jan's hand out of her pants. A ray of moonlight trailed down from a tiny window near the fold of the roof. They were surrounded by decaying leather trunks and unknowable objects draped with sheets. Jan's nostrils were thick with the smell of cobwebs and damp.

Nadya forced Jan up onto her knees by the hair and held her by the throat, twisting her round to face her.

'None of them know about this, do they?' Nadya's eyes glittered with revelry, near-silver in the gloom.

'But Theo said—'

Nadya shook her roughly by the neck before Jan could croak out another word.

'Never tell them. I can't risk it.'

Nadya could not name what they did, or what she feared; 'it' was all that this would ever be.

She forced a finger and thumb into Jan's mouth to open it wide, and drew close.

They almost never kissed these days, not since Nadya's adolescent teasing of Jan had graduated to this. She pursed her lips and spat, hot dust and saliva dissolving on Jan's tongue.

'Swallow it and say nothing. Go to bed.' Jan put out on one hand, grazing Nadya's breast with the backs of her fingers in a gesture of offering.

'I don't want that right now. Go to your bed.'

Jan gulped a little and obeyed, crawling over to the trap-door for her room, scrabbling for the catch and hearing Nadya snicker at her ineptitude. She did not look back.

Standing perfectly still in her room, she listened carefully for the sound of Nadya above her, moving ever so slowly back to where she'd come from. Jan turned to examine her own face in the dresser mirror, streaked with spit and dust, pupils still stretched wide from her indulgences.

Was this the hour of her life in which she was the most beautiful she would ever be? Would she know if that hour had already irretrievably passed? The thought of having spent it on Nadya enraged her, and yet she firmly believed that beauty was meant to be wasted, its whole point was that it could not be used, for then it would become something else entirely.

She swung her bedroom window open past the point where the latch fell away and smoked a final cigarette. The terrible privacy of her affair struck her at times as the most perfect thing in her life, inviolate and known only to one other person, who had far more reason than she not to reveal it. It was easier to imagine murdering Nadya than it was to imagine being with her day to day, not that Jan hadn't tried both. The knowledge that she could love her searchingly, adoringly and furiously, without ever having to truly risk the rejection that was already absolutely certain, sustained Jan in a way that felt too intrinsic to safely ponder. She could sleep with as many women as would have her, do the most degrading things that appealed to her, and never worry that she would be any less in Nadya's eyes, for when Nadya looked at her at all, it was with pure contempt. Held between unreachable longing and despair, she was entirely free.

The Third Day

The light reached its strong thin fingers into the room, distressing Jan as she lay suspended between dreaming and wakefulness, unable to rouse herself or return to sleep. She lay with her eyes closed for some minutes listening to the wood pigeons crooning outside and the wind playing through the trees before giving up. The faint mothball smell that emanated from the light-raked silk curtains cast her back into the realm of memory.

She had been about ten, at primary school, and put in charge of the dressing-up box for school plays, along with another girl who continually engaged Jan in physical fights and then went crying to the teacher when she lost on account of her small stature. The joint responsibility was presumably intended to transform them into fast friends.

They had been chattering on about something while folding the raggedy feather boas and testing the brightest colours from an old palette of face paint when the girl proclaimed, 'My daddy says Jews don't go to Heaven.'

Jan had been so startled she dropped the palette, magenta, turquoise and viridian blocks crumbling onto the laminate floor and pigment smearing everywhere as she tried to wipe it up. The girl had yet again gone running and, when Jan tried to explain what had happened, the teacher began telling the girl off for saying something nasty and then made them apologise to each other.

One night, Jan had asked her grandmother, Ruth, whether Christians did indeed go to a different Heaven and the whole story had eventually come out.

Ruth asked, 'This little girl, what does she look like?'

And when Jan had answered that the girl had blonde hair and blue eyes and all the teachers thought she was so sweet because she sang in a choir, her grandmother had replied with a surprising degree of venom, 'Little Nazi child. I bet she gets it from her parents. Have you ever met them?'

'No, but her dad runs the garage. She brings in chocolates all the time, it's why she's so popular.'

'One day she is going to grow up and start being nice to you, because it looks better for her. But don't forget what she said, not for one minute, Gianetta, because that's what she's really like underneath. You know your grandpa was in the Black Book? The Germans had a long list of names in a book; they were going to find us and kill us if they landed. And sweet, choir-singing people like that would have helped them.'

Jan had heard all about the Germans at school, though the war had then seemed very remote, taking place a very long time ago and very far away. The idea of them coming to London, looking for her family, shifted from impossible to suddenly, starkly plausible.

'What happened to all the corned beef? Dad told me you have lots of beef in the attic ready for another war.'

Her grandmother laughed. 'Oh, I threw it all away years ago. It was so out of date; it would have killed your grandpa if he'd ever tried to eat it.'

Jan's grandfather's decision to hoard tinned food for a forthcoming cataclysm was the stuff of family legend. The larder of the Rubin household was even now crammed with beans and pickled vegetables, a habit born of ingrained trauma and terror that her father had never managed to shake and had passed on to her in turn. When the lockdown orders came, Jan had been perplexed to discover that only she and Ursie kept preserved food stockpiled as a matter of course.

Jan finally managed to convince herself to reach for the glass of water by her bedside and, chugging half of it, sat up to find that her head did not hurt as much as she had been dreading. Knowing that the true hangover would come later, she decided to make the most of the grace period before it hit.

Her dress from last night lay next to her in the bed, like the outline of a vanished companion, and a badly rolled cigarette balanced precariously at the edge of the night-stand next to an open jar of face cream.

She groaned, swallowed a painkiller and went to force herself to drink another pint of water straight from the tap. Looking blearily out of the bathroom window, she thought she saw someone in the orchard but decided it must be a fox. The house was still apart from the clock, not even the pipes were stirring, her friends plunged deep into silence like sleepers in their tombs awaiting the world to come. She dragged on a pair of leggings and a big t-shirt and walked on the balls of her feet out onto the upstairs landing. Perhaps there would be sunglasses in the boot room she could wear. All the doors in eyeshot were closed. One of Ursie's newly adopted house slippers sat in the middle of the landing carpet. She turned wearily to see the door to the end bedroom once again stood open, light streaming through. Deciding she was too fragile to risk another confrontation between Luke and Theo, she went to close it.

With the dream-slow steps of one still sleepwalking, Jan made her way along the corridor. The smell she'd caught a whiff of before had now intensified; the cloying, faecal sweetness filling her nose, its stench rich on her tongue, as if she were enduring someone pouring it down her throat. She was drowning in it. She heard a creak and pushed the door a little further without thinking, swinging it back into the room. Filled with light, the room thronged with dancing dust, motes eddying and rising in every ray. The hinges of the door whined as she opened it all the way, and the currents in the house were such that as she pushed it further, she felt a slight tugging, the air pulling her into the room. She shook her head and yawned to crack her jaw, trying to dissipate the pressure building in her skull. The bed was made up, pristine and empty with an old woollen coverlet spread over it. Opposite the hulking wardrobe, a carved wooden screen obscured the leftmost corner of the room. Through the windows, she watched the lawn unfolding like a cashmere shawl; it looked soft and inviting enough to rest one's head on. It wasn't so bad in here, there was no reason for the apprehension she felt, for the fine hairs on her neck to stand stiff as needles. She was being stupid. She glanced back at the door to make sure it was still open. Where was that smell coming from?

A gust of wind blew in from the window, half-open at the top. She stepped forward around the bed to snap it closed and the cupboard door swung abruptly open. Jan felt a small eddy of air rush past her, almost like a short sharp laugh right in her ear. She began to turn before she saw the edge of the mirror at the centre of the cupboard door, and found herself welded to the spot. She could not look at it directly. Peripheral vision suddenly, unwelcomely keen, she thought she saw movement in the glass as a reticulated section of the wooden screen slid infinitesimally forward into the room, the space behind it slightly larger now as it stood between her and the door. She did not want to see; she could not turn around. She froze there, eyes fixed on the carpet, trapped, trying not to make a sound and rouse the others from their comedowns. She must not make noise; Theo would be furious she'd come in here herself after he forbade it. She must not scream. She must not look to make sure that was no shadow, just a trick of the light darkening the carved-out sections of the screen behind her. And yet despite all efforts she could not look away. The shadow outline intensified; her eyes locked to the mirror's edge.

Out in the hallway, she heard footsteps, Ursie singing wordlessly as she walked downstairs. All at once her feet broke free of the carpet. No longer frozen, she ran from the room, closing the door behind her with agonising slowness so as not to slam it. And even so she feared that it would not stay shut.

***

Jan walked past the Western drawing room and saw Kara stood in silent contemplation of Harold's portrait, her lips moving as if she was speaking, though no words came out. Jan decided Kara must be relitigating another argument with Luke and, not knowing what sort of mood she would turn on Jan, passed on in silence, in search of a different companion. She was gasping for a cigarette but

135

the idea of being alone again unsettled her so much she couldn't bear to step outside for one.

She found Ursie sitting in the dining room and asked her, 'Do you want some tea?' while trying to stop her voice from trembling oddly. Ursie barely looked up, busy sketching out ideas in her little purple book. In between pen strokes, she ran her fingers through her braids.

'I'm alright thanks, just trying to do some work. Got to get back on track today.'

Ursie seemed to hope her emphasis on work would dispel Jan, but no such luck. Whatever had just happened, Jan desperately needed a dose of normality, even if normality was Ursie wishing Jan wasn't there.

'We . . . we've got some nice seed bread for toast if you want, or even croissants?'

She felt wan and crumpled, leaning her hand against the door because she wasn't sure she could keep standing without it. How long had the others stayed up without her? She could feel a migraine threatening to burst out of her skull, vision warping at the edges and tendrils of discomfort curling along the veins in her head.

'I'm fine. You know I don't normally go for breakfast much, my stomach's all closed up like a fist.' Ursie started drawing again, pointedly breaking eye contact.

The headboard of Theo and Nadya's bed began bashing the wall rhythmically above them, the resulting thuds and groans painfully audible in the dining room below. Ursie had put in one earbud and was about to insert the other when Jan asked, 'What are you drawing?' in an attempt to distract herself from the noise.

Her competitive anxiety stole over her. It pained her to watch others doing anything creative when she herself couldn't or wouldn't commit to it on a regular basis, her thesis blocking out all other possibilities of self-expression in its bloated immensity.

'Just some bits for my website and Insta. You've got to make time for your art every day, it's like weightlifting. It gets easier the more you do it.'

Jan nodded, searching for a way to keep the conversation going. 'When did you start writing visual essays? I realise I never asked.'

Ursie sighed and put her pen down, though the earbud stayed in. 'They're not essays exactly, more like imagery with some words or an artist's journal. I don't know, I guess I've always done it. Mum has all these photos of me scribbling away when I was just a kid; she'd get everyone to give me Smith's vouchers for birthdays and Christmas.'

'Even during uni?' Jan plonked herself down on an empty chair in front of the french windows and stretched, trying to rid herself of the crick in her neck. 'I don't understand how you made the time; you were always so busy.'

'You're blocking my light, please.' Ursie gestured to the battered silver jug and a cut glass bowl she'd plucked from the dresser. 'Anyway, that was the most time we'll ever have to ourselves. If you want something done, ask a busy person. I can take a look at your writing if you want to do an exchange.'

'Oh no, I couldn't. I just have weird phone notes and then my fucking thesis. I've not really been able to focus much, I can barely keep up with the papers I'm supposed to have read. I feel like my understanding of what a book even is has been stretched so much over the last four years.'

'Nothing wrong with writing on your phone, I do it all the time. And maybe it'd be nice to get back into more contemporary stuff, see what you've been missing. There's so much great queer lit out there . . . not that that's the only thing that would interest you, but maybe it'd be more up your street if you're sick of the Vikings.'

'There are the classics and a handful of good new books,' Jan said, 'but a lot of them are about coming out and that's not a stage of life I ever want to revisit.'

'If you can't find exactly what you want, write one of your own. Everyone who isn't a straight white toff goes through this.'

'I suppose so. I just feel very alone.'

Ursie took the bait and closed her book. 'That's just not true. There's loads of queer women and trans people making exciting things. If you want community, you actually need to go looking for it, instead of waiting for it to come to you. What about doing some activism?'

Jan snapped, 'You know why I can't do that.'

Ursie looked at her, confused. 'Sorry, what?'

She knew she was venturing into dangerous territory again, but couldn't stop without first trying to offer some explanation for her loneliness. 'They're all literally obsessed with Israel. I stopped going to any LGBT Soc meetings because it got brought up every single time as a test and then they would all look at me to see how I reacted.'

Ursie sighed deeply and said, 'Do you not read the news, Jan? I get that it's probably very uncomfortable, but the violence is unbearable. Do you not see all the awful pictures of the bombings?'

Jan, exasperated, asked her 'Did I do that? Do you seriously think I'm enthusiastic about bombing Palestinians?

I can't even vote there. And it's not like I can move there and get involved in changing things without people condemning me even more for that.'

Ursie stood up, facing Jan across the table. 'Okay, so join a Jewish group then, if talking about war crimes makes you that desperately uncomfortable.'

'I went looking. They're all religious, and I still don't know if I believe in God. I probably never will.'

'I don't know what you want me to say. This doesn't seem like it's about your writing.' Ursie threw her pens back in their case in exasperation.

'It's about everything, writing is a part of that, but . . . do you not ever feel like you don't fit in anywhere?'

'What do *you* think, Jan? That first day, when we all met, and everyone seemed to already know each other, because you'd all been to the same schools and I thought we were going to be talking about our favourite books, not Horatio the Third who passed out in Chelsea or whatever? Like, there are teachers and nurses on my estate, but half the people I met at uni barely expected a Black woman to be literate let alone better at translating Virgil than them.'

'I'm sorry, they really were such dicks, even after you won the prose comp prize.'

'My friend Monique got into Cambridge on a full scholarship for Maths and had people constantly offering her money to buy them drugs when she doesn't even drink. I had to go looking for *my* people and the ones who do get it are worth hanging onto.'

'Why do I feel like by "my people" you don't mean us?'

'How about, you know, this place?' She pointed up at the ceiling, Hephaestus still tumbling eternally without ever hitting the ground. 'This stupid pandemic holiday you all roped me into coming on, and now Nadya's society wedding we're all going to be expected to attend. Did it ever occur to you that I might be alienated too?'

'Society wedding? Come on, you know she hates that sort of thing. It'll probably be about ten people.'

'That's not the point. I love you guys, I really do, but increasingly it's like you live on a different planet to me. The year we met wasn't the beginning of our lives together; it was the very end of the good times, the conditions that allowed people like me to even be in the same room as you lot ended when austerity got going. That was the last year of the old tuition fees and none of you seem to have noticed how everything changed except maybe Kara, though she still goes on about privilege like she doesn't have any herself. And don't you start. Any time I want to talk to you about anything real, I have to ever so gently manoeuvre your self-pity and defensiveness out of the way first so you can hear me and by the time that's done, I'm mostly too exhausted to speak.'

After a long pause, Jan said, 'For what it's worth, I think if you don't fit in, it's because you're head and shoulders above everyone else. I do get what you're saying, but in any conditions you would still stand out as exceptional. Just don't forget we still love you, okay?'

Ursie drew an exasperated breath. 'I won't. Is there any coffee going?'

'I'll go make some.' Jan put off her smoke and bustled away to the kitchen. The room was piled high with wine-stained glasses, plates smeared with unidentifiable gunge, and loose grapes strewn about. Jan's posy wilted in the centre of it all. Every cupboard door hung open and the tap was dripping noisily.

She could not now ignore the truth that Ursie was indeed avoiding her, however justified that might turn out to be. She felt her eyes prickling with tears and swallowed heavily. Any noticeable reaction to chastisement would just provide further evidence of Jan's unworthiness and her own problems were apparently irrelevant rather than the basis for solidarity between them.

'Actually . . .'

Jan turned away from the pot she'd been dumping spoonfuls of coffee into to see Ursie standing in the doorway of the kitchen. She hoped her nose wasn't too red.

'Yes?'

'Theo's family's been here a while, right?'

'Centuries, he said. How come?'

'This sounds mad, but while you've been here, have you heard stuff? Like things you couldn't explain?'

Dread goosepimpled Jan's arms and tightened her gullet with nausea. It was so cold in the kitchen; she couldn't bear it any longer. When had the temperature dropped? She went to open the door to the garden in hope of welcoming in warm summer air.

'What kind of things?'

'I was probably dreaming, but I swear last night I heard something dragging across the ceiling.'

Jan breathed out. She was imagining it after all, but now there was another problem.

'Oh, that was probably just mice. Old houses like this always have them.'

'Vile. But this was bigger than a mouse, it was person sized. And I heard a voice say something really creepy, like

141

"Does it hurt?" Do you think something bad happened here?'

'Nothing that I know of. Why don't you ask Theo?'

'You know how he is. Did he ever say anything about noises to you?'

Ursie went to light the stove, her face turned away from Jan's. Her braids fell forwards, fringing her hunched shoulders black and royal blue. For all her conviction and solidity, she seemed frail. For a moment Jan wanted to wrap Ursie in her arms and squeeze her tight, breathe in her familiar smell. She stopped herself. Even if the gesture were welcome, she was too afraid that getting close again would simply be the prelude to further abandonment.

A cupboard door yawned open loudly, startling them both. Jan slammed it shut. 'You see? Look at that. Old houses make weird sounds all the time. There's a door upstairs that won't close properly, but I think that's because all the windows are so warped. If you see it open, make sure you shut it? And please stop suggesting something else is going on, you're giving me the creeps.'

'But I remember Theo saying something about how his parents didn't like visiting this place,' Ursie said. 'Maybe someone died here.'

'Parts of the house are more than eight hundred years old; of course people have died here. Harold was a lonely old man and they were probably sad about that. I'm not sure what you want me to do about this? You're acting like we dragged you here at gunpoint. It's not like I can call someone to come and fix the draught.'

'I don't know, I just wanted to ask you about it and now you're being really aggressive.'

142

'If your room is bothering you, how about we ask Theo about making up a bed in one of the drawing rooms? The sofas are easily big enough to sleep on.'

'No really, it's fine.' Ursie retreated to the corridor, not looking back.

Assuming Ursie was off to whip Kara into a nervous frenzy as well, Jan set angrily to work on cleaning the pots and pans. After their previous conversation, she was disinclined to offer any comfort to someone who refused to give it to her.

As if Jan did not keep up with the news, as if she had any choice about the Israel–Palestine conflict being brought up continually out of the blue, as if she could avoid hearing what people really thought about Jews when they imagined themselves in sympathetic company. But perhaps Ursie's keen interest in the papers stopped before she got to any articles aggregating statistics of anti-semitic hate crimes, which kept rising every year, perpetrated in imagined retaliation for a disaster dragging on intractably thousands of miles away. Every time Jan saw a guy in a kippah on the Tube she found herself feeling protective of him and then worrying that she too was staring in a way that seemed threatening from a big, pale woman with no immediate markers of identity beyond the cast of her face and the curl of her messy dark bob, which some people recognised immediately and others not at all. Ursie was who she was all the time, with no room to hide from friend or foe or kin. While she was the best placed of all the others to understand, it felt tactless to talk to her about Jan's creeping paranoia at being recognised by the wrong people or, alternatively, being rendered invisible, without being confronted by the reality that Jan often had the privilege of discretion too.

As the pot began to whistle, Theo sidled in, picked up two mugs and poured in great sloshes of coffee. 'Quis?'

'Ego!' Kara bounded in next, and took the pot from him.

'Whu—?' Luke was knuckling the crust from his eyes. 'I called dibs, I was right after you on the stairs.'

Theo said, 'Sorry, I forget sometimes. Your accent's tipping back to British, you know.'

'It's such a twatty private school thing. I can't believe you still do that,' Kara complained and offered Luke a sip of her milky coffee. He wrinkled his nose.

'You still knew what I meant, though,' Theo said and smiled.

Luke asked, 'Jan, is there *any* tea that isn't Lady Grey? I've been here too damn long.'

Nadya came in, taking the full cup of unsugared black coffee from Theo's hand. Next to the poison ring sat a chunky pear-shaped diamond which looked like it could easily pay off Jan's student loans.

'What are you looking so miserable for?' she said. 'Put the kettle on and come outside.'

Still pondering her earlier argument with Ursie about community and isolation, Jan filled up the kettle and glumly flicked the switch. She said, 'I don't know, I was thinking I might finally do my bat mitzvah next year.'

'Our little girl becomes a woman at last!' Luke cried, in a bad imitation of Chaim Topol, riffling through the pantry for teabags while Jan watched him from the corner

144

of her eye. Then she shooed them all out onto the terrace where the sun had broken through into late morning radiance.

Nadya said, 'I can see you getting to thirty and converting hardcore. Can you even be lesbian and Orthodox?'

'I wouldn't be going full frummer. I'd just be doing it for the Torah lessons, connect with my heritage a bit more, you know.'

'Why? It's not like you're going to have children.'

This had never been a topic of discussion between them, but as Nadya assumed correctly, Jan didn't bother to counter it. She watched through the open french windows as Ursie foraged in the dining room for a yellow-handled grill lighter, lit her cigarette with it and then came to stand outside.

Theo said, 'I'm going to start learning Russian for Nadya. I always said I'd do it if we got engaged.'

Kara looked sceptical of Theo's newfound diligence and was opening her mouth to ask a question when Nadya cut in, 'My parents speak perfect English.'

'I know, but it would be good to learn a little. All I know are swearwords.'

'Your "mat" is impeccable, I must admit.' Nadya went to sit in Theo's lap and began lacing her fingers through his half-buttoned shirt, pulling him in for a long kiss.

'My dad learned some Italian, but I don't think he still speaks it,' Kara said. 'It's not like he has much of a relationship with my mum's parents.'

Theo asked, 'Do your parents really still believe in all that stuff?'

'Yeah, basically. They're not as involved as they were, but they're not out of it either.'

145

'What stuff?' Nadya had swivelled round to look at Kara.

Jan kept her lip buttoned but Ursie said it for her: 'They're in a cult.'

'Really? Jan never told me that.'

Kara said, 'It's not a cult, it's a belief system. My grandparents think it's a cult, though.'

'Why do they think it's a cult?' Nadya asked.

'Well, my grandfather's a Communist, but obviously growing up in Italy meant he had Catholicism shoved down his throat since he was a baby, so he thinks all religion's evil. My mum got quite into drugs in the eighties and started going to these meditation sessions where she met my dad. He was an alcoholic at the time. The guru advised them to get married. It helped both of them a lot.'

'Sorry babe,' Ursie said, 'but every time you explain this, it sounds even more culty. You had that picture of the guru in a frame in first year. I still remember coming in to see it turned facing the wall every time you'd been fucking Luke.'

Jan said, 'I still don't know what you actually believed.'

'Love your fellow man, meditate every day for an hour, we can attain physical peace and then world peace by accessing our chakras. Nothing scary or bad. Well, apart from the time we were doing astral projection and I came back to my body to find there was another being already in there.'

Jan said, 'Um, what? Someone from the group was touching you?'

'No, like another entity. It's hard to understand if you're not spiritual too. We're supposed to be open to contact with beings from other planes of existence, but it just

146

went a bit too far. To be honest, I don't really remember what happened, it was so long ago. There was a lot of chanting and the teacher helped me return safely in the end. I really miss meditating, actually.'

Ursie said, 'I think that would put me right off.'

Theo said, 'But you can still meditate? I meditated this morning.'

Jan hated it when Theo went on his pseudo-Buddhist self-improvement jags, but suspected with his engagement now announced, another one would fast be approaching.

'You have to live a pure life, filled with love. It's not enough otherwise.' Kara sounded genuinely sad for a moment, before Luke started asking her about whether it was possible to get phone signal at Holt House, clearly having completely forgotten discussing it on the first day.

Jan felt her irritation building steadily at all of them as the second pot of coffee reached its boiling point. She silently lamented not having brought her one-hitter to Holt House.

Nadya said, 'I can get a couple of bars in my room if I lean out of the window, but you're round the side, right?'

'Yes, looking out at that big tree. My old boss said he was going to call me later,' Luke griped. 'It's really not ideal.'

Jan said, 'You could always try going back through the gates, it's probably better out there.'

At this, Luke brightened. 'We passed a little pub on the way here which I think was open, how about we make a day trip out of it? We could sit outside, get some pints in, maybe they'd even sell us some real food.'

147

'I was just about to start making a salade niçoise.'

'No offence, but I need a bit more than rabbit food after last night.'

Jan said in acid tones, 'I suppose you need more potatoes or something like that.'

'Great! I'm starving. I'll definitely have room for both. Coffee anyone?'

Eager for a chance to swerve further complaints about the menu, Jan said, 'I'll get it! Theo, can you come help me in the kitchen for a moment, please?'

He ambled in behind her and as she closed the door he said, 'What do you need a hand with? I'm sorry I'm being so useless. I feel like I haven't rewarded you properly yet for all your hard work keeping things together for us.'

He pulled out a bag of white powder and shook it temptingly. Comedown in full force, Jan recoiled from the offer.

'Please no, it's barely noon and I haven't had anything to eat yet. You've already been very generous indeed. It's about the pub thing.'

'Oh, Luke's just being a prat, I wouldn't take offence.'

'No, no, not that, though that was pretty rude. It's the letter. If we're being watched, then we shouldn't be going in and out all the time.'

Theo rolled up his linen cuffs and started washing the salad leaves as Jan assembled all the ingredients. 'Come on, it was just a bit of paper. We'll be fine.'

'Please, Theo. You know Luke will immediately get up to something stupid like trying to do a bump off the picnic tables. The police are probably so bored that it's just asking for trouble.'

'Fine, I'll keep him distracted. I suggest you enjoy it while it lasts. I just got it in the neck from Nadya about letting Kara run up a tab as well. She says I'm a soft touch.'

'A soft touch would not keep tabs at all. Just how much has she had off you, if you don't mind my asking?'

The salad having proven simpler than expected even with a hangover, Jan began prepping the coq au vin for that night, knowing she would likely be too rushed later to get it started properly on time. She diced the mushrooms and shallots and hurled them in the pot with some butter. She knew she shouldn't pry, but the realisation that the seemingly relaxed, open-handed Theo had them all on different tabs was too compelling for her to resist probing a bit further.

'I try not to let it run above five hundred quid, makes it less painful to call in for both of us. I know she'll pay me back eventually; she's just having a rough year with every-thing that's been going on.'

'I'm assuming Luke's debt isn't part of that?'

'Luke and I came to an arrangement. That was never the problem, though. Do you remember João?'

'I don't think so.' Jan frowned. 'Wait, was this the guy with a bunch of different names? Johnny, Jack or Joe depending on the year?'

'That's the one. Luke owed him three grand.'

'What? How did he even manage to get that much without paying?'

'He bought in bulk to sell on, but then did most of it himself. At one point João threatened to have him beaten up if he didn't repay at least five hundred of it in a week.'

'Hang on, was this right before Luke ran away? That explains a lot. Why did he keep biting off more than he could chew?'

149

Jan downed a glass of tap water, her mind racing with this new and unexpected information as she prodded the rapidly sautéeing vegetables.

'He tried. He came and asked me for help selling something else instead to try and make up the money, but it was during revision season and no one was really buying anything much except Modafinil and Valium, which are pocket change, and all the other student dealers already picked their spots in the library months ago. I also told him if he was serious, he should pick a drug he didn't enjoy but he likes everything except for heroin, which is a market neither of us wanted to touch with a bargepole, so that wasn't much use either. It's a good thing he ran away when he did.'

'Holy fuck, poor Luke. What an idiot, but poor Luke anyway. Do you think João spiked him that time he had to go to hospital?'

'Nope, that was a dark web fuckup. It was all clumpy, but we thought it was just research chemicals and tried a line each. Nadya and I got really sick, but Luke went for it and *Pulp Fiction*ed himself. I had to call the ambulance even though both me and Nadya were vomiting into separate toilets while they triaged us. I managed to flush the rest. I think they had to resuscitate him on the way there, but they wouldn't let me see him.'

'I had no idea.' Jan looked Theo in the eye. 'I knew he overdosed but I thought it was just palpitations from doing way too much bad coke.'

'He was so embarrassed afterwards; he asked me and Nadya not to tell anyone. I probably shouldn't have let it slip now, but this is just between us, okay? I wrote the dealer a stern message on Silk Road saying he could have killed someone and the guy was so apologetic, he sent me a bag of top-shelf coke the next day with a handful of Es thrown in.'

'No wonder he left the country, poor Luke.'

'The whole episode really freaked Nadya out, she's still rather angry about it, I think, even though it was ages ago. But between that and these stupid friends of hers who came knocking at our door at 4 a.m. about a fortnight ago shouting at us to let them in because they wanted to buy some pills, she says she's had enough of me selling even to people we know.'

A silvery glimmer of hope that Nadya might yet leave him surfaced in Jan's dehydrated mind.

'But what are you going to do? I'm sorry to be so blunt, but you haven't done anything else for ages.'

'That's not strictly true,' Theo told her. 'I worked in my second cousin's antique map dealership for a summer a couple of years ago. Anyway, Nadya's dad said he could set me up with something; one of his companies has a subsidiary here and they need someone to do bitch work in their office. It's an easy job, I just need to answer the phone and take deliveries; I can read at the same time.'

Jan noted silently that Nadya had never made this role available to her, though she could have done it efficiently without a second thought.

'Papa Stoyanov saves the day. What does he think you've been doing all these years?'

'I think Nadya spun him a tale about how I wanted to set up my own business and become an entrepreneur, but it didn't work out. I'd intended to finish up in a couple of years anyway, it was never a long-term goal to keep doing this.'

'Aren't you worried about becoming Mr Nadya?'

He laughed and plucked a stray mushroom slice off the board, popping it in his mouth.

'I'm already Mr Nadya; it's a very comfortable role. I'm just glad there's something I can do for her at last, she takes such good care of me.'

Should she anonymously tip off Oleg Stoyanov as to how Theo really occupied his time? Would such a betrayal achieve anything except driving Nadya away forever? It was as if the three of them stood tied together at the top of a steep ravine and Jan was so keenly aware of the vertiginous drop, she could not move a single inch away from certain danger nor plunge at last over the edge.

'Are you sure you'll be okay?' she asked. 'I'm really happy for both of you, but you can talk to me. This all feels rather sudden.'

'It's a wedding, not an execution. You and Luke are both being really strange about our engagement. Anyway, what I actually wanted to ask you, since we're on the topic of work, is whether you'd consider catering our engagement party as your wedding present to us? I know you're rather hard up at the moment because of the marking stuff and Nadya just thought of it this morning.'

Jan whacked the chicken with the flat side of her cleaver, breaking its spine ready to be jointed for the pot. Of course Nadya had come up with that; she was probably in fits of silent laughter outside right now at her stroke of genius in drawing Jan further into servility in aid of the wedding. Jan, horrified and enraptured, felt hot wetness grow between her legs. She asked, 'Are you sure? It's a really big responsibility, and I'd be terrified of messing it up.'

'We'd pay for the food of course, and the wedding catering would be done professionally, but it would be lovely to have a more intimate party some time and Nadya is such a fan of your cooking.'

'How could I turn you down when you put it like that? Let me know numbers nearer the time and I'll see if I can draft someone in to help prep if it's more than twenty people.'

'You're an angel, Jan. Of course we will, and we want to keep it small. Are you alright though? You've had a weird look on your face all morning.'

'Oh, it's nothing, I was being petty.'

'Come on, tell me.'

She ransacked her brain for a palatable reason, something that wasn't *well the woman I love is about to marry someone else and now I will have to think about you putting your dick in her forever when she was mine first and I hate myself for hating you for it.*

She put the cleaver down.

'I'm a little embarrassed to say this, but yours and Nadya's news made me start thinking about my own love life and how I haven't been dating at all.'

'You want a Mrs Jan, hmm?' He punched her in the arm. 'And I thought you were a committed womaniser; I was enjoying living vicariously through you.'

'Well, not necessarily a Mrs Jan quite yet, but a few good dates wouldn't hurt.' Jan tried to inject some levity into her voice. 'Who's going to be my plus-one to the wedding otherwise?'

Theo cautiously inclined his head towards the table outside, but Jan snapped at him, 'Dream on. It's off. Has been for ages.'

'Hmm, pity. You'd probably have made each other worse, though, you're both rather neurotic. Now if you don't mind, I'm going to tell Nads you said yes to the party idea.'

After Theo left, Jan checked on the chicken, which was beginning to brown satisfactorily. The meat was filling the kitchen with the golden, comforting smell of home. She began to sharpen her knives, more out of habit than necessity. They were beautifully well-weighted Japanese steel, the tang and the blade all one single piece of metal. On a whim she hovered one over the cedar chopping block and let it fall. The knife sank into the wood like she'd dropped it into the butter pat instead.

Again, she turned her future prospects over in her head. She had a first-class BA and a distinction at MPhil but even if she passed her PhD with no corrections, a funded post-doc felt vanishingly unlikely. Even in the best possible scenario, she could not expect to earn much and the horrors of the academic job market would stretch out ahead of her. She knew she was not appealing to any woman who wanted a luxurious life – or really anything more than subsidised penury. She couldn't face a long-distance relationship with no end date, which ruled out fellow academics, which in turn ruled out a swathe of the queer population who would understand her perilous life choices because they had made the same ones. Someone who could support herself and also remain fairly mobile felt like a big ask indeed.

Jan could not think how to solve the problem of her own life, how to come up with a solution that promised reasonable stability, fulfilment and independence. A small handful of people she knew seemed to manage it with far fewer resources, but she could not quite see how to follow suit. Were all the friends who didn't supplement their income like Theo did being secretly bailed out by their parents or working so hard at something boring that you never saw them again? Would she be sparring over the fridge with her father and going down on other people's girlfriends forever?

The salade niçoise was devoured almost as soon as Jan brought it out and Ursie refilled the jug of Pimm's several times over the course of lunch. They gradually wandered over to the lake for a quick swim, though Kara refused to get in, saying that dark water made her nervous. She sat in a patch of sunlight on the shore with Nadya, gossiping about people who both of them knew from the vast and frighteningly well-informed London school network that persisted well into their collective adulthood.

Jan swam in a t-shirt to cover the scratches, keeping one ear open for names she recognised. Nadya was always very well up on all the latest news about people who'd been at Oxford, but the extent of Kara's knowledge surprised her. Ashamed at not having made the cut for Oxbridge, Jan had more or less faded from view – or so she hoped – during her time at university, as nights with her new tribe had replaced most of her standing commitments to see schoolfriends other than Nadya. She would now be remembered solely for the things she'd got up to as a teenager, perpetually drunk, combative and covered in piercings. These days the only updates that reached her were of weddings and disasters.

Luke and Theo started to play some kind of adapted water polo with the ancient football, while Ursie and Nadya packed themselves into a diminutive wooden canoe that lay concealed in the trees and ferried their things over to the lido to smoke in the full sunlight now playing over the water. Kara stayed lying prone on the flowery bank with her hair strewn about her face, as if she were hoping for Millais' *Ophelia* comparisons.

Jan swam a little closer to the lido, not turning her head as she heard Nadya complaining that Kara had immediately asked to try on her lipstick when she'd seen Nadya reapplying it and wouldn't take no for an answer, despite the fact she got cold sores.

'It's still so weird seeing her and Luke together again. I forgot how pushy she is when she's not all depressed without him.'

Ursie said in an undertone, 'I thought you told her she shouldn't put up with him any more? Do you remember when Theo came and got her from that awful place she was living in with Luke in third year before she and I moved in together?'

'She never listens. Anyway, that was before Theo and I were together. He has an open-door policy for his friends, but it's not always so appropriate. She really took the piss when she was staying with us. She kept borrowing my clothes and I'd come back from the library to find them snuggled up together on the sofa watching Miyazaki films and doing ketamine.'

'True, true,' Ursie murmured. 'I had to keep telling her to stop eating all my cheese and peanut butter and she'd always bring people back for afterparties, even when I told her to keep it down. To be honest, I was kind of relieved when the rent went up and we had to move out of that place.'

'Do you remember Ayesha?'

'Vaguely, I think she was in Climate Soc at uni.'

'You know how she and Theo slept together a few times before we started dating?'

'Yes, but never seriously, I thought.'

'Well, for the first year we were dating, she kept on coming round, saying she'd lost her keys or was depressed and asking to sleep in his bed. I had to have a word with her and she got really angry. She stopped speaking to him after that.'

'I didn't know. That is pretty cheeky.'

'Yes, well, Theo needs to watch himself. He loves waifs and strays, but not everyone understands that help has limits.'

'I don't think Kara's like that. She just needed her friends when Luke ran away, the dickhead.'

The ball landed with a smack next to the lido and sprayed both of them.

Nadya shrieked, 'Guys!'

Jan paddled away briskly so they wouldn't realise how close by she'd been as they were gossiping.

Theo called out, 'Throw it back! Come on, Ursie, skill us up!'

With a martyred air, Ursie got to her feet, balancing herself on Nadya's shoulder and did an impressively accurate kick that landed the ball right between Theo and Luke, who both dove for it. Luke won and for a few minutes everyone but Kara was drawn into the game. The patch with the bullrushes became a makeshift goal, and Jan found herself on the same team as Theo and Ursie, facing off against Luke and Nadya, who surprised them all by diving underwater fully dressed to snatch the ball just as Theo was powering towards it.

Jan's team gracefully withdrew after losing 3–5 and the group extracted themselves from the lake, drying off on the bank.

Ursie was sitting to one side of Nadya, looking at her closely as she pulled off her sopping shirt, tugging it as it caught on the chunky diamond still glistering on her long thin finger. Ursie asked, 'Are those what I think they are? Are you okay?'

Nadya turned her body away from Ursie and said in a tone of voice that belied the anger obvious to Jan, 'Yes of course; they're very old.' Her forearms, silver-laddered with old scars bulged a little in the places where one cut had crossed another. She could have asked for money to get them lasered, but that would mean admitting to her parents they were there in the first place, so she just wore long sleeves and bracelets year-round.

Kara asked Ursie, 'You really haven't seen that before? We all have them.'

'Yeah true, you all do. They really weren't so common at my school; it was just the goth kids. The nuns got so freaked out, they kept going on about taking care of God's creation.'

Jan said, 'We WERE the goth kids. Well, the emo kids, though same difference really. Everyone did it, though. This girl Annalisa used to burn smiley faces into her arm with a lighter and a metal stamp.'

'I wonder if her parents ever caught her,' Nadya said. 'Remember when she got her first fiancé's name tattooed on the back of her neck in Hebrew and they made her laser it off.'

Jan laughed. 'That was so fucking stupid. She went to camp every year; you'd think she would have known.'

'I don't get it,' Kara said. 'Was it stupid because they weren't going out very long?'

'You aren't supposed to get tattoos full stop, so getting a tattoo *in Hebrew* is even dumber.'

Nadya said, 'Finally something the Jews and the nuns agree on. Did they teach all your lessons, Ursie?'

'Luckily no, though they were responsible for PHSE. They showed us that video from the eighties where an aborted foetus screams in the womb.'

'It can scream all it wants,' Jan said, pulling a face, 'it's still getting evicted.'

Ursie laughed and said, 'Sadly for the nuns we had Google . . . though the image of you shoving a Section 21 Notice up your pussy will never leave me now.'

Jan mimed licking and sealing an envelope before rolling it up for insertion and Kara giggled as well. She had a few faded silver scars of her own up one arm. Most of Jan's had healed almost to the point of invisibility.

Kara linked arms with Luke and said, 'Come on, it's so bright out today and now the clouds have moved we're wasting it in the shade. We have to go back to the lawn and sunbathe some more.' She walked him away.

'We don't *have* to go anywhere, we're here on holiday.' Nadya wandered over and stood behind Jan, playing with her wet hair.

Ursie said, 'I thought we were retreating from a plague?'

159

'Why not both?'

Nadya grabbed the tufts at the back of Jan's neck and started twisting them viciously, while continuing to talk about a trip to the South of France she'd had to cancel. Jan felt her nipples hardening like two little bullets and hoped neither Ursie nor Theo could see.

Eventually Nadya said from above, 'Let's dry off and find the other two, where are the towels?'

'They're all upstairs, why did no one bring one?'

'You are literally turning into your father.'

Jan pinched Nadya's delicate wrist between finger and thumb until the pressure at the back of Jan's neck forced her to let go lest the hair be ripped out at the root. Nadya had won again.

Jan said, 'I'm going to take a shower.'

She walked off into the woods, crossing the drive to take the long route round the other side of the house, in the hope she might calm her racing heart. She promised herself she would go easy on the coke tonight; increasingly, it left her breathless, shallow-chested and filled with dread. The path Jan had run between the trees yesterday morning was still visible, grass weighed down by her springing footsteps and dandelion stalks crushed here and there. No sound from the distant motorway, nor even the querulous voices of her friends, pierced the quiet. Ursie had come so close to discovering them; Jan would have to be more careful, so would Nadya – that surprise game of mercy must surely have been noticeable. But Jan knew if she mentioned Ursie's line of questioning, Nadya would find a way to blame her for the noise and perhaps cease to come when knocked for.

Now Jan plunged deeper into the trees, where there was no path to follow beyond her own ever-shifting inclinations. She had to think of another place for her and Nadya to meet, if the attic was no longer safe thanks to Ursie's sleeplessness. Stitchwort lay in a thick cloak over the ground, with patches of bright pink campion dotted further off. As the shade thickened, the ground grew barer and the muffled sound of Jan's footfall against dry earth rang out at each step, with a mounting echo as the ground sloped downwards into a bowl shape. She peered through the trees for the wall that marked the edges of the Mortimer domain, but could not see it. The sound got louder as she pushed further in, trampling dead leaves into powder and trying not to trip on loose pebbles.

Just as she was about to put down a cautious foot to avoid some brambles, she paused but the echo came again, close by her. She started, caught her trainer on a protruding loop of root and fell, hands flailing and trying not to seize the brambles. She hit the ground heavily on her hip and tried to scramble up, spine burning with the force of the impact, anything to keep herself from sliding down, down into the stone-studded gully where the giant gunnera plants grew thick and dark. She knew with absolute certainty that she must not fall down there. The sense of an additional presence, unaccounted for and unseen, yet keenly expectant of she knew not what, intensified the further she slid towards the bottom of the gully. She was awaited, she knew it.

She clutched at a young tree, heaved herself upright and now Jan was running, shoving foliage aside and trampling through the flowers that shot up in the lighter dells, leaping over fallen branches, anything to get out and away from the rushing noise and crunching twigs behind her, the sound of blood rushing in her head confusing all her thoughts. She did not look back.

Jan sat panting on the front lawn, doubled over, sweating, hands clasping her thighs. She tried forcing herself to breathe in a circle like she'd read about, but it didn't work. She longed for a glass of water, but the shrouded quiet of Holt House repelled her and so she stumbled, trembling, round the side of the house hoping that the others would be on the lawn bickering and joking and drying off in the sunlight. With luck they wouldn't see her clothes were covered in mud down one side, grazes streaking her shins.

Not quite ready yet to hold a conversation, she spotted the hammock at the edge of the lawn and slumped down inside it. Ursie and Kara sat at the table on the terrace, Kara's tarot cards spread over the lichened surface. Kara was flicking her lighter on and off against her palm, a nervous tic she insisted could help cleanse one's energy. Jan had never known her to be without a lighter, even during periods she was trying to quit smoking.

They were too focused to notice her and with relief Jan tuned into the sound of their laughter, praying it would soothe her nerves. She must still be drunk from lunch, that was why she'd got so worked up back there. She felt sick and cold despite the sun's rays filtering through the boughs above the hammock. Kara lit a joint and began cajoling a reluctant Ursie to accept a reading.

'It's a pagan thing,' Ursie announced. 'I won't have anything to do with that.'

'You aren't even a Christian these days.'

'That's between me and God, you know.'

162

'Aren't you the least bit curious? It's not satanic, lots of people just use it as a tool to understand their state of mind better. You could look at it as pure randomness if you wanted to.'

Jan poked her head over the hammock's edge for a better view. The two were drinking coffee and Kara was collecting the cards into a neat little oblong between them.

'Some people think it comes from the Ancient Egyptians. You can take whatever meaning you want from it, go on and let me do yours.'

'That sounds like some hotep nonsense. I've always avoided this sort of thing, but I can try everything once, I guess.' And Ursie tilted her head with the grin that Jan had longed for so often and very seldom saw any more.

Kara passed her the cards and told her to reshuffle.

'Can't you do it? I thought you were the expert on all this?'

'But it's your reading, it's just part of the—' Kara clearly caught herself before she could say ritual '—process.'

'Okay okay, my days, there's a lot of naked people in here. If I get one of them is that the sex card?'

'Some of them could suggest that, yes. Have you really never done this before?'

'One of the girls in my year was really into it, voodoo dolls and prayer candles and all that stuff. Super creepy; she kept saying she was going to hex people. One of my friends told on her to the nuns and she got suspended, asked not to come back after the end of term.'

'Well, we're not doing any hexing. Okay, that's nice and thorough, now pass them back to me. I want you to think of a question, not too hard, just the first thing that comes to mind.'

Ursie screwed up her face, deciding, then she opened her eyes and took another glug of coffee.

'Okay, I think I have one. What now?'

'Pick a card, from anywhere in the deck that suggests itself to you.'

Jan watched her put out a beringed hand and pick a card, gingerly placing it on the table.

Kara turned it over. 'Oho! This is the card for your past, it's a very luxe one.'

'All I see is a white lady with a bird and some circles.'

'It's the Nine of Pentacles, it's a card representing wealth and abundance. She's in a little garden having a grand old time.'

'Is that it? How about we stop there then?'

'We're not done yet, take another.'

The process was repeated and Jan continued watching intently from her berth in the hammock.

'What does a Moon mean? That's a good one too, right?'

'It depends,' Kara said. 'It's a sign of things hidden, that deep water is the subconscious – it's a card of vagueness but also sometimes a sign that the truth will be unveiled.'

'I'm confused. How can it just mean vagueness?'

'It's pretty much THE confusion card. If you pick the next one maybe it will clarify things a bit.' Kara waited and turned the next one. 'Oh. This one is not so great, I'm sorry.'

'I thought they all had double meanings or whatever?'

'It's how you look at it. I got the Nine of Swords once too and I got sacked from working in a café the next day. But I hated it there, so it wasn't all bad.'

164

'You don't sound sure,' Ursie said. 'If the picture means anything, it looks like a bad card to me.'

'It's more of an anxiety card, it's not indicative of what's definitely going to happen. Do you want to pick a last one for confirmation?'

'Do I have to?'

'Of course not, but it might clear some things up.'

'Can you stop talking like that, Kara?'

'Like what?'

'Like you're on some sort of Mystic Meg hotline. *Your call is very important to us. Please hold while we consult the Oracle.*'

'Fine. It's just how I learned to do it to avoid freaking people out when they don't get the answers they were hoping for. You do seem very nervous, Ursie. Can I ask what your question was?'

'Does that make it not come true?'

'It's not like the candles on your birthday cake. It's just a way of making sure I don't overfocus on answering your question and stop paying attention to the actual cards. You can tell me if you want.'

'It's about that thing . . . you know I was telling you.'

Ursie leaned in close to Kara and Jan couldn't catch what was said next. She had never been any good at reading lips, much to her chagrin.

'What?' Kara said loudly. 'Oh right. Have you talked to her yet?'

'I was going to earlier, but she was in a shitty mood and kept taking everything the wrong way. I was trying to give her some friendly advice about writing, but she got so offended. Stormed out and everything, though now she's acting like it never happened.'

Jan sunk down among the canvas folds a little further. She was definitely going to need to remain in the hammock until they went inside lest she be accused of spying.

'She's always been oversensitive,' Kara said. 'You should still stand up for what you want, though.'

This coming from someone who once threw a week-long tantrum over not being invited to dinner at a steak-house in Farringdon by Jan and Theo when she didn't eat meat. Jan bristled with irritation at the both of them, but could not stop herself from continuing to eavesdrop.

'I just don't want to be here, Kara. I thought it might be a good break, but this house is even worse than I imagined. I don't feel comfortable and I want to leave. Everything's so complicated with me and her, though, I can't just walk away without making it worse.'

'Talk to her and tell her how you feel. Or say you have work or something.'

'I don't know, we basically just got here and I feel so bad. We even got into a fight about Israel somehow.'

'Yeah well, she's just too brainwashed by her upbringing to see the truth. We had a massive argument in St Pancras once about the time I said Israelis are like the Nazis.'

'Kara, you're missing the point.'

'What? They are, you know they are.'

'I'm not defending the IDF and occupying the West Bank and all that, but human suffering isn't a game of Top Trumps.'

'I—'

'Enough. I don't like it when people compare the slave trade and the Holocaust either. It's not a competition, there's enough misery to go round. And none of it is your misery. Now, what does the final card mean?'

Jan was positively surprised at how consistent Ursie was, both when fighting Jan and defending her, though she knew full well that the eavesdropper's punishment was that one could never reveal the source of furtively acquired information. In the midst of frantic mental calculations on how she could possibly initiate a different tenor of conversation with Ursie without revealing she'd been listening to them, she heard Kara saying, 'Wow, maybe you should stay put after all. You asked me to be honest with you and the Tower's a really bad one.'

'What kind of bad?'

'It's a disaster. Well, it's total change, everything comes undone and you with it. Doesn't mean you're going to die,' Kara said hastily, 'just that everything will be different.'

'Fantastic. And I thought the lockdown was bad enough.'

'It could just be more of that, you know. Let's put these away.'

'Are you not going to do yours?'

'Not today, I'm not feeling like it.'

'So I just have to sit here with the knowledge of bad news coming my way and you get to live in blissful ignorance? I don't think so.'

'The future's still coming, Ursie.'

'Pick a card.'

'Just one and then let's have a drink.'

'Deal.'

Kara pulled one and flipped it.

'Oh bloody hell.'

'What? What'd you get?'

'Ten of Swords. Even worse than the Nine.'

Ursie started cackling as Kara frantically packed the cards away. 'Looks like we're in it together,' she said, gleefully. 'Maybe you're going to get shouted at by Jan as well. Where even is she? Probably sulking and watching her secret stash of Czech porn.'

'Oh god, no wonder she's being such a moody cow, she's not getting any sex because of the pandemic. Do you think that's why she's being so weird with you?'

'God knows. There's always some agenda with her; I don't need that drama in my life right now, I'm getting too old.'

Jan watched them return indoors before she snuck out of the hammock and lit a cigarette. Surprisingly, nothing in her waist-bag had been broken by her fall, except one torn rollie which she bandaged with a second layer of paper before lighting it.

Jan reached a nadir of curmudgeonliness, deciding her strategy for the rest of the afternoon would be in fact one of avoidance. Any hope that things could once again be as they had been was now well and truly thwarted by the last comments Ursie had made. With each day that passed, Jan had enjoyed her friends' company less and less, was feeling decreasingly motivated to get out of bed or even pull a brush through her hair. The only thing that still existed as a constant was the obligation to prepare the meals and keep her promise to Theo.

Before all of this, she and Ursie had slept freely in one another's beds, hair bound in matching silk scarves, drunk as lords and full of chips. Ursie had reached for her often, her soft touch on Jan's arm soothing her in a way she had never allowed anyone else to do. They had shared confidences about their depression, the worlds of art and academia, failed dates they'd been on. That innocence was long gone. Now, in all the hours that Ursie did not reach for her, and might never do so again, Jan reached instead for Nadya, whose form of rejection was at least consistent, or she trawled FetLife in search of other women who might be persuaded to kick her in the ribs.

As Jan turned to head indoors, she spotted Theo through the french windows. He was sitting sprawled at the head of the dining table, legs draped over the corner and drink in hand, explaining something while Luke stood at the far end of the room, examining the silverware on the dresser. Luke turned quickly when Jan came in, and asked her, 'Did you bring any cash, Jan?'

'A little, why?'

'Oh, just curiosity, you know. I'm getting rather restless. Want to go for a walk?'

Trying to come up with an excuse not to re-enter the woods, she said, 'You can come and hang out with me in the kitchen. Do you want me to make you a sidecar?'

Instead of answering, he turned to Theo and asked, 'Where's the nearest cashpoint?'

'The village post office, I should think, but it's probably closed by now.'

Jan shot Theo a curious look but he gave nothing back.

'You know I'm good for it. Come on, I'm dying of boredom here,' Luke whined. He took a step closer to Theo, who sat unmoved, shoes dangling. 'You brought so much; I saw you take the scales out of your bag. Were you going to do it all yourself?'

Theo turned to Jan. 'We were sort of in the middle of a conversation, Jan. Do you think you could give us some space?'

'Fine.' She prepared to leave, stung by his discourtesy in spite of the disclaimer, when she spotted the silver goblet resting on the dresser between some candlesticks and an engraved silver plate.

She picked it up. 'Did one of you bring this in here?'

'Of course not. Now could we have a moment, please?'

'I keep finding it out. I put it back in the kitchen every time, but if it's an heirloom, you should really—'

'I don't care about the fucking cup, Jan. It's some old thing that's always been here. We were having a conversation; can't you just take it away? Don't you have anything better to do in the kitchen?'

She peered into the cup and saw flecks of dried red beeswing. She couldn't believe Theo rudely shooing her out after he'd asked her to look after things. He was literally sat at the head of the table giving commands as if she were a menial.

'Actually, I don't think I will. The chicken's already well underway.' She pulled out a chair at the opposite end of the table and sat stiff-jawed, glaring at both of them. She could not work out why Theo had suddenly gone so cold after they had confided in each other only hours before. She wondered whether Nadya had been berating him again for not cutting Luke off.

'It really doesn't matter,' Luke said, 'Jan can stay. I don't believe in secrets anyhow.'

'I don't have the patience for this right now, but if you insist.' Theo's tone was uncharacteristically short, and he sat up straight, brow furrowed. 'I'd really rather you not keep asking me for this, Luke.'

'Is this about last night? I don't even remember taking that. I must have been super crossfaded and you were asleep, so I couldn't check with you. I would never want to finish the whole bag, I just overshot.'

Jan snorted. 'Mate, come off it. I saw you pick it off the floor.'

He shot her a look. 'I won't do it again, I don't even like speed that much.'

'It doesn't matter what you prefer, I'm not giving you any more for the meantime.'

'Why not?'

'You know perfectly well why not.'

'How could I forget? My debt? The one you've been holding over my head for years? You'll get it all back, with interest. I've got a plan. I just have to get some things sorted first, you know. It's nothing urgent, anyway right, now you're getting married to Nadya?'

Jan looked from one set of large, discoloured teeth grinding to another.

'That's not relevant, you can leave her out of it. I told you no more.'

'Why now, though? What's the next week or so going to do? Just live a little.'

'My answer is final. I've let this go on too long.'

'How much is it now? You know he keeps it all in a spreadsheet, Jan? Mr Good Time over here, pretending to be so relaxed, the life and soul of the party. He ever shown you yours?'

'I've always paid him back, so I don't see why he would. Why don't you read a book instead, Luke? Or there are some old tennis racquets you could try out if you're that bored.'

'Read a book? You haven't even read *Ulysses* and you're lecturing me about reading. I shouldn't be surprised; you've always sided with him. I haven't forgotten that you—'

Jan saw Theo rise slightly; he was about to interject when Nadya burst in.

'You have got to fire the gardener!'

'What's happened?'

'He's such a creep!'

Jan went over immediately, stroking Nadya's shoulders and pulling out a chair for her to sit down, which she refused, walking over to Theo with a trembling gait.

Tears dotted her smooth, angular cheeks, one beading and rolling mesmerically down her jaw as she said, 'It's not acceptable.'

'Where is he? What did he say to you?' Theo was rubbing her other shoulder and pulled out a cotton handkerchief to wipe away the teardrops before they fell.

'I don't know, I don't know, but you need to get rid of him.'

Theo pulled her onto his lap and held her. 'Start from the beginning.'

She gave a little cough and said, 'I closed all the doors before we went out because even though it's summer, it's so cold in here all the time for some reason. The draught is terrible, it's going to make me sick, and I don't trust the door handles after Ursie got stuck yesterday. You need to get the decorators in as well, all the frames are uneven, the wood is so old.'

Jan straightened up, confused. 'What has this got to do with the gardener?'

'When I came back from the lake every single door and window was open again and it was freezing. There was earth spread all over the floor in our bedroom, like from a really dirty pair of shoes. My new silk dressing gown was all ripped up and trampled. He was clearly looking through my things, like a pervert.'

Jan asked, 'Why do you think it was the gardener, though?'

'Well, who else could it have been?'

They all looked up and looked around, thinking. When Jan's gaze fell on Luke, who had listened to the whole story without participating, he merely said, 'I can't believe this,' and left, slamming the door behind him.

'What's got into him?'

Theo said quickly, 'The usual.'

'I really don't think it was him, Nads,' Jan said. 'He knows we're watching him. I mean, he got so annoyed with me yesterday for suggesting he'd been moving the big vase upstairs.'

'Well, it can't have been Ursie or Kara.'

Jan quietly resolved to keep a closer eye on Luke if she was able.

'He *is* pretty angry with you right now, so I suppose it's possible. Anyone want a bump?' Theo said.

Clearly, Jan thought, nothing could distract him from his determination that they all enjoy themselves as much as he saw fit.

He levered Nadya off his lap. 'You're going to be fine, stop crying now,' he said, before taking a book from the shelf.

Jan saw 'Geheimnis' stamped in red on the cover and asked, 'What is that? It looks really old to me, are you sure it's not valuable?'

She reached for it but he put the book back quickly and said, 'You've got to stop treating this place like a museum, it's kind of tragic. Houses are like dogs, if you don't take possession of them, they take possession of you.' He flipped one of the little silver salvers on its back and asked her sarcastically, 'Will this do?'

'Up to you, really.'

He and Nadya hoovered up their portions, but Jan demurred.

Nadya said, 'You need to call the agency or whatever and get to the bottom of this. You can't have someone working for you who just comes in and out without you seeing them, it's a security risk.'

'I've never had any contact with him.'

'Well, figure it out. If you're paying him, you can stop and if you're not, we need to call the police.'

Jan said, 'We can't call the police, we're not supposed to be here either, remember?'

'My parents' lawyers' office should still be open,' Theo said in a conciliatory tone. 'They're essential workers and I can give them a call. We can't have him traipsing in and out of the house and calling the pigs on us with no notice, though I do think it's far more likely that our dear Luke was searching for this and got frustrated.' He patted his breast pocket.

'But we don't want to tell them we're here,' Nadya insisted.

'So, I can frame it as a hypothetical. They're our lawyers anyway, they won't do anything to us.'

174

She said, 'I just think it's unacceptable. None of us have even seen him going in and out.'

'Do you especially want to see him?' Theo asked.

'No, but—'

'Let me deal with it, then. Enough now, Nadya, this isn't interesting.'

Nadya stood up and reached for the packet, stretching out to do another bump, but Theo snatched it up and held it above her head until she gave him a begrudging kiss in exchange. Clutching the powder, she said, 'I need a drink.'

'All the spirits are in the Western drawing room.'

The three of them went in search of the drinks cabinet only to find Ursie and Kara curled up together under a blanket on the small sofa, both drowsing gently. Undaunted, Nadya set to noisily mixing old fashioneds with a bottle of the sugar syrup she'd brought to Holt House in her car and singeing the orange peels she insisted Jan fetch from the kitchen with a match.

Nadya said, 'Change the music, Theo, this is crap.'

'I thought you liked Dark House. We saw Timo Maas live, remember?'

'Oh yes, but it's crap for right now. Put that Lounge Lizard playlist on you found for me the other day.'

Theo got up and went to wrangle with his speakers, while the Bluetooth connection kept dropping. 'You girls look very cosy, what are you doing under there?' He goosed Kara for a moment and she squealed, until Ursie slapped his hand away.

'I think we smoked a bit too much,' she said. 'What was in that joint earlier?'

'Just a bit of Purple Devil, it's a headier high than the one you're used to, more THC-heavy. It's good for sleeping.'

'Why did you give us that one and not the other?'

'It was what I had to hand, and it's nicer towards the end of the day. How much did you put in the joint?' Ursie gestured a rough quantity. 'Oh dear. Caveat emptor, I suppose. Dinner will sort you right out. Do you want a drink?'

'I can't. I feel like my mind's made of wool, why didn't you stop me?'

'I just gave you what you wanted, what you do with it is up to you. It'll pass.'

Nadya said again, 'Theo, the music. It's still shit.'

Kara disentangled herself from the blanket and stood up, shakily. 'Do you still have that ket I was asking about earlier?'

'Sure, sure, it's upstairs, I can go and grab some for you now. Want to come along and do a line?'

Nadya put down the shaker and stormed over to Theo's phone, which she held out to him to unlock then angrily changed the music herself. Fatima Yamaha's voice welled up out of the speaker, bouncing oddly off the high ceiling. 'Can't you just sit for a moment? There's no need to go right away.'

'Oh really, it's no trouble.' He turned back to Kara. 'I can mix you a little CK One if you like? I think coke pairs really well with that ket, they smooth each other out.'

Nadya said, 'No, you can go later. I just mixed us drinks.'

Kara laughed and said cattily, 'Looks like I'm going to get you in trouble with your fiancée.' She leaned against the side of the leather armchair and asked Nadya, 'Can I have one?'

'Can you have what?' Nadya was mixing the sugar syrup vigorously, spoon rattling her irritation to the assembled room.

'An Old Fashioned . . . please.' She jutted out her chin, challenging Nadya to react.

'All the things are here. Come and make one.'

Kara got up, mouthing a scandalised 'Okayyyy' to anyone who cared to look, snatching the bourbon and clinking the cocktail spoon loudly in the glass once Nadya was done with it. Nadya sat dwarfed by a velvet button-back chair, arms crossed as she stewed in her annoyance at her fiancé, a man from whom she could no longer quite so readily expect obedience in all things.

Theo said placatingly, 'Shall I go and get your cigarettes from the brick, Nads? I notice you've run out.'

'Stop fussing like a grandma. Just be normal.'

He excused himself to go upstairs for what everyone in the room knew perfectly well was another private line.

Ursie said, 'I have such a bad headache; do you think there's going to be a storm?'

The sky outside was still bright and cloudless. Jan jumped as a horrible creaking wail broke the silence as a door opened several corridors away. The noise had come from the opposite direction to Theo's departing footsteps.

Jan said, 'Guys, we have got to start closing the doors properly. It's not safe and I'm really worried in case something happens.'

Ursie asked, 'What sort of thing?' at the same time as Kara said, 'It's fine, we're in nature and there's the big wall round everything.'

'I just feel really uneasy, someone could walk in at any time.'

Nadya fixed her cold agate eyes on Jan and asked, 'Why are we talking about *your* feelings again, when you don't have any real problems? Get a grip.'

'But I thought you—?'

'Now isn't the time for that, Theo already said.'

Kara took a sip of her Old Fashioned and said, 'Honestly, you're so paranoid, Jan. It's really bringing down the vibe.'

Trying not to appear like she was storming out, Jan excused herself to finish up the coq au vin, promising to bring Ursie some aspirin if she found any in the boot room. Coming across an old bottle of iodine and some cotton balls instead, she finally cleaned the grazes on her shins and forearms from her fall in the woods, choking on the rank smell of the liquid.

She took the opportunity to quickly chop up some more bunches of herbs in preparation for the dish, then found herself recutting the vegetables more finely to keep her hands busy while her mind ran through the events of the day.

Jan had never thought the few scars that still remained from adolescence might be an object of innocent curiosity to Ursie, or indeed anyone else. They seemed like something private, a shared language between her and Nadya that others would read only as an admission of instability and failure. There was the lumpy one made with a penknife after her father had read a story about two doomed lovers she'd written for an upper-sixth English class and then stood over her shoulder shouting instructions at her on how to rewrite it, until it was impossible to tell where her ideas ended and his began. The dot of tissue where she'd stabbed herself with a fork in a fit of drunken pique after a boy she'd tried to con herself into liking at Nadya's suggestion had not shown up to a party. Then there were a couple of faint ones near the crook of her elbow from particularly bad mornings at school when Nadya was ignoring her. Nadya had seen Jan's cuts when they were undressed together and pronounced them to be mere 'chicken scratches', a declaration that disheartened her so much she'd quit entirely, knowing that to compete with Nadya, who always kept a razor blade stashed in her compact and had graduated to her legs after running out of space on her arms, would be madness. When her father had discovered what Jan had done, he'd shouted at her for ruining her beauty and, fearing that she could not be left alone, spent several weeks making her go everywhere with him while berating her on the basis that 'misery loves company but company hates misery'.

As Jan recalled these scenes in detail, the knife she was using to dice the onions slipped, cutting deeply into her left index finger before she could stop it. Tiny scarlet beads welled almost immediately, the discomfort of severed nerves itching and shrieking along the route of the blade.

Her father and Nadya had told her the same thing in different words, that she must learn to suffer less noisily, to constrain her feelings within narrower bounds if there were to be any hope of people continuing with her. But even in the present day, she could not learn. And standing in the dirty, dingy kitchen at Holt House after a day of discord between everyone, Jan knew with certainty that she would lose her friends, lose them all if they were not half lost already. They had more past than future together now, and if she had any sense she would leave first to avoid the brunt of it. But still, she wanted them to retain something of her, whether they knew it or not.

The flow of blood from her injured finger wasn't stopping. It wasn't strong enough to concern her, but she was tired of it almost immediately. The claret drops swelled and spilled and slowly she held her hand out over the hob, letting the blood fall into the pot. Just enough to give it additional savour, she thought, and besides, the original recipe called for blood. Still in a half-trance of sadness, she tidied herself and the knife, poured another glass of wine and stared into the pot blankly for a few minutes while the sauce reduced.

***

The atmosphere in the dining room was so unpleasant, Jan found herself opening the french windows to encourage the circulation of some air, until Nadya got up and closed them all again. She took a tablecloth from the drawer and laid it over the polished wood surface before bringing the coq au vin from the sideboard, mostly for something to do in the absence of good cheer. Luke had still not rejoined the group and on being asked whether they should wait for him, Kara merely shrugged.

'I can't eat this.'

Jan realised that she'd neglected to make the stuffed mushrooms she'd planned as an alternative for Kara. 'I'll go fry something up for you right away, it shouldn't take long. You guys start without me.'

'Honestly, it's fine, all this rich food is making me kind of bloated. I'll just grab some salad leaves from the fridge and take extra bread.'

Jan watched Kara's lanky figure wander off down the corridor in pursuit of sustenance, leaving her to face the other three arranged down one side of the table like interviewers for a position she would never be offered. She thought with an absent and dreamy horror of what she'd done in the kitchen and cursed herself for her idiotic lapse of control. But the others, perhaps relieved to have something new to focus on, made short work of their plates, and Nadya even got a laugh when she asked if it would be possible for her to have a glass of white wine with the coq au vin 'for the contrast'.

Theo said, 'This is so delicious; I feel like a French peasant settling down after a long day of herding sheep to something my wife has been keeping on the fire.'

'Sheep are so disgusting,' Nadya said. 'I touched one once and was really surprised. I thought it would be soft like wool but they're so dirty.'

'To think I was going to find a suitable sheep and ask for it to be our ring bearer.'

'Please no. My friend Oksana had doves last year and it was so tacky.'

Jan watched Theo wince for a moment before he ladled more of the sauce onto his plate, wondering again with delusional hope whether he would really be able to go through with the wedding. She had always seen Theo and Nadya as each other's future major ex.

Ursie asked, 'Is Oksana the same age as you?'

'A year younger, I think she's twenty-six. Why?'

'I just can't get over everyone being so young. What do they do with their late twenties?'

'Enjoy being married. Have babies, some of them. It's good to have kids while your parents are still young

181

enough to be involved. You're talking about marriage like it's a life sentence, instead of just being lucky enough to find your person and then get on with the rest of your life together.'

Ursie said, 'I'm so single right now, the idea of being with anyone forever seems mad. I'm used to doing everything on my own, on my terms. I don't even want to text after I've slept with someone, you know?'

Jan fought with every sinew not to say, 'Oh I know.' She merely watched Ursie's cherubic face drop a little as she registered Jan's staring at her across the table.

Ursie added, rather weakly, 'I just don't know what to say.'

Jan watched Nadya watching the exchange, and any feeling of moral victory dissipated into pure abjection.

Nadya asked Ursie, 'Do you really want to be alone forever?' and then took Theo's hand as she added, 'That seems really sad to me.' She slid a bare foot along Jan's bruised ankle, toes inching up her calf with tantalising slowness.

'I didn't say that. Just that even with everything going on right now my life is so full, I have loads of work to do, and my friends, and that's enough. I can find guys if I want a fling, but I'm busy. And if it doesn't happen, it's not a big deal.' She paused and speared a potato. 'Dealing with clients already takes up so much emotional energy. My gallery told me there's this guy who's bought three of my paintings so far, but keeps clamouring for a landscape with figures, something he can hang in his house. I need to find a way of making it look like I just decided to do it, rather than painting it for him.'

Kara, returning with her plate now piled high with salad and olives, asked her, 'Why do you have to pretend?'

'No idea. He's rich and neurotic, so I'm just taking their advice and hopefully taking home the money.'

Nadya said, 'I suppose he doesn't want to be catered to; he wants to feel like he's just come across the perfect thing by chance.'

'Don't get me anything for my birthday, I hate surprises,' Theo said in a falsetto. 'Why didn't anyone get me anything?'

'Is that supposed to be me?' Nadya asked. 'I always tell you exactly what I want.'

The foot had moved to Jan's crotch, probing the thin fabric of her leggings. She stared into her wine glass, face flushing as Nadya began to stroke her ever so gently without breaking the flow of conversation.

'You do. I suppose you get it from your father.'

'He's not so bad, really, he's a teddy bear.' Nadya poured herself another measure of wine.

Booze stocks were running worryingly low already, but Jan feared pointing this out in case it triggered a mass exodus. She was not sure exactly why she felt it important that they stay longer, but the conviction had attached itself to her and swelled, like a tick grown so fat on blood that removing it would be more trouble than waiting for it to fall away on its own.

'The last time I saw him he bought me a brandy and told me that if I ever cheated on you, he would find out about it and that I would not enjoy the outcome,' muttered Theo.

'Naturally he would say that. What a hypocrite. And if you do ever humiliate me like that, he won't be able to find you because I will have gotten to you first.'

'What a bloodthirsty little psychopath you are, my beloved Nadechka.'

Theo seemed entirely unmoved by the threats against his person, alternately cooing over his future bride and levering another chicken leg out of the pot. Jan was trying desperately to keep her expression neutral as the toe increased in speed and pressure.

Nadya added, 'What my father did to my mother was not only cheating, it was an insult because he was so sloppy. If he really wanted to sleep with someone else, he should have taken the secret to his grave.'

Ursie said, 'So you think it's better not to tell someone?'

'What is the point of confessing? It won't make your partner feel better, it's only so you can absolve yourself,' Theo replied for her, complacently.

Jan choked out, 'Maybe your parents have an open relationship, Nadya? Plenty of couples do. It's not that much more extreme than having threesomes.'

Nadya extracted her foot from Jan's lap just before the point of climax to find her shin under the table and kick it, hard. Jan disguised her little shriek as a cough, then drained her water glass.

Kara rubbed her on the back absentmindedly and asked, 'What if they're poly?'

Theo reclaimed the potatoes from Ursie and poured himself the last of the wine. 'Polyamory is a bunch of nerds who've taken sex, something that should be simple, and made it the most annoying, complicated activity you can imagine.'

Kara rolled her eyes. 'You aren't saying they're wrong.'

'I'm not, just that it's deeply uncool.'

'The vocabulary rubs you up the wrong way,' Jan said, 'so you've decided to write off an entire subculture?'

Kara said, 'Why are you being so weird about this? It's not like you're even dating one person at the moment.'

'Thank you for reminding me that I'm going to die alone. Does anyone want pudding?'

Kara muttered, 'Always so dramatic,' into her wine glass as Ursie asked, 'What have we got? I'm stuffed.'

'Just chocolate, I think. I'll get it.'

Ursie stood up and helped Jan gather all the plates, decanting the last portion of coq au vin into a bowl for Luke in case he got hungry later. Kara began a second-hand story of Luke's about the wife of a plastics million-aire back home in Nyack who was well known for propositioning her sons' friends when they turned eighteen.

As Jan left the room, she heard Ursie say, 'She sounds like a predator to me, if that was an older man and teenage girls, we'd all be disgusted.'

And Nadya answered, 'I don't know, women are just different.'

<hr />

Jan was charting a course back to join the others in the Western drawing room, with the chocolate and a lime rickey, when she heard a crash from upstairs. The glass nearly leaped from her hand and she left a trail of diluted gin splashed over the tiles. She set it down carefully on a little lion-legged side table and bounded up the staircase to the source of Luke's bellowing. Peering around the corner in the dim light, she saw pieces of vase strewn all over the floorboards and a dishevelled Luke scrabbling among them, hands covered in blood.

'What did you do? We told you not to go in the end bedroom!'

'I can put it all back together, I swear. Just bring me some glue.' His words were slurred and when she got closer, his pupils were shrunk to half their usual size.

'What did you take, Luke? Were you looking for more ket?' She grabbed his hand and turned it over. 'Oh for god's sake.' His fingertips were pierced by several fine porcelain splinters. 'Just stop it now, I'll tidy it.'

'I'm so sorry, I'll make it right, I swear.'

She looked about her at the bright-coloured fragments; picked out in gold, a group of deer peered at her from one huge shard still rocking gently on the floor. 'It's probably worth a fortune.' Jan heard the ice enter her voice and tried to dispel it; he was still bleeding even if he was an idiot. 'Hopefully it's insured. What were you doing?'

'I was just trying to open my door and I couldn't. Something was blocking it.' He gestured to the chaos around them, flinging beads of crimson over them both. 'I gave it a shove and—'

'What's going on?' Ursie had run out of the drawing room and up the staircase to join them when she heard the crash. 'You okay, Luke? What happened?'

'This THING was in the way. I wasn't going in the other room; I don't know what's in there that Theo's so worried about and I honestly don't care. I couldn't get out from here.' He jabbed a grisly finger back towards his door.

Jan whispered in her ear, 'He's on something. Look at his eyes.'

Ursie glanced at him and nodded, then darted into her room.

'Where are you going? Don't leave me with him like this! Where's Kara?'

'Tweezers! We need tweezers!' Returning with her washbag, Ursie yanked Luke by the wrist into the bathroom between his room and Kara's and flicked on the overhead light.

'Take off your shirt, it's filthy.'

He tried pulling at it, head nodding forward for a moment. She and Jan shoved him onto the loo seat, leaned him back against the old white pipe and unbuttoned the shirt so as to clean his bloodstained cuffs, yanking its hem free from his trousers as they took it off. Several foil-backed packets of dihydrocodeine fell out, ragged holes punched where he'd scarfed three big pills. Jan examined the packet.

'These are ancient, they must have been here for years. Bad luck he found them, but at least it'll hurt less getting the shards out.'

'Just hold his hand up for me so I can get it in the light.'

Quickly and skilfully, Ursie pulled out the splinters and scrutinised the flesh. 'That'll do.'

She turned on the hot tap and shoved Luke's hand under it. He moaned, the sting of the water reviving him.

'I'm so sorry, I made such a mess. I promise I didn't move it; it was just outside.'

'I've got this,' Ursie said. 'Do you know where the hoover is?'

'I think I saw one downstairs in the games room. I'll go look.' Jan backed out of the bathroom, trying not to step on anything. She looked over at the mess in front of Luke's door and spotted the base of the vase amid the detritus, midway up the hall between his door and the end bedroom, among the other, larger pieces, which lay spread out around the spot where it had toppled, or been flung, over. Who knew what Luke, in his addled state, had been doing up here or whether he had tripped and become confused? The door to the end bedroom gaped open, moonlight creeping around the frame.

The largest and bloodiest pieces glinted in the warm lamplight of the evening, sharp points arching up towards the ceiling. Ursie was right, she couldn't leave those lying out while she investigated what else he'd gotten into.

She bounded back down the stairs again, landing heavily on the bottom tread with all her weight, a mighty step that jolted the rickey from the edge of the table where it was balancing, to shatter on the hallway tiles. The glass skidded everywhere, spikes slaloming among the ice cubes. She groaned and dragged a chair over the worst of it to stop anyone from cutting their feet and raced on. Another sticky mess to be resolved and this one was squarely her fault. Though she distinctly remembered placing it closer to the middle. She must have been distracted by the commotion.

She heard Kara saying through the open door, 'Whatever it is he's done this time, I don't give a shit.'

Nadya asked, 'Will you not go to him?'

'No, I've had enough, honestly.'

Jan strode round the corner into the Eastern wing, not bothering to flick on the lights. The glass lampshades jittered as the first door swung shut behind her, they were loose on their sconces and she prayed they wouldn't come crashing down as well. The corridor stretched out ahead, elongated by the dark and bending slightly. The air was moist and heavy, smelling of heat and dust. She pushed open the second door that divided the passage and kept going, feeling her way along the raised paper above the dado rail, like throbbing varicose veins beneath her hands. It was damper here and pitch black, the window at the end obscured by a heavy curtain. Her nose caught a hint of that curious rancid sweetness, and she felt unable to stop herself breathing deep to puzzle over what it could be, but it faded after a moment. She kept one hand on the wall, trailing desperately for the doorframe now. The wallpaper stretched out an impossibly long time as she edged forward, fingers tracing the ripples, ears straining as her eyes stayed blind. There it was! She reached down for the handle, found it cool to the touch and sticky, though perhaps that was just her sweat. It turned stiffly in the door as she pushed.

The room was all shadow, with the barest sliver of light creeping in from the night outside to turn its contents into a jumble of grey. Before she could reach for the switch, she stopped, her eye drawn inexorably towards a mass of blackness at the centre of the room. It did not move. Had there been a chair here before? Darker than the dark around it, she thought she could discern a seated figure, waiting. She tried to call out, but her throat was dry. She was suddenly aware of the dark pressing in around her from all sides, and felt too afraid to turn back into the house behind her.

'Hello?'

It was still there, motionless. She called out the most likely name.

'Theo?'

No response came.

A quaver in her voice, resounding pathetically in her skull as she clung to the door. 'Theo, this isn't funny.'

She felt her eyes adjust minutely; the head tilted as if turning to face her. She heard a soft click, like bare bones turning in a neck and she was running, screaming, not caring what or who pursued her. She hurled herself back into the corridor, bursting through the first door, running to the next one and finding that she could not turn the handle to escape back into the great hall, screaming without breath, bashing against the wood with her whole shoulder, trying to force it open, but it was stuck, stuck, stuck.

'Jan? Jan, what's wrong? Calm down, I'm trying to get to you. Let go of the doorknob.'

Theo was there. He opened the door smoothly and briskly and enveloped her in his warm wide arms where she burst into snotty tears.

'It's okay. Shush. I heard you calling for me but I was half-asleep on the sofa after all that chicken. What's wrong? Why is there broken glass everywhere?'

'There's someone in there. I saw them. They're waiting in the dark.'

He pulled back and looked at her. 'Did you hit your head?'

'Luke-broke-a-vase-and-I-went-looking-for-the-hoover-and-someone's-in-there.'

'Come and show me.' He was laughing now, one hand still on her shoulder. 'I think you should get some sleep after this.'

She hated herself for letting a man comfort her like this, even if it was Theo. She couldn't breathe, choked out, 'I . . . I don't want to go back in there.'

'Come with me.' He darted into the Eastern parlour, Jan shaking as she lost sight of him for a moment, before he emerged holding a heavy iron poker.

'Even if it's the mad old gardener, now we're prepared.' He found the lights and turned them on easily, the yellow glow blooming over the wooden dado rails and making the wallpaper posies bloom. Jan, still wheezing, followed him, retracing her terrified steps. A moment's pause before opening the final door, poker raised aloft. His hand went swiftly to the switch.

The room was empty, a battered leather button-back armchair pressed innocently into the space between the two floor-to-ceiling windows. The huge billiards table opposite it was covered by a film of dust, while an old hoover rested against the far wall.

He put the poker down. 'See, no one's here, Jan. It must have been a trick of the light. I can see how the hoover might look like a man crouching if you squint.'

'But it wasn't crouching. Someone was sitting just here in the chair, looking at me.'

'How much have you had to drink, Jan?'

'Only a sip of gin! And that wine at supper, but no more than anyone else. I saw it. I saw someone.'

'Go to bed, Jan. I'll clean up downstairs as well.'

'I'm so sorry about the glass, it was really pretty.'

'Don't worry about it. There are always breakages with this many people.'

The tears came again. He was being kind to her, kinder than she deserved as usual, ridiculous high-strung, silly Jan, frightened of an armchair in his beautiful old house.

'There was a clicking noise and it really scared me.'

'I'm not surprised, it was pretty dark in here.' He went over to the billiards table and examined it. 'It must have been the balls moving in the sudden draught.'

'But I'd already opened the door when I heard it?'

'I don't see what else it could have been. Now I'm going to grab this'— he cleared his throat —'*haunted* hoover and finish up down here and upstairs. Nadya's going to have an early night and so am I once this is cleared away. Kara's downstairs drinking her feelings, but I suggest you get some rest.'

'I thought it was you. Trying to play a trick on me.'

'You thought I would hide in here in the dark, just in case you came in? To scare you?'

'I suppose not . . .'

He pulled open both sets of damask curtains decisively, dislodging scraps of sun-tattered silk as he did so, then took the hoover under one arm and steered her out ahead of him.

As Jan was trudging up the stairs back to her room, ashamed and too shaken up to go for another glass of water from the gloomy kitchen, she realised she'd forgotten once again to ask him about the prank with the photo frames. Feeling stupid, she wondered whether he had turned them around not to unnerve her but to preserve her sense of privacy.

Ursie's face popped over the top of the banister. 'You've been gone ages. I put Luke down in Kara's room because all the broken bits are in front of his. What was all that commotion just now, running around screaming your head off?'

'Just a minor upset!' Theo called up from behind Jan.

Ursie narrowed her eyes. 'He's very heavy. I had to drag him by myself and keep an eye on all this mess. Where were you?'

'I was trying to get the hoover,' Jan said.

'Be up in a minute!' Theo added, trying to defuse matters.

She would cook him a giant breakfast tomorrow, apologise again for panicking, stop playing footsie with Nadya – at least when he might catch them at it. Looking around the landing, Jan noticed with an intense weariness that almost every framed painting was slightly askew.

'I flushed those pills down the toilet, the whole lot of them. In fact, I dealt with everything, no thanks to you.'

All Jan could say was 'Thank you', before pulling her door to and collapsing into bed.

Jan lay on the large, soft expanse and stared at the ceiling, waiting for the impulse to do something, anything to distract her from her impotent anger and worry about Luke. It had been a long time since she'd seen him that bad. How on earth had he managed to get entangled with the vase? He'd seemed so convinced it had been barricading him in his room.

She regretted the loss of the lime rickey. One avenue of comfort still remained. When she wanted it that badly, every other thing under the sun came second. Decency, morality, practicality all scattered by the encroaching juggernaut of her need. It would frighten her, except she knew men to be just as in thrall to it as she, women too, though too many had been taught to ignore themselves, or call it something else. What would it be like, to become so divorced from your own desires that you could regard those of others as something alien, even pitiable?

As slowly as possible, she stripped, put on more perfume and her good lingerie, covered up with loose-fitting clothes that would be easy to manoeuvre in. She considered going downstairs again to find a better dressing for her finger, but the thought of looking at the results of her own clumsy idiocy was beyond her and she did not exactly relish the thought of returning to the dark hallways of Holt House after being terrified half out of her wits by a room Theo insisted was empty.

She pulled the little stepladder out again and ascended into the now-familiar filth of the attic, before realising she had not bolted the door to her bedroom. She could not be bothered to climb down all over again to go and secure it, so she closed the hatch in case someone came looking for her to continue one of the arguments she'd become embroiled in over the course of the day.

Crawling over to the section of ceiling above the linen closet in Nadya and Theo's bathroom, she pressed her ear against the floor and listened. No conversation rumbled up from below, but she did hear the sound of a hairdryer. She waited, measuring the time in her head for the wailing whoosh to subside if it was being used to dry a man's shorter hair. It continued. She knocked at the ceiling near where the light fitting must be. Three short taps, a pause, three short taps again. After a few moments, the trapdoor opened with a blinding rush of light from the bathroom below.

'What is it?' Nadya's face, mascara semi-removed and smudged around her lower lids, peered up in irritation.

'Want to come up?'

She disappeared for a moment and Jan heard her switch on the extractor fan and turn both taps on full.

'I've had a long day. I'm still finding bits of all my things the gardener ripped up. What have you got up there for me?'

Jan gave her the first genuine smile of the day. 'A mouth, hands, and some other things. You got me so wet already at dinner, come up the ladder.'

'I've already had all of those, I'm tired of them. I want something new.'

Craving the all-consuming distraction only Nadya could bring, Jan said hurriedly, 'You know you can do whatever you like to me.'

'Perhaps you should play harder to get, then. I don't think I can tonight, he's barely asleep. Last night was a big risk.'

Right then, Jan heard a voice from below saying, 'Nadya? Stop messing about in there and come back to bed,' and the cupboard door closed swiftly. Enclosed by darkness, Jan pulled the bathroom trapdoor shut. She waited in the pitch black, counting down from a thousand before crawling as slowly as she possibly could back to the area where her own trapdoor must be. She tried to remain calm, as eddies of dust wafted into her open mouth and made the temptation to cough almost irresistible. Shapes emerged from the darkness as her eyes adjusted but not enough to be certain of what they were. It was far too hot up here. Why didn't she bring her phone as a torch? What had she been thinking? Only Nadya and the promise of temporary oblivion at her hands could propel Jan from one dark and daunting room to another as if her mind weren't still wild with fear and confusion at what she'd seen downstairs. Scrabbling for the ring in the floor that marked the edge of the door, her hands brushed repeatedly over nothing but boards. Where was it? Perhaps she wasn't in the right place.

Wheezing from the dust she had stirred up, she crawled left as far as she could bear to go, then back the other way, swiping the floor as she went, searching and coming up with nothing. Then forward, painstakingly repeating the process, palms filling with splinters. Why wasn't it there? Her chest constricting, she tried to breathe slowly but began quivering, tears beading her eyes. Was she going to be trapped here? Now slapping the floor around her, through the haze of her panic she heard the ring resound against its metal setting, and she placed her hand back roughly where she thought the noise had been and felt for it. Seizing the iron, she turned, trying to twist it and undo the catch that kept the door in place. She felt it give a little, but it was stuck. Even pushing all her weight down against the trapdoor frame didn't help to force it open.

She wondered whether she had it in her to crawl back to Nadya's door and calmly let herself down into the bathroom to wait and sneak out when Theo was asleep. But there was no way Nadya would permit that; she'd tell Jan to stop being pathetic and try again here above her own room. She couldn't use the trapdoor into the end bedroom either, that was out of the question. Something in the far corner rustled and she heard a piece of furniture nearby move slightly against the wooden attic floor. Yanking the ring, not caring now it if came off in her hand, she tried brute force one more time but still it refused to budge. Weeping and gasping on the attic floor, she was too afraid to resign herself to being stuck there until the morning. The shape from the billiards room still fresh in her mind, she could not bear to hear that clicking noise again.

But Nadya had told her about another way, if she dared to take it. The Mortimers had initially only built one priest hole, to shelter persecuted clergy from Elizabeth I's purges, but successive generations had bored further and deeper into the marrow of the house itself, until it was riven with passageways. Jan crawled back over to the Western wing, past all the shrouded family memorabilia, brushing against swathes of filthy velvet and mouldy cardboard, unsure if the sounds around her were that rustling again or the disturbance she was creating. She passed over the bathroom trapdoor and set her course for the far wall, trying to go straight ahead but utterly uncertain. She put her blind hands to the damp, bulging wall and felt all along it. Nestled almost in the corner of the attic, there was indeed a little door, though she had to heave aside a rotting armchair to have a chance at the latch, recoiling at the rotted, spongy mass in her hands as she did so.

Jan pulled the door open, and she clambered down into even deeper darkness, heard the door snap back shut behind her as if on springs and regretted the decision immediately. The air was freezing cold, and the passageway so tight that she was crouching in terror of hitting her head. If she concussed herself in here, or worse, no one would find her. Nadya might not even think to look. She might imagine Jan had left in a huff back to London after being rejected. The walls were wet with who knew what and the steps no wider than half a foot's length. Jan was far taller and broader shouldered than any of those long-ago priests had been. As she descended, it got tighter and tighter: a new fear, what if she got stuck? Twisting her shoulders to dip low, she proceeded downwards in an ever-smaller spiral. Had she gone too far? Nadya had told her how Theo had proudly shown her one tunnel that led below the house and out into the grounds beyond. Jan could feel a cold draught intensifying, the smell of mildew and earth filling her nostrils as dank air rose from the passageway beneath.

She pushed at the walls around her, starting to hyper-ventilate, she could not help it. One palm caught on nothingness and in her panic, she overbalanced, falling to her knees in a hollow alcove that seemed to be cut out of the stone. Perhaps this was the original chamber that she'd been told was behind the panelled dining-room wall. She lurched further into the restricted space, scraping raw nails against the wall for a final catch and twisted it, deter-mined to escape. Leaping out, at last, into the light she saw too late that the room was not empty.

Ursie was standing back from the table where she had been writing in the lamplight, mouth moving in silent, baffled terror, about to scream, a gold plastic rosary clutched in her fist. Jan leaped for her, pressing a sweaty, dust-smeared hand over her lips.

'Don't say anything, I can explain.'

Ursie dug her nails in tight to Jan's arm and forced her off as Jan tried not to shriek in pain herself.

'What the fuck? What the actual fuck are you doing?' She wiped her face and looked at the muck thick on her palm. 'You're disgusting!'

'I'm sorry, please don't wake the others, please be quiet.'

Ursie's mouth was smeared with dirt from Jan's grey hand. 'You scared me so much, when that little thing,' she pointed at the carved loop in the wooden panel that hid the underside of the catch, 'started turning and then THE WHOLE WALL OPENED. I thought I was going mad; I didn't know what was going to come out of there.'

Jan closed it and speedily turned the loop back into place, sealing the door again.

'I got trapped. It was a mistake. Don't tell anyone about this, please, Ursie.'

Ursie looked at her, the fear that had seized her features increasingly supplanted by rage.

'It was you. Wasn't it?'

'I'm sorry, what was me? I don't understand.' Jan was peering over the top of Ursie's head to make sure no one else was in the corridor outside, while frantically trying to brush off the dust and cobwebs that covered her from head to toe.

'The noises. I thought this stupid house was haunted, especially after I got locked in the bathroom. I heard something last night as well, and when I asked about it you let me believe it might be a ghost. All that thumping and those voices and footsteps overhead, obviously that wasn't mice. It was you all along. What were you doing crawling about up there?'

'I . . . I couldn't sleep, I went up to have a look. And then I got stuck tonight and had to use the passageway.'

'Bullshit. If you were just going up there randomly to walk about you could have told me earlier when I was asking about the noises. What were you really doing – last night and tonight? Tell me now or I'm going to start screaming and wake the entire house up. Then you can explain to them why you're covered in dust.'

Jan kept patting her clothes, trying to come up with a quick lie but nothing presented itself to her.

'Out with it. I want to go back to bed now I know I'm not going to be woken up by demons or whatever.'

'You don't seriously believe in demons, do you? You need therapy.'

'Grew up Catholic, didn't I? I'm waiting.'

'Promise me you won't tell anyone about this.' Jan swallowed. 'I'm really sorry for waking you up, I thought I was being quiet.'

'Okay. Go on.'

'I was going to visit Nadya. She was . . . very upset and needed to talk about some things.'

Ursie paused, rolling the information around in her mouth like a wine taster before spitting it out. 'Oh my god . . . You're fucking her, aren't you? No one goes sneaking about in an ATTIC because they're upset . . . Does Theo know?'

'Shhh, please be quiet. No, he doesn't know. It will never happen again. You promised not to tell anyone, this would ruin a lot of things if it got out, it was a mistake.'

'So that's why she orders you around, I thought she was just rude. Are you like her slave or something?'

'It's never been formally discussed,' Jan said, then cursed herself for contradicting her own suggestion of it being a one-time thing.

Not even pausing to gather up her notebook and pens, Ursie rushed to the dining-room door and then turned to face Jan. 'You really are the most entitled person I've ever met. Theo thinks he has a loyal fiancée – they're getting married. Only today he told us he wants a family with her. You're supposed to be his friend and you're going behind his back to mess that up for him. And what about her? How are you going to live with yourself if he calls off the wedding and she gets deported? How is that right? You're so careless, you think you can just sleep with anyone you want on the downlow and act like it never happened. *You* just keep living your life.'

'It's not like that,' Jan insisted. 'Their relationship is a lot different to whatever he's been telling you.'

'And you'd know all about that, would you? Get your own girlfriend and stop messing up other people's lives because you can't keep it in your pants.'

With that, Ursie strode out and away upstairs, leaving Jan alone in the low-lit room, gasping like a stranded fish.

The Fourth Day

Jan lay face down, arms spread wide, mind still possessed by dreams. A great storm had transformed the fields beside Holt House to coursing rivers and washed vast tree branches into the path of the car. She sat in the back seat, small legs kicking and singing a made-up song. In front were a faded blond man and a tall, exasperated woman, both in their fifties. It took her a while to recognise the two as Theo's parents, much younger than she had ever known them, conducting a whisper-shouted argument. Theo's father was insisting that they had to go home now and his mother was steadfast that leaving would be impossibly dangerous and so the family must remain at Holt House that night. A drab, scavenged meal of reheated baked beans and crumbling old crackers in the dining room. Harold dozing at the head of the table, barely looking at them over his plate. The draughty bedroom in the Eastern wing, a big bed for Theo made up inexpertly with musty sheets seized from the airing cupboard next door, Theo's father muttering under his breath before standing outside the bathroom as he got ready for sleep.

Theo's father put her to bed, stroked her hair and tucked the sheets around her tight before telling her to be good and stay put. He'd sat in the armchair, instead of lying down next to her or going to another room, and he waited with the bedside lamp still lit. The world outside was pure black, everything steeped in darkness like the wind had blown out every light but theirs. In the dim grey-yellow of the bedroom he had read from an old book of fairy tales and encouraged her to be quiet, go to sleep, yet he had slept and the child had stayed awake, or at least not fully slept. The time after that was jumbled in the dream, there was a knock at the door and she freed herself from the bedclothes to answer it. She was searching, not for a bathroom, but something else, she could not remember quite what.

The carpet was damp and prickly underfoot, her feet were bare and she was warm, so warm. Just a little further, and she slipped silently round him out beyond the door, knob rolling backwards at her touch. The walls loomed high, unrecognisable, they had stretched and shifted in the night, the sickly brownish glimpses thrown out by the lightning were warped and strangely faded, out of time. The knocking came again, though all the doors were shut but one and she saw no hand rapping. At the end of the corridor, darkness waiting. The door was open wide to greet her, she was going there, step by childish step, knocking growing ever louder; aware of the scent of rot, sweet and putrid, filling Theo's nose, seeping into the pores of his skin permanently, infecting him with its long-drawn-out decay. Theo was so close now, he was expected and he was coming, one foot already over the threshold into nothingness. Later, unknowably later, perhaps an eternity, his father caught him by the middle, pulled him out of the room and roared. Bashed every one of the light switches on his way down and out of Holt House to drive them home through the storm, jaw locked tight with fear and fury as Theo sickened in the back seat, temperature rising and rising, worsening with every jolt in the road.

Jan woke gasping, clutching at her head but the knocking sound continued, drawing her further out of the nightmare. Two sharp raps and then a third, just above the head of Jan's bed.

She had to be somewhere, there were tasks she had to accomplish, if only she could remember what they were. Filled with drowsy uncertainty, she was a speck basking on the surface of deep waters, still facing downward into her dreams and half-grasped notions from the night before. Another knock. She must pull herself upright, come to do her duty to the House. It knew exactly what was needed and what was superfluous.

Jan pulled on a defiantly summery dress in the hope things might improve and then she stepped out into the silent house, determined to take on the day, resolutely quelling her panic at the thought of Ursie's discovery in the dining room. She'd tell her that Nadya and Theo had an open relationship and let Ursie fill in the rest. What mattered now was coffee, ice, painkillers, anything to soothe her aching head.

Rounding the main stairs on the way to the ground floor, the breeze from the open front door took her aback. It gaped wide, wind whistling through the house all the way to the terrace where every french window stood unfastened as well. Little white flecks were strewn across the black and white tiled floor, skittering in the draught that blew through the house. Jan picked one up and groaned, realising it was paper. She knew that penmanship and that handwriting intimately. Ursie had left her purple notebook downstairs the night before and someone had torn it to shreds. There was no way she would believe that it had not been Jan; she would be livid, not to mention devastated. In the light of morning, Jan was most inclined to Nadya's theory of malicious action by the gardener, or perhaps Luke working off the frustrations of withdrawal. Whatever was causing it, this had to stop.

She closed the front door, went racing over to the hall-way table where the notepad sat with a name and scribble on it and dialled a few digits of the number labelled 'Adam' before realising her phone was still virtually useless inside the house. She tried the landline but it was not connected, the receiver nothing more than an inert block of plastic in her hand.

Morning had broken unevenly over the grounds; the air was cold with buds of moisture threatening rain. The birds poked out their necks to sing and thought better of it, while newts and fish slid over one another glumly in the pond. A nest of baby mice had been discovered in the night by an owl and lay strewn across the lawn, some still and mangled, while others breathed in terror at the open expanse, waiting for the fox to come. In the far corner of the wood, a solitary muntjac chewed on the roots of the young trees, ready to dart into the shadows whenever it heard human sound. The thick brambles of the briars stretched to encompass a little more of the verdant under-growth, thorns glistening in the early light.

She strode out into the mist, rabbits darting away into the flowerbeds and back into the forest. Jan traced the long drive back towards the gate, staying on the left-hand verge to avoid the crunch of gravel that might give away her position to any lurking officers of the law. A single bar flickered in and out of existence at the top left of her phone screen. She reached the iron gates and found them still locked, with the envelope stuck to the railings. No one else was in sight. What was Ursie going to do with her revelation? Why did she care so much about what Jan was doing when she clearly hadn't given much thought before to how their own entanglement might affect the group? The scene in the dining room last night looped endlessly in Jan's mind and she cursed herself for confessing so readily after all these years of deception. A worn grey gatepost near the wall stood as tall as her knee. She looked up at the nearest tree, judging the handholds, then hoiked herself up to sit in the crook of two large branches, the cut on her finger threatening to pop open again as she did so, and narrowly missing an abandoned nest of tiny broken eggs. At last, two bars. A message from her parents, telling her to enjoy herself and not stay too long. Her dating apps, minimal new activity. Nothing from Nadya.

She wrote, 'Are you awake?', then remembered there was almost no reception at the house.

She followed it immediately with, 'Come find me by the lake when you get this, I need to talk to you.'

She hoped at some point that day Nadya would wander into one of the unpredictable spots in the house where their phones sometimes worked and briefly considered putting a longer message through Google Translate into Russian but decided that would look suspicious if Theo saw her lock screen. Nadya was going to be furious with her, though these days that was almost the status quo, so perhaps it would hardly make a difference. Nadya had been so sweet and tender in her better moments, reaching out with compliments or inviting Jan to lavish parties so she felt less alone, but this was now largely the preserve of memory. It wasn't just the inconvenient fact of Theo; even before they'd met Nadya had increasingly accused Jan of smothering her if she asked where Nadya was or tried to come over at short notice when she was feeling low, but then would show up to her door at three in the morning after a night out in London with her Oxford friends, wanting to be let in. To love her now felt not unlike being the last adherent of a secret religion, tending to a dwindling sacred flame in hope of the return of a ravenous and uncaring god.

But who had let themselves into Nadya's room to rip her clothes into pieces? Irritating as she found Luke's light-fingered ways, she had to admit that wanton and spiteful destruction was not really his style. He was too driven by his cravings to bother expending energy on that. She needed an answer she could bear to consider and still call herself somewhat sane.

Jan finished keying in Adam's number and called it, waiting as it rang for so long she was sure she'd gone to voicemail. The dial tone filled the tinny speakers of her battered iPhone. She clutched at the rough bark of the tree to position herself more securely between the branches and waited for someone to come back to her with anything, business hours or an alternative phone number for the man, another name, perhaps. Through the lush green leaves of her perch, she saw two teenage girls on horseback wearing padded pink jackets trot past along the road outside the walls, pause when they heard the sound of the phone ringing and then move on, one girl saying to the other 'fucking weird house' before they picked up to a trot and sped away.

Eventually a confused voice with a West Country accent answered and asked what she was calling about. Jan found herself choked up as she struggled to explain why she was calling, but the voice was patient once she had said 'Holt House' and 'Adam' a few times.

Jan heard the flick of a cigarette lighter and the voice said, 'It's a tough house to manage, that one, isn't it? If you don't mind my saying, you sound like you're quite young and perhaps you've never worked somewhere so big before?'

Jan agreed that she had not.

The cigarette crackled with a large inhale and the voice said, 'I haven't been there myself in years, but I remember it from when I was a little girl. Beautiful big woods. Adam Trenarren was my father, he worked there on and off most of his life and on other things besides.'

'Was?'

'He died last year, my love, the cancer took him very quickly. I moved in to look after him – this is his landline you're calling on. I've had so much trouble getting everything transferred over.'

'Oh. I'm so sorry for your loss.'

The voice went on to ask whether Jan was looking to get in touch with the family about something? No, the voice didn't know who had taken over the garden after Adam passed away. In fact, she didn't think anyone in the village had been asked to do it. But if Jan wanted, they could send their son Mike over, he had his own mower and though he wasn't officially a tree surgeon, he was good with the smaller branches. She could recommend a nice cleaner as well. Would that be everything now?

Jan took down Mike's number mechanically and ended the call. Not knowing what else to do, she slowly climbed back into the grounds of Holt House. Unable to lever herself down using just the thin springy shoots that stuck out from the trunk, she tried to rest a foot on the mossy stone post, but slipped and fell onto the grass. Humiliated but uninjured, she decided to walk back through the trees, hoping her face would look less despondent by the time she reached the door. How on earth was she going to explain any of this to the others? The figure lurking in the billiards room, Nadya's destroyed clothes, Ursie's ripped notebook: none of it could have been Adam, and so there must be another explanation.

In the woods, the day was encroaching on the morning, tidying the clouded early summer sky to a perfect blue. She came to a little clearing in the trees, not far from the point where the woods gave out and became lawn, with a partial view of the lake. She watched in bafflement as Kara walked across the lawn unsteadily towards the dark water. Had Ursie already told her what she'd seen? Jan thought at first Kara was looking for her to confront her, but as Jan stood among the trees, watching Kara stumble past purposefully, she either didn't notice Jan at all or totally ignored her. Confused as to whether this could be a deliberate snub or some retaliation for her noisy panic the night before, Jan followed at a curious distance.

Kara was walking barefoot, paying no heed to the broken twigs and pebble-strewn ground that must be piercing the soles of her feet. Loosely dangling from her hand was the tattered remains of Ursie's purple notebook. Jan once again saw her mouth moving but no sound emerged, she heard only the chatter of the undergrowth

210

and distant rustling of the trees. Kara took another swig from a bottle of gin she'd clearly been working on intermittently since last night. Her steps swayed but she followed the winding path with a determination that suggested some fixed if inscrutable intent. Jan did not call out, afraid to interrupt in case Kara was angry or in the midst of something that might somehow explain why she'd taken the notebook. Peering anxiously through the gaps between the trees, she thought she caught glimpses of a figure weaving on ahead of Kara and wondered if it was Luke. She had not spotted him from the house crossing the lawn – but maybe they'd had another fight about the pills and Kara was chasing after him. *Had* he destroyed the notebook? She resolved to keep on watching, in case he was in trouble again. Jan could speak with him, find out the truth, if only he would slow down a little. Ahead of her, Kara started trying to run, tripping over roots and hillocks and Jan picked up speed after her. She lost sight of them both for a while, only a skinny form darting in and out of view, and further beyond them both, the edge of a dark coat flapping. But Luke did not look round, just kept evading them, racing deeper and deeper into the dripping trees.

Kara had reached the edge of the lake and Jan dropped back, hoping some cold water would sober her up. Still holding the notebook, she thrashed out from the shore, taking one step and then another, feet sinking into the mud, wading until it reached her knees, then racing, churning against the rain-chilled water which slapped back at her. As she went, she ripped the final pages loose and strewed them over the surface of the water, iridescent and rippling like a great beast basking under the heavens. She hurled the carcass of the book into the depths and plunged thigh high, waist high, chest high as the water soaked the skirt of her dress and weighed her down. Jan stayed rooted to the spot, hoping Kara could paddle to the lido unaided. But the black water parted, pulling her in up to her neck as she splashed, trying and failing to propel herself forward. She attempted to keep going but seemed to find herself sinking, panicking, beating at the water. If Jan went to her unaided, Kara would surely drown them both, she needed the little wooden canoe. She crept round the water's edge, searching for it in the reeds. Where had Luke gone? Jan could no longer see even a distant form. She listened out for his footsteps but couldn't distinguish them from all the forest sounds of chittering and rustling. She was about to call for him when she heard a splash.

'Don't panic, just grab on here.' Peering back through the reeds, Jan saw Theo crook one thick arm around Kara's neck.

'Stop it! Stop!'

'Calm down, I've got you.' He dragged her forcefully back into the shallows then grabbed her around the waist as she tried to wrestle free, scrabbling at his wrists to get back into the water. They tussled for a while before he seized the back of her neck and dunked her face under for a brief moment then pulled her up to face him.

'Where, where did he go?'

'Kara, calm down, it's just us here.' Theo pulled her free of the lake, then led her to a patch of dry ground under a tree and sat, stroking her back. 'Were you looking for Luke?' This question pushed her over the edge, into streams of tears.

Neither of them noticed Jan, watching from behind a beech tree, filled with guilty relief that Theo had jumped in while she was still deliberating over Kara's bizarre lone ritual.

Theo bit his lip for a moment, seemingly about to say something.

'What is it?' she said. 'What are you not telling me? Is it about Luke?'

'I shouldn't . . . Not when you're like this.'

Kara seemed wide awake now, turned back from the dark undercurrent that had been drawing her away to depths unknown. Jan heard the panic in her voice. 'Is he in trouble?'

He wrapped one arm around her shoulders. 'I should have told you ages ago; I just couldn't stand the thought of how much it would hurt you. Come here, you're freezing.'

She drew closer, turning inwards to him. 'What is it? You have to tell me, I'm so worried about him after last night. I know I said I didn't care, but I was angry.'

'That was very messy, I know. But it's much bigger than that, I'm afraid. Really, it's just between me and him.'

'Come on, Theo, he can barely look after himself at the moment.'

'You know Luke was in a lot of debt,' Theo started, 'and he had to run away before it got worse . . .'

'Yeah, he told me.'

'But do you know how he got out of debt?' Theo was looking intently at her face, as if watching for a sign that did not come.

'He's not . . . he's still in debt, isn't he? I'm sorry about all the money he owes you, I'm not sure what to do about that, I'm in the bottom of my overdraft as well.'

'That's all fine, it can be a gift, though I can't afford to give him any more right now. I meant his debt to João, you remember? That short Brazilian guy we picked up bigger batches from, I think you were in the car a few times.' Theo drew Kara in tighter and chafed her arm to warm her, then peeled off the jumper he'd been wearing and draped it ineffectually around her shoulders.

'You're not serious? Luke barely knew him.'

'I'm afraid he did. And he owed him several thousand. Jan had to loan Luke the money to pay him off in the end. He was very angry and he was going to get violent. Broken legs were mentioned.'

'Oh god, I told Luke he was bad news . . . hang on, I thought Jan was skint? She's always complaining about not being paid.'

'She just wants people to think that. It's a secret, okay? Anyway, she paid it and I sorted things out.'

From behind the tree, Jan listened in baffled shock at this outright invention. The only thing preventing her from springing out to ask a thousand questions was her determination to know what Theo would say next regarding her imaginary involvement in Luke's finances.

'That's so kind of you,' Kara snuffled. 'But you didn't have to do that, there must have been some other way. I should thank you both somehow.'

'There was no other way. But there was a condition to the loan.'

Kara startled and edged away a little. 'He's not going to go to rehab, I've had so many arguments with him about this, you wouldn't believe. If that's what she wanted, I'm not surprised he ran away, he just won't go. He thinks it won't work on him.'

214

'It wasn't quite that. Jan told him to leave.'

'SHE DID WHAT?'

'It's rather awkward having him here, you see. Jan didn't want him to come back at all, she thinks he should still be in Cambodia, Asia, anywhere but here really. He causes so much trouble. She was even talking about calling João herself to let him know Luke is back. A lot of other people are still very angry with him, you know. Last night she was so furious she was running around screaming, and she threw a drink at the wall.'

'What the fuck?' Kara's voice rose in indignation. 'I have to tell him it's not safe. No wonder she was so pissed he came here with us.'

'Well, you know what she's like, she's a control freak – and she hates it when she thinks that she's been cheated. And to be honest I wouldn't hold it against her if she did call João. Luke didn't choose you, Kara – he chose the money instead. He's a liar and thief, and he couldn't even keep his promise to stay away.'

Kara propelled herself back even further, but Theo moved towards her, hands outstretched.

'He was ruining your life; everyone could see it. Jan just wanted him to leave you alone so you could pass your finals and he took her up on the offer because he's a coward.'

Kara was suddenly crying hysterically in his arms, as he rubbed her sodden back and stroked her head. He paused for a moment, then said in an urgent voice, 'You won't tell the others anything about this, I wasn't supposed to share it with you.'

Jan stood blankly, still hidden behind the tree, trying to wrap her head around Theo's story. The dimensions of his

215

lie about her and the money felt troublingly familiar, though she could not immediately say why.

Kara, calming down a little, began trying to extricate herself from the hug, but Theo pulled her closer again and said, gently but firmly, 'Speaking as your friend, he's not good for you and you should leave him.'

He was about to say something further when she shoved him, yanking his fingers from her shoulders one by one and wrenching herself away.

She sprang back, half-falling, and shrieked, 'Stop it, stop it now! I don't want to hear any more!'

Theo said, 'Please, listen to me!' and, as she ran away sobbing into the woods, 'Come back!'

Scarcely wanting to breathe in case he heard her, Jan waited for Theo to pick himself up. Letting out a long sigh, he kicked ineffectually at a clump of wet earth. Then he extracted a little phial from his pocket and tapped out a bump onto the web of flesh between finger and thumb, inhaling with a guttural snort. He walked back towards the house and, once he was out of sight, Jan set off herself, taking the gravel path as she saw him wend his way towards the kitchen doors. Mind ablaze with questions, she struggled to put one foot in front of the other.

The lawn free of Theo, at last she picked up speed, gravel clattering about her as she cleared the front of the house. She had been torn between guilt and covert pleasure in cuckolding a man like Theo, someone who had everything. But if he had been ready to lie so wholeheartedly about her like that almost from the beginning of their friendship, then she would take everything she could from him, Ursie's fine scruples be damned.

She took the steps up to the double doors in two strides and pushed them wide, expecting to find the hallway still littered with torn paper. The fragments were gone. She cast about under the ottoman and round the side of the hall table for any remnants of the notebook but without success. Now more uncertain than ever about the true culprit behind the other strange incidents, Jan's fears swelled and multiplied. She still clung on to the hope that it had been Luke, making his dissatisfaction known. It had to be him – even if it didn't seem to fit his personality, surely there was no one else? Luke called to her now, ambling down the corridor from the kitchen in a holey vest and tracksuit bottoms, holding a steaming bowl of the coq au vin, scooping meat into his mouth as went. The purple shadows under his eyes were stained so dark they rendered his pale face more like a death's head than ever.

'Hey! I was just trying to find you,' he said. 'I can't figure out where everyone went. Look, I'm really sorry about last night, I was fiending but that's no excuse.'

Jan's mind was filled with revelations, swarming like a jar of hornets. She had no further words for him, just staring blankly instead at the stubble on his chin because she couldn't stand to meet his eyes.

Luke took her silence as an invitation to come closer. He put one sweaty arm around her and said, 'I know I'm not supposed to be here, but I'm really happy we could spend more time together anyway. It's been so good to get out of the city.'

She shrugged him off, recollecting as she did the folded note with Adam's number still secreted in her bra, one pointed corner catching at her side. There was only one way to be sure. She asked him, 'Did you go into Nadya's room yesterday?'

'This again? Come on, Jan, I feel bad about the vase, but you've got to stop accusing me every time something goes missing. How am I supposed to get better when you still all treat me like I'm scum?'

'Nothing went missing. She found a dress of hers all torn up and muddy. Did you do it?'

'What? No? I thought you were having problems with some old gardener guy?'

'There is no gardener any more. I checked. Did you do it?' she asked again, desperately. The look of genuine hurt on his face made the buzzing of the hornets intensify until Jan was afraid her skull might really split open with the terrible suspicion she found ever harder to deny.

As Luke was spluttering his denials, Ursie popped out from the Western drawing room, holding a sheaf of torn pages that looked worryingly familiar.

'What the hell is this? What have you done with my note-book?' She wheeled to look at both of them. 'You know I need it for my socials. I've had just about enough of this, throwing my things about and messing up my room, creep-ing about keeping me awake.' She jabbed a finger to Luke's chest. 'And I haven't forgotten about last night, not a word of thanks from either of you for clearing up your messes.'

Luke looked like he was about to burst into tears.

Just as Jan was about to explain what she'd seen in the forest, Kara walked through the open door behind them, still in sopping wet clothes, her hair lank about her face and eyes pink with crying. Ignoring them all, she went straight into the drawing room and threw herself down on the sofa, knees drawn up to her chest.

'What happened? Kara, why are you all wet?' Ursie, pages forgotten for the moment, rushed to her and felt her cheeks. 'Did you fall in the lake?'

Kara nodded glumly, not saying anything.

'She needs a blanket and a hot tea,' Ursie commanded. 'Don't just stand there, you two, go and do something for once. Luke get the tea; you should be capable of that at least.'

'I'll find her some dry clothes. I saw a blanket in here yesterday, it should still be behind the sofa over there,' Jan offered.

'Fine.'

Jan bounded up the stairs and along the corridor to Kara's room, now heavy with Luke-fug, and rummaged about inside the rat-king of clothes in Kara's holdall until she could separate out a clean t-shirt, underwear and leggings. She returned to the drawing room to find Ursie wringing out the damp hoody and nightdress she'd managed to strip off Kara, who was now wrapped only in a scratchy-looking eiderdown. Ursie held the hoody up to her face, scrutinising it. At first Jan thought it was one of Kara's myriad charity shop pieces, gathered and discarded as the mood took her, before she recognised the design on the front.

Ursie examined the wet clothes, looking appalled. 'This is my limited-edition Basquiat X Supreme hoody. And it's stained. Did you know she had this?'

'No, I've never seen her in it before.'

'It was downstairs and I was chilly,' Kara mumbled. 'I didn't realise you'd mind.'

'Here, Kara, put these on, I'll turn around.' Jan shoved the clothes at her and faced the wall. 'She's drunk out of her mind and upset about Luke relapsing. I don't think she knew what she was doing.'

Ursie continued to study the wet, pondwater-stained fabric. 'Nah, I'm leaving. Sorry, guys, but this is the limit and then some. And I'm not playing nursemaid any longer, none of this is restful for me. This was supposed to be my holiday, too. Kara, you can drive us back when you've sobered up, you owe me for this.'

'Maybe, I need a nap first. I'm really achy.'

Luke came in with the tea, which Ursie took from him. 'Is there sugar in it?' she barked.

'Yeah, loads.'

She forced Kara to drink half, then put a pillow under her head. Luke shuffled onto the arm of the sofa and stayed there, stroking Kara's hair and looking concerned. Jan reflected that even though Luke was not faithful in the strictest sense, he really did love her for better or worse. She watched him pull the eiderdown over Kara's shoulders and look over to Ursie as if for further guidance.

Ursie said, 'Stay there and try not to do anything else stupid. I'm out. If she's not well enough to take me then it will have to be Nadya. Theo can drive the rest of you back if he ever sobers up.'

Luke said, 'Come on, Ursie, we can get it dry-cleaned for you. We've barely had any time here yet.'

Ursie looked at them, face lined with disappointment, her dark eyes watering with disgust. 'I want to go home.'

Jan could not think what else to do but trail behind her along with Luke to the terrace, where Theo and Nadya were eating American pancakes with blueberries and maple syrup and looking far more cheerful than Jan felt either of them had any right to be.

'Nadya, how much petrol have you got? I've realised I need to start heading.'

Theo laughed; his usual baritone had a manic edge to it that made Jan's stomach writhe with worry. He said, 'We've both just taken some 3iTR, you know the research chemical I was telling you about, it's going to really hit in about an hour. I'd catch up if I were you.'

'Kara is sick and I need to go,' Ursie repeated.

Nadya asked, 'What sort of sick? Does she have Covid? Oh god, we're all going to get ill, I knew it.'

'Nothing like that. She just got soaking wet and caught a chill. She's wrapped up on the sofa dead to the world. She destroyed my favourite hoody.'

Jan kept her eyes locked on Nadya as Ursie said this, praying she was not quite angry enough to reveal her additional reason for wishing to leave.

As Jan held her breath, Theo thought for a few minutes, cutting up his pancake into very small pieces and chasing the smears of syrup around his plate in a trance.

He came to. 'Alright, we can help you leave tomorrow. I'll figure out the details then.'

'But you're going to be way too wrecked to drive tomorrow, Theo.' Ursie was pacing back and forth, still agitated not to be immediately springing into action.

'Actually, there's no comedown from this stuff,' Nadya said. 'Please sit down, you're putting me on edge.'

'I am on edge. These idiots keep getting themselves into situations and my notebook got ruined as well.' She lit a cigarette. The smoke curled away from the table and hung like heaped ribbons on the heavy summer air.

Jan's hungover brain had been crammed with more new information than she could process, but the opportunity to share at least one thing leaped out at her. 'About that, I—'

Ursie snapped, 'I've heard just about enough from you.'

Theo got up and pulled out his chair for her to sit down in. He looked tired. 'Ursie, we all understand you have things to do and you need to get back, that's been agreed on and it's not a problem, it's already settled. Anyone who wants to can try the 3iTR with us, but I'm not going to push it on you, you've done a lot already and you deserve to relax before the journey tomorrow.'

Nadya poured a fresh mug of steaming black coffee and pushed it towards her. Ursie began heaping sugar into it. 'Okay. But actually tomorrow, not the day after.'

'I can go turn the cars round now while I'm still lucid if you want. Do you have the keys, Nads?'

'Wait, no, no, it's okay. You shouldn't be anywhere near those if you're coming up. I'm going to go upstairs and pack. Don't want any more of my things getting thrown about and destroyed.'

She stubbed out her cigarette and threw back the rest of the coffee so fast Jan wondered how she didn't scald her mouth, before walking back into the house and closing the door firmly behind her. *They mustn't leave.* Jan felt herself flooded by the strong sense she had to persuade them to stay here with her just a little longer, even though she did not know why. *It wasn't time yet.*

She checked to make sure the windows above them were closed before leaning in to ask quietly, 'How did you do that?'

'I didn't do anything at all,' Theo sighed. 'Most of the time when you two lock horns it's because you mistake her anxiety for aggression and then get angry yourself. I was on my way to bed last night and saw her sitting in the dining room saying the rosary; she's obviously got something on her mind.'

Nadya gave an amused sniff at the mention of the rosary. 'What did you do with the stuff? Do you want to do it with us, Jan?'

'Can I eat first? Is it nil by mouth?'

Theo said, 'Nothing that extreme, but maybe something light like bread or fruit. Do we still have raspberries and whatnots?'

'Oh yes, plenty, and I have a huge lasagna in the freezer ready for after we come down. I can just bung that in the oven later. It lasts about ten hours, right?' Jan was already making further food-based calculations.

He replied, 'More or less, depending on body mass. Women tend to come up slower. It's better if you swallow it after something acidic like orange juice.'

'Have you tested this batch, Theo?'

He didn't meet her eyes, mechanically scraping little curls of butter from the pat for a new piece of pancake. 'Right. I did those strips, it's definitely what it's supposed to be.'

'That's good, but I meant have you personally done this one?'

'I did a controlled dose of the last batch and went to Hyde Park. It was pretty weird but enjoyable, you'll see. You in, Luke?'

Luke had come outside to lean weakly against the wall of the house. He gazed at the bees in the kitchen garden persisting with the damp flowers, nudging their way despondently into each one. She was surprised he could still stand, though after all this time she probably ought not to be.

'You sure? I thought . . .'

'It's on me. My treat.'

<hr />

They reassembled ten minutes later in the Eastern drawing room, watching as Theo measured out the dosages with the small silver set of scales he'd brought with him. Nadya lay stretched out along the smaller sofa, legs splayed, yawning theatrically as she waited for him to be finished. He dusted carefully calibrated lines of golden powder into tiny heaps before nudging each one into a separate tumbler of water, making a dose each for Jan and Luke, plus two spares in case he or Nadya wanted to re-up later in the day.

Ursie came in and sat on a low divan, not meeting Jan's eye. Jan had to get her alone and talk, though without being able to prove that Kara had taken the notebook it might not do any good.

'How's Kara?' Luke asked her, swooshing his glass of 3iTR about tentatively.

'Fast asleep. She'll be fine, we got her dried off pretty quickly. She was talking in her sleep. I think she was dreaming about boats; she said something about a submarine.'

Luke said, 'Cute, I'll go look in on her later. Don't want to wake her just yet.'

'So, you're really going for it, then?' Ursie asked, looking sceptically at the 3iTR.

Theo, holding a spare glass, asked, 'Sure you won't join us?'

Jan caught Ursie smiling despite herself. 'What does it do?'

'It's a bit like 2CB just with stronger hallucinations and a smoother body high. It's so new it's barely even illegal yet. By midnight we should all be back to normal.'

'And it doesn't do anything else weird?'

'Tingles, chills, mild nausea if you're unlucky, that's about it, I think. I can show you the Erowid page if I can get it to load.'

Ursie made the uncertain moue that Jan recognised as a sign she was about to do something reckless. She said, 'I don't know . . . I guess I am stuck here. Do you absolutely promise to take me home tomorrow?'

Theo said, 'Of course, on my honour.'

She opened her mouth and closed it again. Then reached forward. 'Go on then. Let's finish with a bang. I'm going to down it before I change my mind!'

Luke clinked his glass against Ursie's and Jan's, then knocked it back. Jan took a long drink of the water, swallowing hard as it caught in her throat, releasing a horribly bitter, chemical taste that lingered even after she finished her glass.

'Yeurrgh. Now what?'

'Entirely up to you, I don't care. Personally, I'm going to go enjoy the swing.' Theo, who had seemed pretty lucid up to this point, walked over to the drawing-room window and opened it, half-climbing half-falling out into the flowerbed. He picked himself up and raced over to the lone oak tree that stood on the lawn, with a wooden swing dangling above the grass, hooting loudly like a giant, ridiculous bird. Luke crowded in behind Jan as she hung out of the open window to peer at Theo swinging frantically and doubling over with hysterical laughter in a way that looked almost painful.

'I guess he was only just holding it together till now?'

Unsure of where to turn, she began tidying up the glasses, before Nadya put a hand on her arm and said, 'Come on, not today.' She produced a joint from her shorts pocket and, though clearly considering the window, lead Jan round and out onto the terrace. The sun had regained its strength, shining brightly at last over their surroundings. They strolled to the centre of the lawn and Theo called to them to push him, but Nadya said, 'I want to go look at the tennis court. I've been dying to go in all week, but Theo hasn't been sober enough for a game. It looks locked, though.'

'It's just rusty.' Then, remembering she had much to discuss with Nadya out of earshot from the others, she brightened and said, 'Do you want to play?'

'I thought you'd never ask.'

Jan tried the door of the little outbuilding that held things like mowers and part of a croquet set, selecting the two least ancient racquets and wiping the cobwebs off on the grass.

Jan asked her, 'Are you feeling anything yet?'

Nadya said, 'Nothing. You? You aren't supposed to have any effects for about an hour.'

Jan paused, trying to extend her concentration to the body she usually ignored. She felt faintly tingly and nauseous but that could just as easily be the near-overwhelming desire to take Nadya in her arms and press her up against the rusty old chain-link fence. Instead, she meekly followed in after her.

'Impossible to tell.'

Nadya took a ball and ran over to the far end of the court, daintily hopping over the cracks and ripples in the weathered surface, before hitting an impressive serve that took Jan completely by surprise.

'Fifteen—love to me. Get on with it!'

Jan ran over to pick up the lone ball and soon they were rallying back and forth, though Nadya was so obviously the superior player that Jan suspected she was holding back to keep things fun. The sun was getting warmer and the remaining cloud was thinning to white wisps overhead.

'Where did you learn to play like this?'

'School. I didn't have any friends in England before we met, remember? I was the weird Russian kid who went from a system where I was expected to memorise Yevgeny Onegin and be really good at piano to be respected to one where you were supposed to be really good at piano but never mention it and also give head like a porn star.'

Nadya fired the ball back again and, after hitting it deep into the corner of the court, Jan said, 'Oh school. I still remember having to tell someone what a blow job was and wondering how the fuck it had fallen to me to explain that; the same year Sophie B got caught having sex with a twenty-two-year-old gardener's assistant on the geography teacher's desk after hours.'

'They really didn't tell us anything about men, no wonder we were so obsessed.'

'Well, most of you.' With that, Jan hit the ball again, this time so hard it cleared the rusting fence and flew away into the woods behind the court.

'Do you have another?'

'Not an intact one. I'll go look for it.'

Nadya came with her, leaving her racquet neatly by the gate of the court. The ball was nowhere to be seen, so they walked further among the trees.

'Never even a little bit?'

Jan was baffled for a second until she realised Nadya was still talking about men. She groaned and said, 'Come on, you know this. Sure, at some points when we were younger and you were off with Dimitri all the time, I would have liked the social status of having a boyfriend. But nothing more than that.'

Nadya shot her a look, eyes almost closed in the dazzle of the sun. 'I think Theo suspects something. He was acting really weird this morning before breakfast, like he wasn't meeting my eyes and was in a foul mood. He must have heard more than we thought last night.'

'I really don't think that's it, Nadya—'

She stepped closer, stroking Jan's upturned cheek, grazing the curve of her cheekbone with the edge of one nail. 'We should have a threesome, it's the perfect cover.'

Jan felt her stomach twitch dangerously as if she might need to run indoors at any moment. 'You can't be serious.'

'You wouldn't have to touch him; he could just watch us. We could tell him that's what we were plotting all along.' Her lips were tantalising, hovering so close to Jan's that all she had to do was close the distance.

'I can't believe I'm hearing this from you of all people. Do you not know how often this has happened to me? Do you know how insulting it is?' She stepped abruptly back, dropping her racquet in the long grass and leaving it there.

'Please don't get too emotional right now, I can't handle it. It would just be a bit of fun. I thought you liked making me happy.'

Jan had been determined to reveal to Nadya what she had overheard in the forest, to tear away her illusions about Theo's honesty the moment she had a chance to do so. There was also the problem of Ursie, though Nadya's reaction to her slip was such a terrifying prospect that Jan had decided it could wait. On the way back to the house she had even pondered sitting Nadya down and asking whether she could talk to Theo and propose sharing Nadya openly, come to some kind of arrangement, so long as she didn't have to deceive him any more. But if that truly was how Nadya saw her, as a 'bit of fun', despite everything that had passed between them, revealing her newfound knowledge of Theo's lie about the money would do nothing except drive Nadya further away from her as she moved to defend him.

'Just think about it. It would be the ultimate submission.' Nadya smiled then beckoned her. 'Come look at this leaf, it's moving by itself.' She'd run forward to look at something on the ground, but it was just an old dead husk. Jan hoped the phantasmagoric rush of the 3iTR would loosen Nadya's grip on this new and terrible idea. She extended a cautious finger and prodded at the leaf. It did look startlingly yellow. 'It's only moving a tiny bit, it's just the wind.'

Jan looked up to see if there was a breeze, but the trees above them were still, though she heard a slight rushing sound coming from nearby. Then, ever so faintly, she saw the branches begin to curl and wave, stretching up towards the sun while roots slithered around underfoot. 'Are you seeing what I'm seeing? It's all alive!'

Daisies popped into being across the path like stars winking in the heavens and patches of bare earth glimmered with minerals.

'It's kicking in! You're so lucky, I'm still just getting tiny hints at the corner of my eye. Do you have the body high yet? Theo said it was really strong; a lot of people get nausea but then they feel amazing.'

'Why did you tell me that? You know I'm really impressionable!'

Already Jan was feeling strange and shaky, still groping the ground for the lost ball as all the dead leaves skittered about like mischievous crabs, settling into formations best known only to themselves. Her skin was too tight and yet very delicate, an overripe nectarine that the wrong touch might burst. She sat down heavily on the earth and Nadya pulled her up again.

'You need to walk it off, let's take the long route back to the house. I'm all tingly too, I think—'

Nadya promptly covered her mouth and ran over to a blossoming apple tree to vomit noisily.

Jan watched the sky overhead curling subtly like smoke, the clouds tessellating slowly as if they all dwelled within a vast lava lamp and just hadn't noticed until now. She was too warm and suddenly afraid that she desperately needed to shit.

'I found it!'

Nadya wiped her mouth on the back of her arm then dived down again to seize the ball from beneath some brambles that trailed through the fence and back into the woods in a deeply suspicious fashion.

'Stay away from the brambles, Nadya, they have bad intentions.'

Both of them looked back at the bush, which seemed to cower like a scolded dog, then burst out laughing.

They walked away through the woods, stroking the bristling lichen on the trees and greeting the shy violets that sprouted from corners to wink hello at them. Jan felt the entire moment suspended in a giddiness that could easily tip over into terror. When she looked too closely at the trees, she saw them twist into faces and bodies, each one ensouled with a wailing man or woman, reaching out to pull her into their despair, clasp her with their wet-leafed hands and restrain her there forever. The pair pushed their way out of the wood at the point where Jan had thought the swing would be, only to find they had overshot and were standing on the long gravel drive. They heard Theo's faint whooping pierce through the trees. The path back to the house glistened and made a rushing noise, as if they stood on the bed of an invisible river. Nadya pointed up above them at a hawk gliding on an updraught and shouted something in Russian.

'What was that?'

'I was telling him that the forest is full of mice. He needed to know.'

'Yes, it's very important.'

Nadya peeled away to go in search of her toothbrush. Brushing her teeth when she was coming up was one of her favourite things. Returning to the lawn, Jan found that all of the sofa cushions from the games room had been dragged out onto the grass, along with an inflatable mattress someone must have found in a cupboard.

'Want one?' Kara was now awake and holding a tray of glasses filled with mysterious pink froth. 'I made strawberry daiquiris.'

'Hey, are you alright? You were in a bit of a state earlier.'

'I'm fine. Just needed a nap, I think. Sure you don't want some hair of the dog?'

'God yes.' And she darted in to hug Kara's spindly body really tightly, trying not to upend the tray of drinks and wondering why she'd ever been annoyed with her. None of this was her fault, really.

'Are you on something? You're so . . . cheerful. And nice.'

'I am nice. And we're all on 3iTR, it's beautiful.'

Luke came round the side of the house, sweating heavily and grinning. He swiped a daiquiri from the tray and kissed Kara with pink foamy lips.

'Your eyes are so amazing, they're like emeralds and . . . what's another green jewel, Jan? Help me out here?'

'Peridots. You do have lovely eyes, Kara.'

'Thanks, guys. Is there any three-whatever left for me?'

Luke led her back into the house to find the last dose and Jan sat down heavily on the pile of cushions as Theo came to join her.

She said awkwardly, 'Kara was pretty soaked this morning. I'm worried about her.' Then she fretted that there'd been an edge to her voice. What would he say if he knew she'd been spying on them?

'Really? She seems fine now. She probably shouldn't go swimming by herself though.'

She scanned his face, looking for any sign he was aware of what she'd witnessed. He was always so calm, so unconcerned.

All she could think to add was, 'I know who it was that ripped up Ursie's book.'

He lay back, stretching out and closing his eyes. 'I'd say that's between the two of them, wouldn't you? No need to stir the pot.'

Theo was so resolutely unruffled by most things that Jan knew she would be wasting her breath in trying to talk to him about the phone call that had preceded her latest unpleasant discovery.

'Something isn't right with Kara, though. Should she be tripping with us?' Jan felt jittery and irritable, as another wave of the drug passed through her, the unpleasant chemical flavour repeating at the back of her mouth.

He opened one eye halfway. 'You've got to stop stressing out about controlling what everyone else is up to. You're on such high alert all the time, no wonder you're seeing things that aren't there on only alcohol. There's plenty more 3iTR if we need it.'

He withdrew a fat joint from his trouser pocket and lit it before passing it to her and they lapsed into silence. The grass around them was studded with tiny buttercups and forget-me-nots. Surely those had always been there? Perhaps this was a drug that made you really attentive to what was around you rather than inventing anything that wasn't. Nature moved, after all. Plants turned towards the sun, objects swayed in the wind, comets made their course across the heavens, all life was animate.

Drinking the daiquiri on the lawn, Jan found herself running her free hand over the curves and divots in the air mattress and thinking about Diana of Ephesus, wondering what it would be like to have sex with a many-breasted nature goddess. Probably quite interesting, though that was how mortals tended to get obliterated. She felt flushed, her skin prickling with the heat of undirected lust filling her body like an overbrimming cup. So this was why men in literature carved out holes in the ground to fuck when they were drunk and stuck in the wilderness.

233

Theo scooted over to sit behind her and started running his hands through her curls, giving her a head massage, which made her tense up in fear that Nadya had already put her plan to him and this was his opening gambit. She batted him away, but when he asked what she'd been thinking about, she found the 3iTR had removed her wherewithal to lie.

'So, you've been sitting here getting horny for the Greek pantheon. I wondered what that faraway look on your face was. Isn't Diana supposed to be a virgin?'

'Oh, come on, she hung out in the woods hunting with a big group of women and took an oath she wouldn't marry. What do you think that makes her?'

'A massive nerd. But if you want to fondle a mattress, do whatever gets you off. Next time we're out together I'll make sure to look for girls with eight sets of tits, they shouldn't be hard to find.'

She felt him scooting closer again and cast about for a distraction. 'Did you bring the cracker for the nitrous balloons?'

'Actually, that's an excellent idea.' Theo sprinted back into the house, re-emerging with two silver canisters, a packet of party balloons and a cardboard box that made a promising jingle. He shouted to Luke, who was lingering behind him, to lift up and bring over the sun umbrella.

An overpoweringly mint-scented Nadya sat down next to Jan and asked, 'Are you getting anything more? I only have little glimmers.'

Jan leaned in as close as possible, not caring who saw; she just wanted to gaze at Nadya's face and touch it. 'Just wait, it gets really good. You know your hair is growing, I can see it.'

234

Nadya pulled back a little and said loudly, 'I want to get to wherever she is.'

'I can help with that. Take one of these. Jan, you pass her that joint and we'll break open the canisters.' Theo was laying out balloons on the ground, dividing them into different colours. 'I also have veterinary ether, if anyone's interested.'

They waited, fingers and thumbs gripping the generous double balloons that Theo was cranking out until he cried at last, 'Done! Let's all go together!'

They breathed in and out for what felt like an eternity, flashes of colour from the balloons bursting into Jan's peripheral vision, the garden around her dissolving into a mosaic and then into fractals before she lay back into the eye of the glittering storm. *Something very bad is coming soon.* She wrested her attention away from the nitrous oxide-induced sense of doom and tried to surf through the disorientation, staring at the distant hills as they re-formed gradually on the horizon to ground herself and it seemed to work. This was fun, she was living in the moment, having fun with her friends. This was fine.

Theo was sitting with his legs crossed, as if meditating, saying to himself, 'I think I've squared the circle,' over and over again and looking pleased.

They lay there in the soft lap of the lawn, laughter punctuated only by daiquiri sips. Someone had fetched a speaker and Portishead was playing on a loop, while they watched the garden flourishing and blooming before their eyes. Every time Jan turned her head, she caught sight of an arcing rainbow at the edge of her vision, as if glimpsing the light distortion in an old photo print. She wondered lazily whether the Vikings had been right that the universe was made of poison and to truly live one must accept that and drink deep, die ecstatic in the attempt to savour every radiant note.

Nadya sat up and asked, 'Where did Ursie go?'

'I'm over here!' A small, quavering voice came from the hammock. They all got up and went over, peering down at her. Jan mechanically passed her a daiquiri and Ursie stretched out a hand to take it. She paused, sipped, took a long breath. 'Thanks, guys. I wasn't doing so great earlier but I'm better now, this is helping. I should have brought some bush rum, it'd be perfect for a day like this.'

Theo asked, 'Did you come up really hard? Nadya vommed. Luke too, I think.' They looked over at him and Kara rolling about on the lawn, making out furiously.

'Gross. No, I didn't throw up. I tried to go back inside the house and track down all my things, but it's . . . it's no good in there right now. I can't. After last night, with the secret passageways – sorry, Jan.' Nadya stared at Jan wide-eyed as Ursie continued. 'Anyway, it freaked me out. I just want to be out here. Actually, I think I need to be on my own a bit longer, I've been looking at the sky and it's calming me down. All the clouds are doing cool stuff but it's not too overstimulating.'

'Okay, Urs, we're around if you need us. Do you want half a Valium just in case?'

Theo handed one to her and she slipped it into her phone case. Jan was furiously trying and failing to catch Nadya's eye and telegraph to her that she hadn't told Ursie on purpose as the three of them backed away from the hammock. She could see Nadya's forehead taut with panic

236

as Theo asked her, 'What was all that about Jan and secret passageways? Nads, did you show them the priest hole already? I was looking forward to that being a cool surprise for later.'

'Sorry, I got overexcited!' If Nadya's eyes were lasers, Jan would have a hole the size of a coin bored through her head.

'Oh well, anyone up for a game of Sardines?'

Before she could reply, Nadya cut in, 'Brilliant idea! The winner gets to pick a forfeit.'

⁂

The paintings were alive and it was extremely distracting. Small birds flitted busily between the Chinese prints and curious tendrils poked out from the still life of a flowering cactus among ruins, while on the opposite wall figures danced in one another's arms, rotating gently under a full moon to music Jan could not quite hear even when she strained. She waited in the Eastern drawing room, each of them having agreed to start from a different place. Theo was to be the first sardine, beginning outdoors as his handicap for knowing the house better than they did. Perhaps if she waited for Nadya to find him first, she stood a better chance of avoiding them both until they forgot about the game entirely.

She kept trying to count to ten but getting stuck at the number 8 because it was an infinity symbol standing upright. An hourglass with her life pouring through its cinched waist. Did she have sand in her shoes? Eventually she just said 'ten' aloud and wobbled out of the door – the long corridor stretched away to her right, but she remembered that it led to the games room and she was not going in there alone again.

She groped along to the dining room to check whether Theo had pried open the hatch and hidden himself that way. If she could just figure out where he was then she could buy herself some time by going elsewhere. She pushed at the heavy door, but saw Kara sitting alone at the table, smiling with the silver goblet held aloft. Her teeth were black with wine.

'Did Theo come through here?'

She sat grinning in silence, not meeting Jan's eyes or acknowledging her. Jan considered waving a hand in front of Kara's face, but after her troubling antics with the notebook, decided to leave her to her own devices if she was going to be like that again.

The door to the kitchen was open behind Kara, and from it came an unbearable screeching Jan felt in the roots of her teeth and all down her spine, tugging at the sides of her cut and probing the soft flesh under her nails. The knives were singing. She longed to draw closer and listen to their piercing song, but forced herself to turn away. Kara said nothing as she left, face frozen in an eerie rictus of triumph.

The only path left to Jan was the sprawling main staircase, which she tottered back towards, trying not to get tripped up by the black and white floor. It was playing chess with itself and she had to use only the squares not currently occupied by the game. She made her way up the staircase infinitesimally slowly, more on her hands and knees than anything else. The carpet was so dusty, and any surface she looked at closely became dangerously fascinating to her – there must be hordes of mites living within the fabric, but if she thought about them too hard, she would start to itch uncontrollably and it would all be over.

<hr />

Early evening crept towards them and Jan snuck back into her room in search of a shawl and a free toilet. She had learned many times over not to look in the mirror while on any drugs, it destroyed the levity with self-consciousness, and yet she was overwhelmingly curious. Her reflection showed her dishevelled and wild-eyed, but not alarmingly haggard, though she could not help but focus on the faint fern-like spread of broken capillaries she had always hated on her own face. They were branching and dividing further, as all the veins under her skin and in her neck became clearer and clearer. The blood pulsed through them and air travelled down her throat, while her skin became more and more translucent. The pinkish red muscles tensed as she strained to see more of herself, this skinless woman, until they strained in such a way that she caught a glimpse of bone shining white beneath the rest. Two round green eyes swivelled in a grinning skull to meet her and she burst out of the bathroom, slamming the door as she rushed back onto the landing to get as far away from the image as possible. She collapsed onto the divan overlooking the stairs, doubled over with panic and struggling to breathe.

What if she had peeled off her own skin like in those acid scare stories and everyone had been too high or too polite to tell her? What if she looked like that all the time? What if—? But she knew her own death was coming without question and it was that which she had seen and tried to flee from, though it could never be outrun.

She wished she could give up and go back outside, but felt it was not allowed. If only she had brought her cigarettes. Eyes glued to the wall for want of another calm surface, she repeatedly traced the moulded dado rail beside her with one finger in an effort to calm down.

Nadya appeared at the edge of her vision, loitering in the corridor by the entrance to her room. Clearly, she had not gone that far either.

'What are you doing over there?'

'You would tell me if I looked like a monster, right?'

'What you look like is a weirdo stroking the wall. Come with me.' Nadya put out a hand and Jan peeled her eyes away from the wall, riven by a surprisingly sharp pang of regret. She tried to keep pace. Nadya shot a quick look over her shoulder then shoved Jan back against the wall and strained up towards her, Jan greeting her greedily with a bite in her kiss, cupping Nadya's buttocks and half-lifting her from the ground in her eagerness not to feel or think of anything else.

Nadya took the lead and pushed open the door next to them, the air full of old perfume and stale wine, Nadya's dresses and skirts draped over every available surface. Jan followed her in, closing the door behind her, only to look over to the vanity and see Theo sat there surrounded by powders as if about to refresh his toilette.

'It's our favourite nymph. You having fun, Jan?'

'I—uh yes, I think so, now I'm away from the bathroom. And the carpet. What are you up to in here?'

'Just replenishing my minerals.' He gave a meaningful snort and said, 'It's my room, remember?'

Nadya said, 'Darling, did you bring the wine up with you?'

'Wine and vodka. Whatever Madam prefers.' He turned to Jan. 'How are you finding the 3iTR? It's good, isn't it?'

All Jan could think of was asking him why he had lied about the loan but her head was so full of colour, texture and sensation she was afraid that she would not understand his answer if he gave it to her now. After a long pause she remembered he had asked a completely different question.

She said, 'It started out well, but I think it's too intense for me. I feel weird.'

'It'll pass, just go with it, don't fight it.' He moved to sit on the bed, leaning back on one hand with the other tucked beneath his shirt. Jan and Nadya took his place at the vanity.

Nadya took a swig of the vodka and straightened up. 'Weird how? Do you mean the physical stuff?'

'That as well; it's such a big rush, I wasn't expecting it.'

Nadya giggled and said, 'Theo had a hard-on for an entire hour, we had to get you indoors, didn't we?'

Theo smirked and Nadya reached out to put a hand on Jan's leg. What was she doing? She was going to give them away . . .

Jan looked at the hand, veins glowing faintly green through the translucent skin, nails arched like a griffin. Theo looked at it too. Then he put his hand on Jan's other leg and suddenly Nadya was sitting on her lap, arms around her neck and tracing her lips with her tongue in the way she did when she wanted Jan to open her mouth for something. Her hair falling loose over both their faces, her delicious, familiar smell setting Jan at ease, Jan's hands reaching under and into her clothes from unstoppable habit, clasping her thighs and pulling Nadya's dress over her head. She took one silky nipple in her mouth and ran her nails along the slightness of Nadya's back, reaching up to wrap her fingers through Nadya's hair and pull her closer. Rough hands yanked the straps of Jan's dress away from behind, unlatching her bra to cup her breasts. She ignored the inexpert fingers rolling at her flesh and continued kissing Nadya's neck, running light, searching fingertips across her thighs. She felt many handed, many mouthed, both inside the scene and outside it all at once.

Nadya fell back on the bed, where Jan swiftly joined her, ready to delve further, kissing her way up from ankle to thigh. Nadya wriggled away to peel off Jan's dress, exposing her to the lamplight. The butterflies in a Chinese print over the bed fluttered and flocked, crowding the frame with their uncertainty. A hand reached out to pass Nadya a thick brown leather belt, which Nadya looped round her knuckles. Jan perched on all fours, hands clenched into fists as Nadya slid off the bed again, took a couple of paces back and aimed.

The leather cracked and bit at a spot at the top of Jan's hip, the harbinger of many more blows to come.

'For god's sake, can't you sit up straight? Theo, hold her for me.'

He curled both hands around her wrists, pulling her upright onto her knees, before letting go of one to turn Jan's face by the chin and make her look him in the eye. She tracked the growth of stubble across his face, the black pits of each pupil. One incisor crossed a little way over its neighbour.

'I know this is what you like, isn't it? You've been a very bad girl. We're going to teach you a little lesson.' Then he grabbed Jan's nipples, pinching each one between forefinger and thumb to keep her kneeling in place, as she looked away from him, down onto the turning whorls of the sheets.

'You really thought I didn't know?'

The belt blows bit at her shoulders, each leaving an icy sprig of sensation that unfurled towards the pain in her breasts. Nadya was giving her a cloak of scarlet feathers, they hung down like ostrich plumes, extending into the air and drifting gently behind her.

'I don't care what she does with you, it doesn't mean anything.'

Theo yanked both her wrists suddenly forward again, propelling her face first downwards into his jeaned crotch. She tried not to breathe in the musty, unfamiliar smell, as he bucked, rubbing his hard-on over her chafed cheek. The belt blows began nipping at her buttocks and thighs, then travelling upward, grazing dangerously close to the softest parts, drenched with renewed wetness. With a thud and clink, Nadya threw the belt to the floor and moved to push Theo aside, planting Jan's mouth on her cunt. Shoulders and legs still burning, Jan lapped eagerly, as if this could put out the fire in her skin. Nadya's thighs wrapped around her neck as she followed her tongue with two fingers to push and curl in just the way Nadya liked best. She felt Theo's hand stroking at her own cleft, circling the hole and she reached back to swat him away.

Nadya said, 'You should let him; I want to watch you.' Jan looked up at her, across the length of her beloved body and shook her head. Nadya gave her the triumphant smile of one consigning her most hated enemy to the pyre. 'Do it for me,' and she reached out to prod Jan's shoulder, indicating how she must turn. 'It's my forfeit. You lost, remember?' And Jan obeyed her.

Now entirely unclothed, Theo advanced on Jan, spreading her legs apart and rolling on a condom, as Nadya cradled Jan's head in her lap and trailed her fingers over's Jan's lips, making her suckle them. It would be no different to a strap-on, she supposed, but he was far too close, the hair on his chest sprouting in random patches like mould, the smell of his sweat in her nostrils filling her with disgust.

She met his gaze blankly, seeing there nothing but conquest and slightly bored lubricity. Nadya laced slender fingers around her throat to choke her. Through the tips of her fingers, she felt Nadya's excitement at the prospect of seeing her so abased, body opened and rifled through, all for Nadya's entertainment. Theo was holding her legs wide now, the hands around her neck constricting ever tighter and suddenly she found herself kicking wildly, catching Theo square in the belly, forcing him to wilt and withdraw. She seized the chance to throw off Nadya's hands, sliding off the bed into a roll and racing to gather up her clothes, the room rocking like the stateroom of a foundering ship.

Clutching at the walls, bent in a crawling walk, with the 3iTR still speckling and subdividing her vision, she hurried as fast as she could back into her bedroom and locked the door, deaf to Nadya's calls to return, calm down, he could just watch instead. She had to get further away from them. She dressed hastily and wondered whether she could fit into the giant wooden wardrobe to rest but found it was too narrow and the camphor smell bothered her. She saw the stepladder already in the centre of the room, reaching up towards the attic like a sign. Ascending shakily, she clung to the hatch in gratitude for its solidity.

The attic was different in the daylight, the dust so thick it sat like grey, velvety fur over everything. Trails of black ran across the floor, stark records of her rendezvous with Nadya. Jan saw the perfect imprint of her bare arse and hastened to rub it out with her foot. She cast about her, searching for footsteps, traces of their nocturnal activities or mislaid belongings to take her back to when she had not known Theo's intentions. She had expected his rage, disappointment, sorrow – but not that.

A cold draught flitted through the space, riffling the abandoned papers and black plastic bags so they trembled with a faint noise that seemed to her almost like whispering. The small dormer window was closed and when she craned to look through it, the grounds below seemed impossibly far away. The woods looked neater than she'd ever seen them, though perhaps that was the angle. The draught curled around her ankles, chilling them despite the stuffy heat of the attic, and made her turn in confusion at where it could be coming from. The whispering grew louder, but she couldn't make out any words, just intonations rising and falling like a prayer or midnight curse. The door down into the dining room was closed tight and so was the hatch to Nadya's room. She put her ear to it but the whispering was above her and around her, not below. She really had been nothing to Theo all along. No threat, no friend, just a convenient pair of hands and a hole to empty himself into.

A second gust of freezing air whipped through the attic, throwing up papers and making the space shake. She looked about her for its source. Waiting in the Eastern corner, the trapdoor over the end bedroom stood wide, dark mouth gaping with intensifying cold. Step by deathly slow step, she walked towards it as if underwater, half-sucked by the force of the wind, the whispering growing louder and louder in her ears. Jan descended, rope ladder uncoiling beneath her.

She was enveloped in darkness. The air grew denser and heavier with moisture as it wrapped around her. It passed over her skin like the cool belly of a snake, twining about her wrists and ankles and over the back of her neck. Her panic intensified as it grew more solid, pressing in on her ever more closely until she could scarcely breathe. She was not certain if her eyes were open or shut.

She heard a wet, glugging sound like a tap dripping near her left cheek. Something was trying to speak but could not. Cold droplets trickled down her ear canal, making her squirm, but she couldn't move. All at once, in several places, she felt a pinching sensation, the fat on her hips and the back of her arms squeezed between two pincer points. Pressure bearing in on her, a force winding ever tighter, almost choking her, a dense and bitter ooze over her lips as the something grabbed at her hair, tugging it straight out in all directions as if to examine it.

The rasping stutter came again, still failing to coalesce into intelligible sound. Unable to make anything of the noise, she struggled against the constriction, thrashing and pulling at the air around her.

Her mouth was prised open, a rough surface moved over her lips, the sensation of thick fingers probing further

246

inside, stroking the sensitive surface of her tongue and slicking over each tooth, reaching inwards, stretching and pushing down into her throat. She kicked out her feet and groaned, trying to force it out, cold sweat pouring off her brow with the strain of trying to free herself. Suffocating.

Then something whispered in her ear, so close and intimate she could swear she'd known the voice all her life. *You are a pestilence, but you can still be put to use.*

With that, the invasion stopped all at once, her jaw clamped shut, clacking her front teeth together so hard it hurt, a terrible pressure building in her head as her temples were squeezed so forcefully, she feared her skull might crumple like a rotten apple. Then nothingness.

Thick ruby drops coagulate and fall, rolling down from the clotted hilt of the dagger and spraying loose. Two red hands stained almost to the elbow with gore and filth grip the bridle of his horse, the cross on his tunic so spattered with blood it scarcely stands out against the white. Under iron-grey skies the young knight rides, galloping through forests and wooded valleys as he races for cover. He dismounts his horse to enter a low longhouse on a sloping hillside dotted with trees and washes his weathered face before sitting to unpack the spoils of his latest skirmish in the city, having ridden hard all night to flee the scene and escape the king's displeasure. He pulls out a bulging bag of silver, ransacked from the house of his dead creditor. The bones burned, the debts incurred by his long absence erased, the coins gleam with new promise. He resolves to fashion some of his newfound treasure into a memento, a medallion or a silver goblet perhaps. He swears an oath to himself that next time he and his brothers in arms shall prevail not only against the Jews but that wicked dog, Saladin, and take Jerusalem for Christ.

Feasting and revelry and booty. War wounds and licentiousness and song. Theo's face reappearing over and over with different beards and new shirts, but every time the same name, one generation giving way inexorably to another, spirit draining into the foundations, lining the roof and clinging to the walls. One mind with a hundred slight shades of distinction, and one true purpose to guide them. There is cold and hunger without the walls, but within is ample gaiety and plenty. The hose lengthen into trousers, the ruffs disappear and doublets become jackets. The thighs of women are still clutched and discarded, and wine is still drunk from the silver goblet, while the vital matters of the day are discussed. The centuries swell and fall away while the house remains, growing, reaching ever upward to the heavens.

A cherubic little boy runs through the corridors of the house, brandishing a wooden sword. He is hand in hand with a small girl of about his age, blonde pigtails bouncing on her shoulders as he thrusts and parries to save her from an imaginary foe. Harold's nursemaid calls for him and Lettice to come back right this instant, they're making such a din. He ignores her scolding. The goblet and the grounds and the ancient Mortimer name are his by right.

Harold in his morning dress at school, learning grammar tables by rote, rushing through his prayers in Chapel and being caned for small acts of insolence. The year Harold turns eighteen, three kings sit on the English throne and electric light comes to more than half the nation, but his letters of complaint still go unanswered by his father, as his own father's letters were before him. The Napola exchange students come from Germany, a generation of future leaders promising friendship, fraternal camaraderie. Their rigid Teutonic discipline in the day and wild abandon after hours appeal to him, a mixture already familiar from home. Their other ideas appeal too, about purity and empire. He keeps in touch with several of them, continuing to write and visit even as relations between the two countries grow strained. He longs for a similar renewal in England, a stripping out of pernicious foreign influence to return to God, King and Country.

He receives the Germans' gifts, and attends the meetings of like-minded countrymen, who see a bold new future for them all, if Chamberlain would only keep capitulating. He even hosts a few of these meetings, though by that time the battles at sea are not going in their favour. Bombs fall on British cities, while he sits and waits, all lights extinguished after dark. But Harold, still young and determined, sends lists and maps and bides his time, enlarging the house just in case. Once a stronghold, always a stronghold, after all.

And when it all fails, the utter ignominy, the condemnation of those whom he knew had believed the same in secret. The reading room of a members' club, replete with soft green leather chairs, vast glass-fronted cabinets of obscure quarterlies and parquet floors laid with dark Turkish rugs, where a smarmy bald man in a suit leans forward and whispers, 'Nothing to be done, I'm afraid, sir, they're all firmly against it.' He will not be admitted.

Then, the view down the long dining table at Holt House, one of his brothers at either side, both chewing merrily on beef and potatoes and talking across him like he wasn't even there. Rising up on foot despite the aches and stiffness to bellow at one of his dull nieces for a minor infraction with knife and fork while she sits glumly in silence, hands poised to resume the meal.

Then, staggering from the end bedroom on crumbling joints and groping agonisingly slowly along the corridor and downstairs out onto the terrace, to look over the sun setting on his tiny fiefdom of Holt House. Here, at least, was still pure, still unsullied by decadence and rot. He lays a swollen, blue-veined hand on the young Theo's shoulder, telling him that all would soon be his to conquer, if not already his.

'Jan? Jan?'

She heard a door opening. A figure appeared far off from her, haloed by sudden light, afternoon sun reaching in to strike her eyes and new air buffeting her back to consciousness.

She was sitting with her back to the wall, unable to get up. The carved wooden screen towered above to her right. Her mouth was drier than sand and her throat ached terribly. Glued to the floor, Jan groped about her, surprised to find that it was solid, trying to return to a present day still hazy with swirling darkness and translucent floating spots of light.

Ursie peered down at her through the doorway to the corridor. 'Were you really hiding in there all this time? I thought we weren't allowed? I was getting worried, no one knew where you went. Come and have a line with me, I'm doing much better now.'

250

Jan could not put into words what she had seen and felt, so she just sat there, stunned, until Ursie held out a hand and Jan heaved herself up, reaching for it desperately. Her entire body was stiff and sore as if she'd walked for miles through a midwinter blizzard, ears ringing and hands fumbling at the doorframe for support. She tried not to put any weight on Ursie in her scramble to leave the room but she failed, almost pulled her down too in haste.

'Steady, steady, you're nearly there. Come with me.'

They traipsed across the upper floor to Ursie's room, hand in hand to stop Jan tripping with every step.

Jan followed her in, closing the door behind them. The floor was thick with clothes, necklaces glistening from their folds and abandoned shoes like capsized boats, careening in the mess. Jan ventured what she hoped was a normal question.

'How are you doing with uh . . . with everything?'

Ursie shrugged and said, 'I only had a sip, to be honest. Spat most of it out.'

'Do you have water?'

Ursie handed her a sports bottle and Jan chugged it while Ursie fished some coke out of her shirt pocket and tapped a little mound onto the surface of the vanity. She then began to use a razorblade to separate it, and swore to herself as it clumped together with moisture from the air.

'Please no.'

'This should wake you up a bit, though.'

Jan crossed the room, eyes averted from the mirror, blankets squirming and shifting on the bed as the rose pattern slid off them to puddle at the edges, plunking herself down on a chair and breathing heavily as she waited for her turn.

251

'I keep seeing movement and uh . . . patterns, every-where, it's fading a bit but it was horrible, honestly. I'm never doing research chemicals again.'

Ursie did her line and straightened up, gesturing for Jan to take her place on the stool. She gave the line a bit of further tidying, wondering as she did so whether she should be anywhere near a razorblade in her current state. Was Ursie not still angry with her? Jan hoovered up her line and said, 'I thought you were going to pack?'

'I'll get to it. I came back from the shower this morn-ing, and it was just all wrong and I was sober then, or sober enough, anyway. Even the proportions of this room were fucked, like I was shorter somehow and looking upwards. It throws me off every time something new happens.' She shrugged, mournful and exhausted. 'I haven't been right since I got here.'

'I'm so sorry about last night with the door. I should have believed you about the other stuff.'

'Did you rip up my notebook?'

'No, that wasn't me, I—'

'Thought not. It's not in your nature to do that to get back at me. You forget I know you and how obsessed you are with preserving things, even when you're mad.' She laughed slightly and continued, 'I don't think it was any of the others either. Something is not right here. Are you not even a little bit scared?'

Ursie clambered up towards the headboard and patted the empty space next to her on the coverlet for Jan to sit there. Jan took a deep breath and climbed in too, their legs stretched out in the same direction, arms almost touching.

'At first I felt like you were being oversensitive, or at any rate I wanted to think that. But no, you're not imagining it. It's so hard to tell what's real when we're fucked up all the time. This morning . . . and just now . . .' Jan struggled to express anything that had happened in the end bedroom which might be comprehensible to another human person and settled on the one concrete piece of information she had.

'There isn't a gardener, Ursie, he's dead.'

'So all the vandalism and the locking doors and stuff like that?'

'And what I saw in the games room yesterday. It wasn't him.'

'Finally! I knew it, right from the beginning.'

'Really?' Jan felt the familiar cold, pooling in her guts. The skin on her arms prickled. This room was too quiet, she should never have dared to speak the thought aloud, not now.

'I'm not as superstitious as you seem to think, at least not without good reason. This is something else, and it absolutely hates me.' Ursie put her hand, clammily warm, but comforting, on Jan's arm, fingers resting on the curve of her forearm as if they had always been meant to sit there. 'Why did you not tell me you were afraid too?'

Jan had a thousand elaborate answers. That she had wanted so badly to believe they were welcome there she had ignored the evidence they were not, that she was scared Ursie would blame her for encouraging the group to come, that she knew they were growing apart and just wanted to have one last fun trip all together. As she was trying to find the least pathetic of these, Ursie's searching

253

fingers encircled her wrist, and she pulled her closer and kissed her.

Baffled for a moment, Jan forgot to kiss back and she withdrew.

'Sorry, I shouldn't have done that. I don't know what came over me.'

Jan seized her face in both hands and went back in, half-falling into her mouth with relief at touching Ursie, so known to her, so solid and indisputably alive. She had missed everything about her so badly. She felt the sensation from earlier, like her body was wrapped in a net of stars, return. Nothing further was said. Ursie's lips were wet and wondrously soft, her limbs stately, slickly sheened with sweat as Jan undressed them, hands wild as Ursie ripped off what remained of Jan's clothes in turn. It was a kind of unravelling, the mental barriers Jan had patched and rewoven between them to better shield herself fell as if unthreaded all at once, coiled uselessly about their feet. Her glory in the lamplight, her soft laughs of anticipation as Jan kissed her sides, her breasts, her everything. Both kneeling, tongues sliding over each other. Her fingers knowing, Ursie traced the welts across Jan's back and thighs, inscribing fresh pain as she transformed them into a means of mutual indulgence. No more the icy mistrust and restraint that had locked them away from one another, no rancour remained in the rush to consume all their joys in this one long moment, not promised to return.

Jan sat astride her thigh, stroking faster and faster, biting and grinding, Ursie moaning underneath as all the walls began to shake, the glass in the windows rattling, bedside light flickering. It was too late to stop now and the little oval mirror fell from the wall and shattered while the two twined closer together, Jan's lips locked over Ursie's, pulling away for the last rush to the finish line, efforts redoubling as the great chest of drawers leaned dangerously as if about to topple.

Ursie's eyes were closed but Jan wanted to drink all of her in, to share the pleasure fully as they reached for each other in the depths of their fear.

'Look at me, look at me please.'

Ursie's lids flew up, her pupils widened before she reared up beneath Jan, looking not at her but at something behind them, though they both were still so close now, still grinding, too far gone for either one to stop. Jan felt hands groping at her back and thighs and there seemed to be too many, but just a little more, a little further and as they finished the current surged and crackled with a lick of flame, plunging the whole house into darkness before unconsciousness took them.

The Fifth Day

Sunlight filled Ursie's bedroom in Holt House, slipping through the tightly drawn curtains and warming the crowded bed. Jan lay curled with her back to Ursie, two parabolas stretching close together without quite touching. Light played over the crushed glass on the floor, glittering on the polished boards, before growing and thickening to illuminate the scene as Jan's eyelids flickered open, not yet fully awoken. A necklace lay torn into three sections, amber beads rolling under the bed, while an old wooden barometer hung sideways, precariously supported by a loosening nail. The door of the wardrobe hung wide open, spewing dresses, hinge cracked. Jan closed her eyes again, thinking drowsily that one of the others must be awake already as the shadow loomed above her, passing over her face and briefly shielding her from the burgeoning day before slinking out under the door.

She forced her eyes open again and silently, carefully, slid a leg out of the tangled sheets and set it on a clear patch of floor. There must have been a small earthquake last night, for everything to have come off the walls like this. Upright and undisturbed, she found her bag and searched around for her clothes in the ruins of the bedroom, but soon gave up and decided to take her chances streaking through the corridor. She placed one foot slowly in front of the other, tracing a safe path across the perilously glass-strewn floorboards. Quietly, ever so quietly, she tried the door and found it opened just enough to allow her to escape without waking Ursie up.

Jan hauled herself back to her bedroom and went to smoke her first despondent cigarette of the day by the window. In the daylight, she felt even less sure of herself, the precise sequence of events scattered into a jigsaw array of images and sensations. She thought perhaps it had been terribly cold and there had been a high wind over the moors, or at least a sort of whistling and howling. Ursie had been warm beneath her as she'd closed her eyes and waited to be kissed, hoping to obliterate all uncertainty with the insistence of her mouth. They needed to leave; she had to pack. But it couldn't last. Ursie would just ignore her again like last time, and then she'd be even lonelier than before . . . Jan's stomach flipped over upon itself, sending her racing to the bathroom, liquid streaming between pursed lips and creeping out of her nose as she heaved clear bile into the toilet bowl, head pounding and hands clutching uselessly at the tiles. If anything, it was a welcome distraction from the rapidly fading joys of memory. She was such a fool to fall for it again, such a fool to set herself up to be rejected.

After a number of apprehensive attempts to clean her teeth and tongue without tickling her throat, she dressed and ventured out onto the landing. Every door was now closed, even that of the end bedroom. She wanted to put her ear to each door but that one, straining for breath or signs of life. The thought crept unbidden into her mind that the others might have packed up and left them here, to wander the corridors forever. She sank down into the middle of the carpet, already given over to despair.

Jan sat there, she didn't know how long, waiting for one of them to emerge and prove her wrong. The corners of her imagination were all blocked off and there were no trifles she could occupy herself with, try as she might. The force of her mind when not directed anywhere must inevitably be turned back upon itself in fear and dread. The remaining Chinese vase loomed behind her, as if longing for its counterpart. The vaulted window over the stairs, plastered with old leaves, let in only a web of dappled light, shadows playing over the stairwell as clouds passed. As she watched the patterns on the floor move gently with the stirring of the wind and sky, she noticed one patch of shade, larger than the rest, emerge from the leftmost corner where the Western wing ended. She looked up at the window, but nothing corresponded to the shape. It travelled swiftly over the floor, before she could clearly make out its edges. She jumped to her feet and saw it pause before resuming its course over the carpet and down to the head of the stairs. With useless heavy limbs she tried to run after it, hoping to herself she was still dreaming but knowing she was not.

The light dimmed as the stairs curved round and Jan lost track of the shadow, fearful she had been outpaced or even run right through it, the thought of which was somehow worse than its changing course to pursue her instead. She almost collided with Kara crossing the floor of the great hall downstairs, heading out of the Eastern parlour door. The same vacant look from yesterday was on her face and Jan's relief at not yet having been abandoned mingled with terror when she realised Kara was sleepwalking. The way she moved was jerky, every so often half-tripping to launch herself back on course. Jan waited on the last step until Kara strode past and away from her, legs rigid and knees unbent so she walked like a toy soldier. Halfway down the corridor, she adopted a more normal posture, as if she had worked out the length of her own limbs. Perhaps with a gentle touch, she might be steered back to bed until she woke again for real. Jan reached out for her shoulder.

'Hey!'

Kara moved the hand forcefully away, as if enraged at her presumption. Jan caught a glimpse of two alert, straining eyes examining her intently from Kara's slackened, absent face. She could not bear to meet them for more than a moment.

As Jan started back, repulsed, Kara set off again. She appeared to be looking for something, though Jan couldn't imagine what. Jan hurried to get ahead of her and push open the heavy dining-room door before she walked straight into it and injured herself.

She saw Kara cast a glance at the half-empty wine glasses sitting on the table and heard her give what sounded like an outraged cough.

Jan tried again, more firmly this time. 'Wake up, Kara. Don't panic, it's all okay. I'm going to take you back to your room now.'

Kara fixed that disquieting alien gaze on her again. She looked well rested, the feverish bloom gone from her skin and no trace of a cold to be seen. She wore a strange combination of old moth-eaten trousers belted tightly about her waist and an oversized woollen jumper, plus a battered fishing vest Jan recognised, which had been hanging on a peg in the hall.

'What are you doing, Kara?'

She walked around the table, eyes half-closed, clipping her hip on the sharp point of its corner yet not seeming to register any pain. She stopped and opened her mouth, but no words came out.

Jan felt compelled to walk round to where her friend stood and continue the desperate attempt to engage with her.

'Please stop it, Kara, if you're in there. I don't like this.'

She pawed at the table, pointing for Jan to assist her.

Jan, now too afraid to do anything but confusedly obey, lifted the white tablecloth to see a thin drawer cut into the polished wood. She tugged at the knob set into it, and the drawer slid out, but revealed nothing inside. It was entirely empty.

Kara turned on her heel and strode out of the dining room, with Jan hurrying after her. As they passed the Western drawing room, she could not help but peer in through the open door. The portrait of Harold that hung on the far wall was damaged somehow – no, it was darker. It looked almost black and she peered in trying to divine what was wrong with it. The background was undamaged, she saw, but Harold had vanished from the frame.

She followed Kara back into the hall where she caught sight of Luke as he appeared at the top of the stairs. She mouthed, 'Help me.'

He did not understand until she'd done so several times, pointing to Kara and exaggeratedly holding a finger over her own lips. He hurried down to join them and put a hand on Kara's shoulder, which she immediately wrenched away with even greater viciousness, though admittedly this would not be unusual on any other day.

'Are you seriously pretending not to know me again?' he griped. 'We were doing so well last night, what's with you? This is really beginning to piss me off, it's just constant mixed signals.'

Kara stepped around him as if he barely existed.

Luke pulled a face at Jan of utter non-comprehension and she grimaced back. All this time, Kara had been plotting a determined course back towards the Eastern drawing room. She steadfastly ignored Jan and Luke's requests to slow down or explain her mission, stumbling over the carpet and narrowly missing the low ottoman on which the silver coffee tray rested, before coming to standstill in the far corner of the room.

A large mother-of-pearl inlaid box rested on a low shelf; its lid patterned with geometric tessellations. Kara tipped over the box, spilling out innumerable keys of different shapes and sizes, scattering them across the carpet, some labelled in neat, curlicued writing and others unadorned by any form of identification. Luke was still trying to hold Kara back, as she scrabbled among the keys, seemingly looking for one in particular.

'I've never seen her like this,' he said. 'I think she's finally gone crazy. Do you think the fever's come back?'

'Does she feel hot or cold?'

'She won't stay still.' He wrestled with Kara for a moment to feel her forehead before giving up. 'Fairly normal, I think.'

Kara shrugged Luke off as if he were not almost twice her weight and returned to the pile before her. Jan watched her closely as she sorted through them, and just as Kara was about to reach for a little bronze key no longer than two joints of Jan's pinkie that was apparently the object of her search, Jan snatched it.

'Looking for this?'

Jan yanked her hand out of reach just before Kara could grab it from her. 'First I want to know why. Tell me what you need it for.'

Kara's face managed half a smile and she slowly shook her head, too slowly to be convincing.

Luke looked at Jan, eyes wide and said, 'So it knows who *you* are.'

Kara moved towards Jan, who took two quick steps back away from her.

'Who are you and what have you done with Kara?' Luke asked.

He tried to seize her again but she wheeled round, with a flash of silver. A needle-sharp knife was pointed directly under Luke's chin, its black and silver scabbard discarded on the floor. Jan noted a stylised, blackletter inscription that read 'Meine Ehre heißt Treue', which ran up the length of the blade, as Luke trembled at the other end. Kara must have snatched it from its habitual place on the wall in the Eastern parlour before Jan had lain eyes on her.

She gestured in a way that could mean nothing else but *give me the key*.

Jan had no choice but to draw a little closer, holding out the key to Kara, who seized it from her at the same moment she lowered the dagger slightly, allowing Luke to back away, hands still raised.

Not knowing what else to do, they mutely followed Kara as she made a lumbering path onward to the library.

Kara held out the little bronze key gingerly and tried to position it in the keyhole of the old wooden trunk but failed, the current occupant not having sufficient control of Kara's limbs for the finer grades of movement.

263

She slid the key back to Jan over the dark wood of the desk, motioning for her to do it.

'What's in there? You can tell me.'

Kara cast a scrutinising eye over her in evident disgust.

Jan picked up the key once more. 'Surely you can let me in on it, if you need my help?' Her heart was beating almost at her collarbone as she resolved to test at last the theory that had now formed in her mind. Luke was just staring, mouth moving inaudibly, hands clasped together, and Jan realised he was praying.

Kara stepped closer, still holding the knife.

'Alright, alright.'

Jan's own hands were shaking now, as she jiggled the key into place, taking as long as she possibly could and finding unexpected new reserves of defiance as she did so.

Luke was still going, next to her, '. . . *even though I walk through the valley of the shadow . . .*'

Jan might not get another chance to ask. 'Was it you? In the end bedroom yesterday? And the billiards room?'

Silence, another step closer.

'. . . *your rod and your staff, they comfort me . . .*'

'Come on now, Harold, I know you wanted me to see. Did you mean to frighten me?'

Luke broke off, screaming, 'Tell me! Tell me now, is there life after death? Is Hell a real place?'

A horrible shrieking, wheezing sound like laughter without air, distorted violins and industrial compaction hissed forth from Kara's parted lips. Its smell and taste was of metal and needles and earth. The frequency made Jan's eardrums start ringing in agony and, when it subsided, she saw twin trickles of blood dripping from Luke's ears, felt the same wetness on her own neck.

Face white and without expression, he turned to bolt up the stairs.

The key clicked in the lock a final time and Kara grinned lopsidedly, motioning her to get on with it.

Jan pulled the trunk out of its corner further into the room, unbuckling the heavy catches and levering the lid upwards, crude metal hinges stiff from lack of use. It was almost empty. Inside lay a dark green velvet cloth, already crumbling with age into dry particles and, bound in black ribbon, a neat stack of handwritten letters.

She lifted them out of the trunk and laid them on the desk, trying to cast a quick eye over the scrawled hand-writing before Kara shoved her aside. She cast about for the fireplace. Finding it empty of all but years-old ashes, she made a gesture clearly indicating matches.

'Can you not tell me what's in the letters first? Surely Theo would want to know his own family history.'

Despite everything, Jan could not stand to see an archive burn.

Kara came very close to her. Jan averted her eyes but she could still smell the sour stench of dehydration and feel the grave-chill clawing at her face. Kara gripped Jan's chin with iron-strong fingers in an attempt to force her into eye contact. Jan could not do it again, she had seen enough the night before, kept her lids clenched tight. When proximity didn't work, Kara slammed down the point of the knife into the wood of the desk, between Jan's splayed-out digits, narrowly missing her index and nicking deeply the web of her middle finger.

Jan, nursing her bloody hand, resolved to take as much time as possible over the task, lest the visitation come to an end of its own accord. She was surprised that he had not yet done anything worse to her and suspected the only reason could be the urgency of this current need. Perhaps whatever was binding him to Kara's body could not hold for very long. She walked backwards around the end of the desk, not taking her eyes off Kara, and made a great show of rootling through the nearby cabinet next to the old, unused fireplace, turning up a silver ewer, a magnifying glass, three fragile lace antimacassars and an ancient orange studded with cloves. In the bottom drawer she caught sight of matches and the ugly, yellow-handled grill lighter, presumably for reaching the candelabra if needed. Just as she began to wonder how sharp Kara's eyesight could be at present, she noticed motion in the doorframe. Nadya, walking on bare feet, was creeping silently behind Kara, holding a small white cloth. Kara hadn't noticed her yet.

Jan began to chatter. 'There's just so much random stuff in here, I'm having a lot of trouble. Did you buy this for the house or is it even older than that?' She brandished the ewer, wiping it on her shirtfront for effect. 'This is ever so pretty; I'm amazed at the craftsmanship.' She could feel herself babbling.

Kara let out another groan that lifted dangerously towards the shrieking sound again.

Jan, noting how close Nadya had come to Kara, cried, 'Look! I found the matches!'

Before Kara could lunge the two paces forward to take them, Nadya clasped the white cloth around her face and held it there. In the struggle, Jan saw the knife still in Kara's hand and, knowing Nadya's strength was no match for Kara's newfound reserves, leaped towards them, knocking back Kara's skinny wrist to jolt it out of her grasp. The dagger skidded across the floor, coming to rest near the corner. Jan kept one eye on it while she held Kara's flailing wrists tightly until she stopped struggling.

Still holding onto Kara, they lowered her to a chair, and Jan directed Nadya to use the sashes from the curtains as makeshift ties and they yanked back her hair so they could stuff another in her mouth, in the hope it would prevent her from screaming like that again. Luke re-emerged and peered around the door nervously.

'How nice of you to show up again. Look at this.' Jan held up her injured finger, from which the blood had just stopped flowing, leaving a trail of red down to her elbow.

'What was I supposed to do? You didn't seem that fazed by it.' He went over to fetch the blade. 'Where did this come from? Is this a replica?'

Jan shrugged. 'Germany, I assume.'

Luke had started casting about for the sheath, when Nadya said, 'Can anyone tell me why the hell I just had to ether Kara?'

'Oh, that was ether? I was wondering about the smell.'

'It's pretty good, an old school friend of Theo's is a vet and they all get high on it together. He was hoping to bring it out as a fun extra.'

Jan said with a shaking voice, 'I can't take any more surprises right now. I think we just met Harold.'

Nadya asked, 'What do you mean?' at the same time as Luke said, 'Oh.'

'I mean exactly what I said. That isn't Kara in there. I don't know where she is right now, but that's not her. It's Harold, I think. He was totally obsessed with getting these old letters out of the drawer to burn them, that's why he was waving that knife around.'

267

'You don't seriously believe that, do you?'

Jan raised her hand again. 'Does this look like a joke to you?'

Luke had put the knife down again and was now struggling with the ribbon round the packet. He was still trembling and his nails were bitten to red shiny stubs, so Jan had to loosen it for him. She took up one of the envelopes at random and noted the address on the front. It had been sent to Harold Mortimer at Holt House, the stamp bearing an image of one of the moustachioed kings who had preceded Elizabeth II, she did not know or care which. Fanning the first few letters out across the table, she could see that all of them were in the same scratchy handwriting, elegant but with thin and faltering ink, still dark after so many years of being hidden from the light.

She pulled one from the top of the pile and tried to pass it to Nadya, who said, 'Don't look at me, I always struggle with messy cursive when it's Roman letters.'

Luke was squinting at the bundle. 'This is almost illegible, how is anyone supposed to read this?'

Jan peered at them. 'I think I can work with this. It's hardly worse than Carolingian miniscule or bastard secretary.'

The two of them looked at her nonplussed.

'Just keep an eye on Kara, won't you? She'll probably come round again very soon.'

Both Nadya and Luke whirled round to check the ties on Kara's wrists were secure enough.

As she went to replace the knife, Jan added, 'Watch her closely and keep her away from those, okay?'

Standing in the Eastern parlour, she turned the knife in her hand, seeing for the first time the little silver eagle on the hilt. It had been turned to face the wall while it was on display. Jan wondered whether putting it back within easy reach would be an unwise thing to do. But where else could it go? Items wandered free from the drawers where they were placed, and storing it in her own bedroom felt like an invitation for more trouble. She had no belt or boot to stash the knife in safely and touching it disgusted her. She reluctantly placed it in full view on the hall table, where at least someone would notice quickly if it went missing. Back in the dining room, Nadya had begun trying to read aloud from the letter, in a faltering voice.

'My dear Harold,

Please allow me to offer you my most heartfelt congratulations on the engagement of your brother, Clarence. I have written to him already at his new address but I thought I should also convey my regrets to you that I will not be able to attend the wedding as your particular guest. I know that it shall be a great occasion for your family and Mother is already very much excited to attend. I have heard of nothing but hats ever since.

Your Lettice has some wonderful news of her own she must im-im-imparat?'

'Impart. Give that here.'
'What is this? It's so boring.'
'Just wait. He must have hidden it for a reason.'

'. . . By the time the wedding is to take place I will be on a boat to Cádiz. Simon and I are to be married! Mother has relented at last and all his family are terribly displeased as well but we are too happy to give a fig for that. You have always *been my great champion and protector since our childhood days and I know that you at least will be pleased for me. I hope that after our return you will dine with us in Bethnal Green, where we have found the sweetest little house to let. Whoever could have foreseen that I was to become Mrs Levy? You may already have obtained them by other means, but I have many other tales of London to share with you . . .'*

Jan paused and asked them, 'Do you want me to read the whole thing? There seems to be a long passage about a motor race and a couple called the Bloomington-Smythes who are apparently obsessed with jazz music. Someone called Cousin Ethel has terrible problems with sending telegrams to the right address.'

'Then not really, no,' Luke said. 'Is there anything else in the pile?'

Jan sifted through it. 'I'll have a look in this one.' She scanned through the gossip and the pleasantries to find a passage at the end which confirmed her suspicions.

'. . . I do not see what you can possibly have against Simon and I had hoped you would know better than to cleave to such absurd and extreme beliefs. I know you wished to bestow a copy of your latest feuilleton on me as a gift but I have no interest in social philosophy or racial science.

I had always regarded you as my dear friend and a beloved brotherly presence. Your behaviour towards me was disgraceful and it is fortunate that Lady Percival came upstairs when she did. I fear that it will be impossible for me to visit you unchaperoned again, though I wish it could be otherwise.

Yours sincerely,

Laetitia'

As Jan read the letter, Kara began to writhe in her restraints, making guttural moans and rocking the chair back and forth. Her eyes remained closed; when Luke peeled back one eyelid to check on her, they were rolled all the way back into her skull.

Jan hovered her hand over the pile and picked up another letter more or less at random. She opened it and began to read intently.

Luke asked, 'So what does it say?'

'Hang on, I'm trying to make out what she's getting at. I think he was threatening her with something.'

'Should we be doing this?' Nadya asked. 'You're getting blood on the letters.'

'We need to know what's in here, it's proof of what he was really like. I think he's still furious about being passed over by Laetitia in favour of a Jew.'

Jan silently asked herself if perhaps her own exploits with Theo's fiancée had woken Harold once more as upstairs, with a clamour, every single door opened and slammed shut from East to West, the walls shaking as if a great wind were sweeping through the house. Kara lay still in the chair, not responding to a single sound, wrists and ankles white from the pressure of the ties but still not regaining consciousness. Luke held a hand to her brow, feeling uselessly for a fever and looking pained. 'What if you're making her worse, can't you do this somewhere else?'

'Do you want to watch her by yourself?' Jan asked him and, when he had no reply, she turned to Nadya and said, 'One more. I think I am beginning to understand.'

But before she could start, the door to the dining room opened and Theo strode in. In the commotion she had not heard him coming downstairs. He picked up the bottle of ether silently and pocketed it, then went to stand beside Luke with his arms crossed, flanking Kara. Jan could see from the set of his jaw that he was furious. He gave a small nod and Jan began to read again.

Harold,

I have been receiving your letters, I simply have not replied to them because I no longer have anything to say.

I have not ruined you utterly, your mother tells me you are in perfectly good health. In such times as these, one should be thankful to possess all one's limbs and a ration book. We still manage to have a gay time between the air raids and all hunker together down in the Underground when we must. It's almost rather jolly if you choose to put on a brave face and get on with life, as we have done.

There are plenty of suitable girls from whom you might choose among. I have broken no promises, but what God has joined together, let no man put asunder.

Kindly do not write to me again.

As Jan read the letter, the banging and crashing intensified once more. The golden-hued mirror above the sideboard cracked and burst in a spray of shards; Jan heard them breaking all over the house. Kara slept on, her jaw yawning open, head lolled to one side, looking for all the world as if she were sleeping at the end of a long day.

Jan moved to the bottom of the pile and found several letters marked 'Not at this address'.

'I think these ones are all from Harold.' She peered at the contents more closely. 'They seem to be a mixture of threats and love poetry. Not good poetry either, rather derivative.'

'I think that's more than enough,' Theo said and went to take the letters from her. He looked at them briefly and shoved them back into their envelopes. He said with an oddly clipped intonation, 'This has to stop. I don't know why you're going through Harold's private correspondence or why it should matter to you that he was having an affair with some woman.'

'It wasn't an affair; I think he tried to—'

The house shook again, with a great rumbling that sounded like thunder, despite the clear daylight outside.

Jan asked him, 'Did you not just hear that? The whole upstairs floor might be destroyed.'

Theo continued, his voice becoming increasingly nasal and warped, like a cassette tape played too many times. 'I don't know what that was, subsidence probably. This house is built over a bunch of tunnels, remember? The foundations are not especially stable, but that's a problem for the insurers to sort out, not you. All of you have got to stop being so melodramatic and just calm down, we've all been indoors too long. Kara was having a freakout, she's not well and it's disgusting that you've gone and tied her up like this. Perverted, if you ask me.'

'It really wasn't her,' Luke protested. 'She didn't even know me. We've had our fights, she's thrown things at the walls, but she's never threatened me like that with a knife or anything and she's had plenty of opportunity to before.'

Theo said, 'She's had plenty of reason, too.'

'How would she even have known the letters were there? Why would she want to burn them?' Jan asked.

'I don't know, she believes in all sorts of hippy bullshit. She once told me that she wanted to give my mum a rose quartz to help her mood, as if she isn't depressed by being

273

in chronic pain from arthritis most of the day.' Theo had his hands clenched round the top of the chairback, his whole manner growing more and more agitated. 'You've got to stop putting this sort of thing into people's heads, Jan. You know how impressionable Kara is, and it's really dangerous.'

'Are you saying she's stupid?' Luke asked, with more than a little edge to his voice.

'Oh, come off it. You don't like it either, you've told me you hate all her cleansing nonsense . . .'

'You're one to talk about cleansing,' Jan said. 'Harold was a fucking Nazi. Or did you not know that?'

'I'm sorry I dragged us all here, Jan. Clearly you didn't really want to come and I shouldn't have pushed you, I can see you've become tired and hysterical. But just say you need a break instead of insisting that you're being pursued by my dead relative and calling him a Nazi, which is incredibly disrespectful and inaccurate, by the way. He worked for the Home Office during the war, he was very patriotic.'

'After everything that's happened, you still don't believe what you just saw and heard?' Luke asked, mopping Kara's pallid brow with the cuff of his shirt.

'No. You forget, I grew up in a different big old house, before we had to leave it. There were thuds and noises all the time; I would have gone mad assuming every single one of them was a ghost. Do you know how many people lived and died in every place we've been? You've all gone completely mad and I'm sick of tiptoeing around it.'

'He was a Nazi! He had a Nazi knife!'

'That knife was a trophy. Lots of people have them.'

Jan brandished the letters in his face. 'He was a eugenicist for fuck's sake! You missed that part because you were

274

off doing god knows what while he was wearing Kara like a glove.'

Before Theo could respond, Ursie pushed open the door, duffel bag in hand. 'What was all that banging and crashing upstairs? What have you been—? Oh, it's happening again. I'm not getting involved in any more of this, I'm leaving. Jan, if you're coming with me, tell me now, otherwise I'm going by myself. Even if I have to hitch-hike, I'm not staying here any longer.'

Nadya straightened up and said, 'You know what, I'm going to go too, I was just packing. Wait outside while I bring the car around.' She had a grim expression of certainty, having anticipated the refusal that would inevitably come next.

'No, you aren't. We aren't due back for another week and you're ruining our holiday over something completely stupid,' Theo told her with an air of menacing finality.

'It's my car. You can stay if you want. I'm out. This' – she gestured to the letters strewn over the table – 'is so much more than I can handle right now.'

Luke said, 'I think Kara and I should go too. I need to think about some things.'

Theo stepped forward into the room and plucked the sash from Kara's mouth. 'You can't just leave like that. The gates are locked, remember?' Then, modifying his tone to a more persuasive one, he added, 'Come on, guys. You've let her get you all worked up over nothing. I'll take Jan and Ursie to the station myself and drop them off, since they're so keen to upset everyone and ruin the party. There has to be at least one train a day. Now you sit down and have a line, Luke, and Nadya can make us some coffee.'

Luke looked resigned and frightened, while Nadya was spluttering with rage at Theo's assumption of total control.

Another crash came from upstairs as Kara jerked her head upright and everyone in the room turned to her immediately. She straightened, trying to stretch but finding herself trapped as she opened her eyes.

'Guys, what's going on? What have you done to me?' She struggled against the ties, twisting her shoulders back and forth. 'Is this a sex thing? Because I'm not really feeling like it right now to be honest.'

Luke asked her gently, 'How much do you remember of this morning, baby?'

'I don't know. I was in my room, and then I was in the woods for a bit. I must have been dreaming. I was just lying down in a big pile of grass and leaves, looking up at the sky. I was there for ages and it was so peaceful but I felt very lonely. Then I was here. Did you carry me indoors after last night?'

'I don't know how to tell you this, but you . . . you weren't yourself for a while. You had us all pretty frightened.'

Ursie said, 'Whatever has been going on you can tell her about it later, Luke. Let's just get her out of here. It's time to go.'

'I don't think you quite understand what just happened,' Luke said. 'She was possessed or something, I don't know if she can go in the car.'

'How do we know this isn't a trick? You saw how strong she is. If she's coming with us, I want her tied down properly.' Nadya had clearly decided to ignore Theo's command, tidying away the letters into a neat stack and closing the window, cutting off the supply of summer air that had been circulating in the room.

276

'Seriously?'

'Yes, seriously, Luke. I'm not driving her without restraints.'

Kara choked a little. 'You're going to make me sit like this all the way back to London? And you aren't stopping her, Luke?'

'Baby, I think she's right. It's not safe for us. Let's just keep an eye on you for a little while, okay?'

She kicked against the table leg. 'I'm not going then; I'll just stay here.'

'Please come home with me.' Luke was close to begging. 'We can go to your mom and dad's place and I can look after you there.'

'Look after me? You've never looked after anything, you couldn't have a pet rock without cracking it, you worthless sack of shit.' She craned her neck to look at Jan. 'I can stay here with you, right? You're not really going to leave?'

'I'm not going to free you either. You were trying to stab us. I can't let you loose; I don't know what you'll do.'

'I guess that's entirely typical for you, Jan, you do love getting people in a bind, don't you?'

'For the last time, this isn't a bondage thing for me. I wish you would all stop staying that. I don't even fancy you, Kara.'

'That wasn't even what I meant, you smug bitch. I *know*. I know what you did to me and Luke when we were going through that bad patch years ago. I bet you thought I'd never find out, but Theo told me.' She gave the table another kick, tilting the chair back dangerously.

Jan wracked her brain for anything else she could possibly be referring to. No, it must be because of what Theo had told her in the woods. But admitting to the room how she had found that out would hardly help her case.

'What are you talking about? What did I do?'

Luke caught her and righted the chair. 'Not now, Kara, come on. We can talk about this when we're back in London.'

'Is it something Luke told you?' Jan could not prevent herself from pouncing on this, the sudden opportunity to confront the untruth without her ever having to admit to spying on them, offered up at the most unexpected moment.

Kara snapped, 'You know.'

Jan replied, 'No, I genuinely don't. What did you tell her, Luke?'

Theo said, 'I'm going to pack.'

Nadya said, 'Oh, so now you're willing to come with us, are you? You just stay right here, I'm not finished. What are you on about, Kara?' Nadya tried to catch at him as he left the room, but he easily evaded her grasp. They heard him charging up the stairs, bounding over the detritus strewn across the carpet.

'You really don't even remember, do you? After everything? I guess that's normal for you, it means so little.'

Jan got down on her haunches and stared into Kara's eyes. 'Just tell me. I'm asking because I clearly have no idea.'

Kara made a noise of rage so high pitched it was almost like a whinny. 'Fine, if you want to do this in front of everyone, we can. Years ago, when Luke was really struggling during exams, you were the one to pay off his debt to João.'

She kept going before Jan could interrupt again to say that in fact she had never done this, that if anything her failure as a friend was in not helping him escape the mess that he had made.

'There were strings attached to the money, though – if Luke took it, he had to leave the country and break up with me, because you thought he wasn't good enough for me.' She leaned back against Luke's stomach and looked up at him. 'Those were the worst years of my life. I almost lost him and I didn't know why.'

It took Jan a few moments to formulate a denial convincing enough that it might bely her lack of surprise at hearing this bizarre allegation that Kara was repeating with apparent total belief.

'What the actual fuck are you talking about, Kara? I never did any of that. You think I bribed Luke to leave the country?'

'Not bribed, blackmailed. You were going to ring up everyone he owed money to. You think I don't remember you bragging that you might tell his parents how bad things were. You kept talking about it, all the time, how somebody should call them and tell them what their son was up to.'

'You were really going to do it, weren't you, Jan?' Luke asked. 'My dad would have sent me to one of those rehab camps in Utah. What were you even thinking?'

Jan was shouting now, all composure gone. 'I didn't do that! I didn't do any of it! I was frightened for you and I wanted to call them but I thought that would just make it worse. I didn't do anything. Luke, I didn't blackmail you – tell them!'

'I don't believe you.' Ursie had been listening from her corner throughout and now thrust herself into the middle of the room. 'You've always loved secretly meddling in other people's lives, because you have nothing going on in your own. You were too much of a coward to even talk to me this morning. I thought you'd changed, grown up a bit, but I see now you'll never change. You can't even admit it when Kara is right in front of you.'

'It didn't stop you from fucking me last night, though, did it Ursula? You don't find me so repulsive when your bed is empty.' Jan was snarling now, ready to throw something, but there was nothing to be thrown. She slapped her hand against the wood panelling and groaned as it opened up the cut between her fingers again, the pain almost a welcome distraction from her hurt at Ursie's disbelief.

'I never "fucked" you. We had sex a few times, and I deeply regret it. I imagine Nadya feels much the same.' Ursie picked up her duffel bag again and walked out in silence.

Just before they heard the front door of Holt House slam so violently the whole building shook once more, Jan asked, 'When did Theo tell you this, exactly?'

Kara replied, 'I knew about the loan for years but Theo just told me the details recently. I was feeling so miserable about the state of things with Luke. Theo's always looked out for me, not like you, refusing to help me yet again. He said it's always about control with you.'

Nadya gave a choked little gurgle, like she was about to say something, but Jan surged in. 'Remind me, was that before or after Luke stole your designer coat and sold it?' she asked. 'You think everyone else is so blind they can't see you're wasting your time on him too? I heard what Theo said to you by the lake yesterday about Luke being nothing but trouble. Like it's not completely obvious why he wants to hurry along the breakup, so he'll have two more craven little worshippers totally focused on him? I really don't give a shit what either of you do. I want to be less involved, not more.'

Realising halfway through her own invective that not only was she wasting her time, but also that she was about to lose Ursie to her own rageful excess, if indeed she was not irretrievably lost already, Jan left Luke and Kara to their misconceptions and sprinted out in search of her.

The house was so wrecked it resembled the aftermath of a hurricane, the light fittings dangling precariously from their sconces, papers from the hall table scattered everywhere and deep black scratches across the tiles as if something hugely heavy had been dragged over them.

Fighting with the vast double doors, which did not seem to want to open, she tried to peer out through the warped panes of glass at either side to look for Ursie's shadow beyond. Finally managing to kick them wide, she ran down the steps and hurried round to where Nadya's car was parked. The brilliant daylight came like a slap to the face, contradicting the darkness of the day. Ursie stood leaning against the car, jabbing uselessly at her phone and scowling. Jan approached cautiously, standing at a little distance. After a beat, she forced herself to speak.

'I'm so sorry, I should never have humiliated you like that by telling the others about last night. Please can we talk?'

Ursie looked up. 'What is there to talk about? You meddle in other people's lives; you lied to Theo and to all of us for years about Nadya and you still can't even admit what you did wrong. You crept out of bed this morning without even trying to wake me, like I was nothing, and you're lying to me again now.'

'I never paid Luke that money. I wouldn't have paid it even I'd had it to hand, you have to believe me. Yes, I think they're bad for each other, but I just don't care that much. Their lives are their own to ruin. What I care about is you, for god's sake, can't you see that I'm in love with you?' The words spilled out unbidden, surprising Jan even as they came forth.

This confession only seemed to make Ursie more enraged.

'In love with me? Where do I even begin with that? Theo warned me that you had a big crush on me and I should be careful about hooking up, but love is something else entirely. I didn't know it was that serious, or that you thought it was anyway.' She let out a startled little laugh.

'I am, I really am that serious. This is the worst possible timing, I know.'

Jan could see Luke and Nadya hurtling towards the place where they stood, faces contorted with rage, hastily packed bags spilling shirts and socks over the drive.

'It is. I see how you act with Nadya; I don't need that kind of obsession in my life. I don't need someone to idolise me. I don't think you know what love *is*, beyond your self-loathing, and you have to figure that out before you try to build something real with anyone. I can't hold the weight of all your sins for you and hate you, so you don't have to do it. It's enough of a struggle to like myself most days.'

Jan was just about to launch into a defence of her feelings when Nadya caught up to them.

'Get out of the way. Now.'

Jan sidestepped her, looking helplessly at Ursie in the hope of continuing the conversation, but Ursie pointedly looked away.

'Do I need to shove you?' Nadya was raging. 'Get out of the way of my car before I get in and reverse over you. I can't believe I ever thought you were my friend. You told Ursie about us when it could have ruined everything. It still might, he's furious after yesterday. I can't believe I invited you into our bed and you messed it all up for me.'

'I thought the problem was that I meddle in everyone's lives? Are you seriously trying to tell me if you get deported it's my fault for not fucking your boyfriend?'

'I don't give a shit, maybe it's for the best. My friends in Moscow, my real friends, would never have breathed a word about any of this. I'm so disgusted I can't even look at you right now.'

She hurled her bags into the trunk and went around to sit in the driver's seat with her head clutched in her hands, door hanging open as she sobbed.

And now it was Luke stood very close to Jan. 'I could have died out in Phnom,' he snarled. 'I very nearly did, you know. I was so lonely I just wanted to disappear but Theo kept telling me you didn't think it was time yet. You didn't even call. Your grand plan didn't fix anything, it got me hooked on meth instead.'

Jan took a step nearer, so they were almost nose to nose.

'Your problem is that everyone who isn't three thousand pounds deep in coke debt looks rich to you, because you can't get a hold of yourself. I never paid. I didn't call you because I was pissed off with you for abandoning Kara and I don't know why Theo told you both that pathetic story, though I suspect I do know why you believed it of me. It's not my fault you fell for that racist lie.'

Luke's hand was balled into a fist and, as Jan spoke, she saw him raising it from the corner of her eye. She moved into a defensive stance, ready to finally have it out, but before he could strike, Ursie asked, 'Where *is* Theo?'

And Luke turned back and groaned, 'We left Kara in there with him.'

Eyes wild and red, Nadya sat up from the steering wheel and said, 'We've got to go back, he still has the key to the gates.'

The four of them turned and dropped the bags, running back even faster than they had come, sprinting to the house, the doors flung wide in its customary, self-satisfied grin.

Jan tried to keep up but found that she could not run; with chest pressed inwards and lungs contracting, her legs were moving so slowly her feet felt glued to the earth. She might as well have been walking through tar. She looked up at the first storey and saw strange movement in the windows, unfamiliar flickering shapes reaching and playing over the glass, with a curious light glowing behind them.

By the time Jan reached the house, the hallway was impossibly clouded, billows of smoke streaming out of several rooms and the distant sensation of a building heat. The moment they were distracted, Harold had seized his opportunity to obliterate all record of the shame and failure that had outlasted even his death.

The others, hearing Kara's distant shrieks of rage, ran blindly up the stairs, but Jan went to the library, fearing what she would find, and there encountered Theo

284

sprawled on the floor, clutching his shoulder. Black blood had soaked his shirt and was coursing freely over his fingers as he lay below the level of the fumes. The chair to which Kara had been bound was empty, the curtain ties neatly cut and lying by his side. The dagger glinted on the table; point sheened in scarlet.

Jan kicked him full in the stomach, possessed by all the rage she had not had a chance to turn on the others.

'What have you done? Why did you set her free, you absolute moron?'

He retched and writhed away from her over the parquet, struggling to catch his breath before he said, 'She's mad. She's gone completely mad. She stabbed me.'

'We told you and you didn't listen, did you? I'll do far worse to you if you don't tell me everything.' She could hardly stand to look at him.

He pointed upwards to the ceiling, indicating Kara was still inside Holt House. 'I don't know where she's gone. She was begging me to let her go and I wouldn't. I lost concentration and she must have wriggled loose, she's so skinny. I was trying to catch her again but she stabbed me and grabbed the letters. Please, I don't think I can stand. Can you drag me out of here?' He was still clutching his wound, fingers tight around the clotted fabric.

'Maybe I will and maybe I won't. But first I want to know why you told that lie about the loan.'

'I can explain everything, just pull me out of here,' he pleaded. 'The smoke is getting thicker.'

'That's more of a problem for you than for me, isn't it?'

Jan nudged him with her foot a little further into the rapidly darkening room and began walking back towards the library door without him.

'Please!'

She turned.

'He would never have left me alone if he knew I lent it to him. I had to tell him it was you. I thought I was doing him a favour.'

She took a few steps closer. 'I don't think that's all of it.'

'I thought . . . I thought maybe if he left, I'd have a real shot with her, but she was so depressed all the time, she wasn't ready to think of me like that. Then I met Nadya . . .'

'That's still not everything.' She stood one foot onto his lower abdomen, testing her weight but not pressing her heel down all the way into his crotch just yet.

'If Kara knew I had that much lying around and didn't help Luke, she'd never forgive me, but she'd believe me if I said that it was you! Listen, I know I messed up, but I'll do anything, just get me out of here please! I'll give you anything you want, I'll pay!'

Jan shifted her weight away, leaning down to take him by the collar and seeing the relief on his face as she did so.

'You still don't get it, do you?' she asked. 'I don't need thirty pieces of silver, or a pound of your worthless flesh. I needed you to be my friend.'

She spat in his eyes then went round to drag him by the legs, gut busting with the effort of his weight, all along the corridor and out onto the steps where he lay for all the world like a sack of spoiled goods, breathing heavily and moaning from the pain in his shoulder. She checked his pockets for the key, but it was gone.

She ran from room to room in search of something, anything, to put out the flames that had sprung up where each burning letter had fallen, but the fire had spread to

286

the carpets, the curtains, all the soft furnishings; she would need more help than the others had to give just to douse it all with water. There were cloths big enough to put it out, but there was no way to open the leaded windows, already scorching to the touch. Down the hallway in the kitchen, one decrepit fire alarm wailed ineffectually.

Dodging and leaping over patches of flame, Jan fought her way upstairs, listening to Nadya calling out her name, all rancour forgotten in the mounting terror of the fire. She could scarcely feel her way along in the dense dark smoke to the source of the sound. The others were clustered together in her bedroom, though by the time she got there the air was so hot and thick that Jan could scarcely breathe; she felt her lungs singeing within her. Flames wreathed the window outside. The old dry branches of wisteria had caught alight, burning like a torch that encircled the whole building. Luke was standing on her bed and holding Nadya by the waist as they reached for the catch in the ceiling, hitting the wrong spot every time as Ursie screamed at them to stop and come back downstairs with her to safety.

From above them she heard footsteps roaming over the floor, banging and crashing with wild abandon as Harold set light to every precious thing the Mortimers had ever stored away up there, not caring if all their history burned with it, so long as every shameful detail of his failures would be erased. Horrid laughter echoed in the space above, sounding more and more like screams as it went on.

Jan seized the ladder-chair from the corner of the room and stood on it, getting the catch open in one go. The trapdoor fell open with a heavy bang. Luke was holding a towel under the tap of the ensuite, soaking it before he draped it over his shoulders and head to form a wet cape.

'It's too late, we can't reach her,' Ursie groaned as she tried again to dissuade them from their mission. 'She doesn't know what she's doing.'

Luke shouldered Jan aside, hauled the ladder over until it was in position for him to climb up. 'I'm not leaving her, so don't ask me again.'

The stumbling footsteps increasingly gave way to piercing shrieks, though whether these were Harold's utter despair or Kara's agony, Jan could not tell.

Nadya said urgently, 'There's a tree, Ursie, if you can get to Luke's room in the other wing, the branches should hold you. Get out of the window and go to safety, then.'

Jan held the ladder base steady as Luke ascended. He disappeared into the burning space beyond. Nadya went after him and waited halfway up. Jan put one foot on the bottom rung, feeling how hot the metal rivets had already become. Poised to ford the burning corridor and try that way out, Ursie caught Jan by the arm and said, 'You can't go up there. Don't do it.'

Every sinew in Jan's body strained to back down, escape the flaming nightmare and flee Holt House with Ursie, out and away from all of this. But there was still a chance they could get through to Kara, shake her out of it again just long enough to save her.

'I can't let Luke go alone. He's not strong enough by himself.'

A crash came from nearby, sounding like part of the stairs had fallen in. Ursie still had not let go of her, her fingers hot and tight around Jan's wrist.

Jan asked, 'What's it to you, anyway? You hate me.'

Ursie said, half-choking, 'I do right now, but we'll never find out anything different unless we survive.'

'Get on with it! We don't have time for this!' Nadya screamed at them with terror and frustration as she scurried up the ladder.

Jan looked up, into the heart of the blaze, where darkness mingled with the light from the flames. She climbed, into the heat and smoke, not knowing what awaited her. Moments later she felt the reverberations of the ladder as Ursie put one hand and then another on the rungs, following up behind. She hauled herself into the smoke-filled attic and reached down to pull her up. The air was charcoal dark, enlivened only by patches of bright fire. Keeping low to try and breathe, she crept along the floor in a squat towards the source of the noise. Kara was still wheeling about, a sheaf of burning paper in one insensate hand, the other jabbing at the air with the long grill lighter, flicking it on and off to keep Luke back from her as he tried to lunge and take it from her grasp.

The smoke in her throat turning her voice into more of a growl, Jan shouted, 'Harold, listen to me!'

She saw the shadow of his ruined, aged face overlaying Kara's, flames twining about his hair and his eyes fixed on hers. Luke paused to bend over, face craned towards the floor, trying to take in more air as Ursie was frantically scrabbling at the dormer window, crying out in pain as her hands burned on the latch. Jan had to try, or Harold would doom them all. Nadya was by the wall, groping for something in the gloom.

'You're destroying everything your family worked for, look around you.'

He croaked back at her wordlessly, hands still flicking the lighter on and off.

'It doesn't matter,' she said. 'You lost years ago, it's time to rest.'

The screeching, ringing sound came again and, with it, words not spoken by any human mouth but instead bellowing out from the walls around them, the foundations shaking dangerously, burning rafters falling from above.

GET. OUT. OF. MY. HOUSE.

With each syllable new pockets of flame unfurled across the attic room.

The bags of old clothes were all ablaze, the stacked family photographs curling in their frames as the glass warped and cracked. Ursie, hand wrapped in Luke's discarded wet towel, punched the window pane and shattered it, shrieking in pain at the shards stuck in her forearm and then in horrified dismay as the flames rose higher fuelled with new oxygen.

Jan tried again. 'Just stop it, put down the—'

Then Luke jumped, knocking the lighter out of Kara's hand and tackling her to the floor. They rolled over and over, each of them triumphing for a few moments but also evenly matched by the other's fading strength. Shorter of breath than ever, Jan went to help him but a new wall of flame had sprung up across that part of the floor where Kara had dropped the last of the burning letters, cutting off any path towards the pair. Ursie tugged at her arm and pointed downwards, covering her mouth: the bedroom below was engulfed as well, the bed consumed by a bonfire licking up towards the ceiling, their route back down now impassable. Through the haze she could still just about see

Luke and Kara locked in their ceaseless fight, neither of them able either to prevail or relinquish their hold on the other.

Nadya called, 'Get over here, you idiots!'

Ursie said, 'Is there no other way out? What about the trapdoors?'

Muzzily, brain drowned in smoke, Jan tried to think. All the other hatches led down into rooms already lost to the flames.

'Hurry up!' Nadya rasped. 'I don't want to die.'

There was only one option left and Jan did not like it one bit. Taking Ursie's hand in hers, they ran together across the scorching floor at a low crouch, terrified at every step the ceiling would give way and hurtle them down into a lethal heap of burning bricks and rubble. Clinging to the attic wall, Nadya had eased open the door just enough for the three of them to slip inside and slam the door behind them. Cold, stale air blew up to condense the sweat on their singed faces. They could breathe again but they had to hurry.

Jan prayed the door would hold long enough as they started the descent, saying nothing, trembling but keeping on in desperation to get out. Beneath them the mile of empty tunnels stretched away into the dark and they stumbled forward, away from the inferno they had left blazing above them and yet uncertain of what lay ahead.

Five Years Later

Nadya's new flat was stuffed with overflowing boxes of trinkets and memorabilia, suitcases full of clothes and trunks ready to be transferred into wardrobes. Jan recognised some of the framed prints and even a couple of the handbags, but most of it was entirely unfamiliar to her. Time had not stayed still; she had been gone half a decade, after all. Jan had deleted her social media, changed her number to a Portuguese one and tried as best she could to forget. But her email address was still the same, and when Nadya had written, insisting they needed to talk in person, Jan's curiosity had overwhelmed her. Flights from Porto were cheap and at least her parents would be pleased by the visit. Jan came back very seldom; it was hard to stay away from the restaurant for too long as she was still working her way up.

Nadya said, 'How was the flight? You can sit down over there, just clear a space for yourself. I can get you some crisps if you're hungry.' She hugged Jan and went to the stove to stir the large pot of red wine bubbling on the hob, perfuming the air with cardamom, anise and cinnamon.

It was strange to see the passage of time across a face Jan had once so dearly loved and which now appeared only in her nightmares and occasionally her prayers. Jan probed at her heart, dreading the possibility that on meeting again she might still feel the same, but found only curiosity and pity. Five years of marriage to Theo was punishment enough, and in order to stay in England Nadya had been

293

obliged to accept his offer, despite knowing full well what he was. Nadya chattered away, explaining how she had found this place, her job working for an art auction house, her plans for Christmas. This was the first time Jan could remember seeing Nadya genuinely nervous and she chose to let it play out rather than swooping in to set her at ease.

So far Nadya seemed only to have unpacked the essentials into her new home. This space was smaller than her last place in Knightsbridge, but still felt echoey without much to adorn it yet. In her email, Nadya had promised that Theo would not be present, but Jan did not know enough about how things might have changed to trust her entirely.

The intercom rang and Nadya checked the video link. She said, 'It's Ursie', and buzzed her up. Nadya moved slowly, her bad ankle impeding her walk to the door to welcome Ursie in. Shattered and expensively remade twice over after she fell badly in the tunnels under Holt House, she had told Jan in her email she could still feel the pins holding it together in the winter cold.

The December slush clung to Ursie's boots, and Jan watched her gingerly shucking them off before proceeding into the main space in her socked feet. She looked Jan up and down, clearly noting her bronzed and faintly laughter-lined face, hair tinted copper from working in the hot sun. Ursie was as beautiful as ever and as difficult for Jan to predict. She said, 'Good to see you again,' in a clipped voice and started removing her big, padded coat.

Jan was not sure whether to approach her or hang back. Ursie looked downcast and almost angry. Jan wondered what she was doing here – Ursie and Nadya had never been close when she knew them, but perhaps that had changed.

Here were the two women whose presence and then absence had shaped Jan's life for over a decade, much as she hated ever to admit that to anyone except her therapist.

Ursie asked, 'Aren't you going to say anything? Why didn't you write? I had to find out from your mum that you'd left the country.'

Jan watched her face for a long moment, trying to find a way to explain herself. Eventually she just said, 'I'm sorry, I was too ashamed. Everything was so broken after the fire.' Then, trying something new, she asked, 'Why didn't *you* write?'

Ursie said, very quietly, 'Because I was too.'

And then they were both crying and Ursie was stepping forward and Jan was embracing her and it had been so long but her perfume was the same and they only let go of each other when Jan had to dig the tissues out of her pocket and hand some to Ursie as well as drying her own sore eyes. Nadya, who had been watching all this from beside the stove, cleared her throat and said, not without a wobble in her voice, 'Guys, come on. Get it together.'

Ursie pulled back and, still dabbing at her face, asked Nadya, 'So are you feeling settled in yet?'

'Hardly. I can't decide where to put anything. And there's still so much I have to talk to my lawyers about.' Printouts were strewn all over a huge pinewood counter dotted with takeaway boxes. Jan cast her eye over them and realised they detailed the process of application for Indefinite Leave to Remain.

Ursie scanned one and asked, 'You're definitely staying then?'

'It certainly looks like it. I've been here my entire adult life. It's a shithole, but I can hardly leave now, can I? We can't all just run off to Porto.'

'It's a beautiful place,' Jan said, 'and I really needed to be somewhere else.'

Ursie said, 'I'm envious, I wish I could have left afterwards too.' She went to sit on the cluttered sofa while Jan stayed standing, not knowing quite where to place herself amid the chaos. Eventually Ursie added, 'The inquest was pretty awful.'

'Yeah, it really was.'

The three of them were silent for a moment, remembering the judge's long tirade about the group's fatal recklessness, which had reduced Jan to a trembling mess in court. Theo had sat through an account of the vital minutes lost to the firefighters trying to break down the gates and said nothing, staring into his hands throughout. The utter destruction caused by the fire and the heavy fine for breaching lockdown orders had forced him to sell what was left of Holt House to developers, though Jan suspected he'd still made a tidy profit on the land.

Nadya gave the pot on the hob a stir, wafting the scent towards them.

Jan asked Ursie, 'Did you go to the funerals, in the end?'

'I'm not sure that Luke's dad did a service for him in the UK. I went to Kara's though. It was painful, but I'm glad I did it.'

'I did think about going, but I wasn't sure I'd be welcome after everything that happened. I still can't believe Luke gave his life trying to save her.'

'I think we underestimated him,' Nadya said and began ladling out the wine.

Ursie said decisively, 'We should never have gone to Holt House, it was so stupid. But nothing can fix that now.'

Nadya said, 'We all know whose fault it really was.'

Jan decided to push a little harder for the update she really wanted. 'How is Theo doing? Where is he?'

Nadya gave a curt little laugh. 'I haven't heard very much from him, unsurprisingly. I don't think he's best pleased. I can't thank you enough for what you did at the restaurant, Ursie.'

Ursie said, 'You owe me a new liver. But it was worth it.'

'What happened? What did you do?'

Instead of answering straight away, Nadya passed them mugs of the mulled wine, and went to put on some music, before realising that the speakers were wedged so far at the bottom of a box it would have been impossible to retrieve them without unpacking everything.

Ursie had been spread out over the sofa, but she moved so Jan could perch at the very end of it and gave Jan her first real smile since setting foot in Nadya's flat. Jan hadn't waited, not exactly, life moved too fast for that, but she found herself wondering whether perhaps after all this time away, things might even be different for them. Jan raised the mug to her lips and let a big hot gulp of wine run down her throat. It was just the right amount of sweet, with none of the bitterness she'd associated with the cups of overboiled grog on sale at ice-skating rinks and festive markets.

Ursie asked Nadya, 'How long were you planning this for?'

'A little while. The last piece of the puzzle only clicked into place very randomly. I was having a beauty treatment and they had lots of pamphlets in the foyer for upscale places. Wellness retreats, all-inclusive trips to Turkey for procedures that aren't quite legal here yet, that sort of thing.'

'And it was just on a flyer?'

'Not a flyer exactly, more of a brochure, and only the one. It's a secure treatment facility for high-net-worth individuals. They were very vague on their website but I called them to check.' Nadya laughed and Jan heard her click the stove off carefully, before she felt Ursie move a little closer to her on the sofa as they told the story.

One Week Before

Bitterly cold and increasingly confused, Theo waited in the alleyway for the car to come around. The dinner at La Balance had stretched garrulously all the way till closing, Ursie regaling him with stories of art world absurdity and her new exhibition, which was rapidly taking shape. They kept drinking in the hotel bar next door, downing cocktail after cocktail with none of the frostiness that usually accompanied their meetings. He hadn't been sure why she would ask to see him, since they had barely spoken more than a few words since Kara's funeral. She had declined to attend his registry office wedding to Nadya, arranged as soon as was legally possible and arguably before it was passably decent.

He supposed Nadya might have asked her to sound him out on something of importance. It even occurred to him that she could be laying the groundwork for Nadya to announce a change of heart about having kids, news of which his family had been pressing him for years now. Nadya had always proclaimed an icy disinterest in children and Theo had professed to feel the same, but he saw the way she sometimes looked at toddlers when they passed them in the park or when she was offered friends' babies to dandle. Ursie had certainly mentioned children, via a long and rambling story about her cousin choosing names for her twins, and when she asked him if he had any plans on that front, he had chuckled and nodded. Ursie ordered another round of

Sazeracs and said, 'But I thought Nadya didn't want them?'

'Well, she says that, but you know how she is. Only focused on one thing at a time. It's not like we're trying all that hard not to, and if it did turn out that way, I think she'd want to keep it.'

'I suppose accidents do happen,' Ursie had said and picked at her arm. The scarring had healed pinkish-brown and puffy there, slashes curling from wrist to elbow in a great wave like a particularly abstract tattoo. He couldn't think why she didn't just wear long sleeves.

The conversation became stilted and died around the time he'd called for the bill and proposed another round of nightcaps somewhere else to top off the evening's drinking. It wasn't as if he had anything much to do tomorrow, but Ursie wasn't keen. She'd always been so ambitious; it was exhausting just to think about her schedule.

Now, back outside the restaurant with its minimalist logo, depicting a recurring set of golden scales, Theo pulled his thin coat tighter around him and shivered as Ursie took her leave, walking off in the direction of the Tube. He felt impatient for the car to come and take him back to Clapham and the comforts of his bed. A larger vehicle stopped at the end of the alleyway and a man got out to open the door.

'This way, sir.'

It wasn't the usual guy; Nadya must have changed the service without telling him. He walked closer and, as he was about to bend, the man grabbed him by the scruff of the collar and smashed his head against the edge of the door. A starburst of pain exploded behind his eyes. Theo felt himself shoved face first into the leather depths, legs bundled up behind him so he lay splayed against the seat. The windows were blacked out instead of tinted as they had first appeared and a thick screen separated him from the driver. Or was it drivers? He heard a murmur of voices in the front seats that suggested more than one man was there. Disorientated and afraid, he heard the locks depress and the car picked up speed, swerving round past Piccadilly Circus and down Haymarket to what he knew must be Trafalgar Square. But instead of making the familiar turn for West London, he felt it keep going, driving in circles until he was too dizzy and sick to keep track of where he was being taken.

Nadya had always warned him something like this might happen. He searched in his breast pocket, but the man had also pickpocketed his phone and now they were careening through the dark, he knew not where or why. Someone must have decided to send her father a message. Could he run away if they stopped to refuel? He didn't think he could fight them both off, his fitness had declined in recent years, and besides, the man's hands alone struck terror into Theo, each one hard like an iron claw, the training palpable in the few flicks of the wrist it had taken to incapacitate him.

At least the car was warm, the leather seats cushioned and comfortable. The seat was so wide he could even stretch out to lie curled up on his side. He knew that he should stay awake, try to retain some idea of where they were driving, but the alcohol and the heavy meal began to overcome him and he started losing the ability to resist. Theo drifted off into a deep and desolate sleep.

When he awoke, the car had come to a complete stop. He heard one of the men talking very fast in Russian, it sounded like a phone call. He had never learned more than hello and yes, had never needed to when Nadya spoke such perfect English. He tried once more to bang on the divide between the seats.

'Please, let me out! I won't tell anyone anything! I'll walk home. I don't know anything about Oleg's business, I'm just the husband. Please!!' He bashed it frantically with his fist, then tried another tack.

'This watch is worth thousands of pounds, I have more at home. I don't have any useful information.'

One of the men rolled down the partition just enough that Theo could see a slice of cheek, and the anaemic first light of day behind him. How long had they been driving for? Were they even still in England?

'Be quiet. Journey almost over.' The glint of the man's eyes sent him spiralling further into panic. They contained not even a pinprick of sympathy. All the terrible things Theo knew could happen in situations like these crowded into his mind. Hanging, poisoning with rare chemicals, dismemberment. Could they be planning to cut bits of him off and send them back home with ransom notes?

'Is it Nadya you want? I'll give you our address, if that's what you're after, just let me go.'

The man chuckled and, without another word, drew the partition back up again.

The car rolled forward and Theo could hear gravel beneath the wheels. They travelled another few minutes and the distance was one he knew well. It was a feature of the nightmares that had plagued him for years, the ones he had tried to stave off with every powder under the sun, awake and red-eyed till the early hours, the insides of his cheeks gnawed to tartare, tongue locked tight in his terrified skull.

But he still did not believe it until the men stopped the car and came round to restrain him, carrying Theo wildly kicking and screaming past the pretty orderly who had stepped to one side as she blithely welcomed him to the Holt House Recovery & Wellness Centre.

When a place has stood for so long and seen so many terrible things come to pass, when blood has polluted the threshold and its very foundations are soaked with iniquity, its presiding spirit does not die so easily as that.

When the inside has crumbled and the roof has fallen and the finery is reduced to ashes, so long as a few stubborn bricks of the old structure remain standing, the house continues. When the name persists and the walls are rebuilt and the ravaged heir returns, it is more than a home, it is a force to be reckoned with.

It does not forget what it was before and may be again. It sees Theo, stirring even now beneath the dose of tranquillisers, and knows him for its own, mind softened and covered in disgrace. Lying prone, in the end bedroom overlooking the lawn, he stretches and stiffens in its familiar grasp. Scarred and diminished but not defeated, the house does not appreciate failure. But what cannot be burned away must be put to other use. He is weak, so weak, and the house is hungry still.

Author's Note

The first inklings of what would become *The Decadence* came to me many years ago while visiting Florence as part of an interrailing trip through Europe before starting university. The beauty of the ancient setting stoked a desire to start reading *The Decameron* and while wandering the same city where the characters first met, surrounded by other pretentious teenagers and twenty-somethings on their own travels, I realised that Filomena, Pampinea et al. were not as impossibly distant as they seemed at first, in fact they were around the same age as us. But surely my own generation, sequestered in a remote country house while the world around them seethed with plague and turmoil, could not be relied upon to behave so demurely? I read on, waiting for one of the noble Florentines to misbehave, but all the truly scandalous action was relegated to the stories with which they entertained one another as their world came crashing down around them – it was not in the frame tale about the characters themselves. What would we do? How would it be different? What might go wrong, with less rigid religious and social control?

These questions continued to burn away in my mind as I went to university and encountered texts like *Sir Gawain and the Green Knight*, which has at its heart a sadomasochistic love game between Gawain, Sir Bertilak and Lady Bertilak, played throughout the castle of Hautdesert and its magical environs. It is more or less impossible to study

307

English literature without encountering the great house as a potent symbol of feudal power and my interest in characters stuck together in a confined domestic space became an obsession with the country house novel, both the traditional variety and modern reworkings. I grew to love L. P. Hartley's *The Go-Between*, Aldous Huxley's *Crome Yellow*, Toby Litt's *Finding Myself*, Martin Amis's *Dead Babies* and Iris Murdoch's *The Unicorn*. Their shared themes of enclosure, surveillance, escape, retribution and clandestine sexuality were a potent brew of everything that interested me most. Donna Tartt's *The Secret History*, while not strictly a country house novel, also informed my understanding of how tight-knit group dynamics playing out in a remote location can lead to violence and madness. Around this point, I tried to write the first draft of this novel several times and yet it continued to feel lifeless, it was not truly mine and had no truly animating spirit.

A new vision arrived unexpectedly, with the help of Isabel Colegate's *The Shooting Party*, a wonderful novel about a group of adulterous aristocrats convening at an Oxfordshire estate on the eve of the First World War. One among their number, a financier named Sir Reuben Hergesheimer, is afforded a heartrending passage in which he reflects on sacrificing the chance to have a family of his own because it would force him to choose between Jewish custom and total assimilation. I realised I was trying to depict a world into which I do not readily fit as a queer, Jewish woman. Looking at the genre more closely, it was easier to see the deeply recherché nature of concerns about inheritance, land and tradition – and to identify places in other novels where these surfaced in disturbing ways. *Brideshead Revisited* may well have been a 'panegyric preached over an empty coffin', as Waugh himself noted in his preface to the 1959 reissue of the novel, but the narrative voice's revulsion at the effete, racially indeterminate Anthony Blanche is something I would prefer buried six feet deep. Questions of racism and homophobia at the heart of the British Establishment are powerfully and inventively explored in more contemporary novels like Alan Hollinghurst's *The Line of Beauty* and Kazuo Ishiguro's *The Remains of the Day*, both of which provoked me to think more deeply about the genre conventions with which I was engaging.

What is exiled is not necessarily absent and one way of squaring the horrors of our past with its traditionalist, much-aestheticised presentation was for me to look over towards the neighbouring genre of the haunted house tale. The great grande dame of literary horror, Shirley Jackson, has much to say about the persistent inheritance of evil in *The Haunting of Hill House*, while Sarah Waters's *The Little Stranger* makes heterosexuality itself the source of the uncanny, in a haunting inversion of the trope, and Helen Oyeyemi's *White is for Witching* made me think again about all ways a home can be terrifyingly hostile and all-consuming. For many years, I had been suffering from recurring nightmares about a malign house leading me deeper and deeper inside itself until there was no way out. Mark Z. Danielewski's *House of Leaves* helped me to understand the many possible valencies of this motif, though it was leaving England for Germany that put a stop to the dreams.

While most of my work on *The Decadence* was completed before 7 October 2023, the long-protracted and deadly conflict in the Middle East has been much on my mind while editing. I find myself drawn back to *The Garden of the Finzi-Continis* by Giorgio Bassani, which begins and ends in the grave. In the present day, I still hope for a ceasefire, the return of the hostages and a longer program of peace and repair, though at the time of writing all seems bleak.

I invoke these texts not in an attempt to claim their glory for myself but rather in a spirit of wonder at the richness of literary creation and in tribute to those from whom I have been privileged to draw inspiration. They have been a solace when I have felt alone, a guiding light when I could not see my own intentions clearly and sometimes a scrying glass as well. The opportunity to read and think is one of the greatest gifts there is, and I must count myself very lucky indeed to have had such books available.

Leon Craig, November 2024, Berlin

Acknowledgements

It is hard to say exactly how long *The Decadence* took me to write because I have tried to write it so many times. Once at nineteen, once again at twenty-three and then finally over the course of four years in my late twenties and early thirties. I wrote an entire collection of short stories to try and escape from it, but knew one day I would have to return. It has been the mirror of my preoccupations and the dark waters into which I peered looking for other distorted visions of existence. Now it is completed, I will miss the visceral connection I once had to its world and characters, but I am grateful that the process is finished.

It is not really possible to do this chronologically, but I want to start by thanking the brilliant Francine Toon, who commissioned the novel along with *Parallel Hells* and therefore finally gave me a deadline and confidence to write it.

To everyone who reviewed, bought or recommended *Parallel Hells* or had me on their podcast to talk about the strange things that go on in my mind, thank you so much, especially Kirsty Logan, most recently author of *No & Other Love Stories* and Adam Z. Robinson who runs the delightful Ghost Story Book Club. I was really worried the short stories would disappear without a trace and instead I got to meet so many fascinating and engaged people during and after its publication. To Hugh Foley, who read an early draft of *The Decadence* and gave me thoughtful and extensive feedback on how to improve it (and his baby daughter who obliged us by sleeping through the entire phone conversation) – thank you for all your wise words. To Geffen Semach, for their friendship and solidarity. To Julia Bell for her generosity of spirit and ongoing encouragement. To the *London Magazine* and the much-mourned *White Review* for everything they have done in support of my work and of other people's too.

Thank you also to all the authors I had the privilege of working with at Serpent's Tail, each of whom broadened my understanding of what it is to care about books in their own individual way.

Huge thanks to my deeply perceptive and patient editor Charlotte Humphery, particularly for her good humour during extensive discussions of scene-blocking the threesome and on a more macro level for her wisdom and insight regarding the nuances of characterisation.

311

Thanks to Nico Parfitt, final eliminator of the troublesome guinea fowls and excellent second editor, to Louise Court, whom anyone would be very lucky to have as the publicist for their work, and to the wider Sceptre team, whom I owe considerable gratitude. Thank you also to Emma Hargrave for her attentive copyediting and to Deborah Balogun, who kindly agreed to be the sensitivity reader for Ursie, though any remaining errors there must rest with me.

Many thanks to the talented Saffron Stocker, who fulfilled all my cover design dreams and then some!

Thank you so much to my diligent and clear-sighted agent Matt Turner for all his good advice and kind understanding and to the Rogers, Coleridge & White team, with all my admiration.

To Victoria Gosling, for everything she taught me about nostalgia through her own wonderful writing – and for allowing me to housesit those difficult first few months in Berlin. To Jane Flett, fabulous author of *Freakslaw*, and the Berlin writing community, for creating a genuinely special and unique world of art, creativity and intellectual exchange.

To the wider Jewish community of Berlin, for their warmth and friendship at I time I really needed it, and many others did as well.

To my friends in London and Berlin more generally, with special mentions for Alice and Ksenya for not only getting me through the worst of last year but always making me laugh, for Leyla for her hair-raising Swedish ghost anecdotes and calming forest walks and Lauri for her enduring good sense and panache.

For everyone who remembers the old times – I do/did love you, and you taught me a great deal. Thank goodness for the possibility of change.

With many thanks to my mother, Amanda, who always knows which plants are in season, which is vital if you're writing in a bucolic mode, and to my father, Robin, for his annoyingly correct advice on a core aspect of the plot. Many thanks also to my brother, William, who patiently walked me through multiple legal scenarios for the inheritance of haunted houses.

With thanks to my beloved extended family, especially my aunt and uncle Constance and Mike and my grandmother Zelda, for their generosity and wise counsel. In loving memory of Gillian Cohen and Kate Saunders, both of whom strongly encouraged me to write and who sadly left us before *The Decadence* was finished – thank you.

And to everyone who gave me advice, assistance or inspiration not otherwise listed above, thank you so much and please forgive me the omission – I am chronically sleep-deprived because I still dream of ghosts far too often.

312